ANTHONY DALTON

RELENTLESS
PURSUIT

BookLand
press

Published by BookLand Press
15 Allstate Parkway, Suite 600, Markham, Ontario L3R 5B4
www.booklandpress.com

Printed and bound in Canada

Library and Archives Canada Cataloguing in Publication

Dalton, Anthony, 1940-, author
Relentless pursuit / Anthony Dalton.

Issued in print and electronic formats.
ISBN 978-1-926956-59-6 (pbk.).-- ISBN 978-1-926956-60-2 (epub).-- ISBN 978-1-926956-61-9 (pdf)

I. Title.

PS8607.A473R44 2013   C813'.6   C2013-902534-0
                                               C2013-902535-9

Canada Council   Conseil des arts
for the Arts   du Canada

We acknowledge the support of the Canada Council for the Arts, which last year invested $157 million to bring the arts to Canadians throughout the country. We acknowledge the support of the Ontario Arts Council (OAC), an agency of the Government of Ontario, which last year funded 1,681 individual artists and 1,125 organizations in 216 communities across Ontario for a total of $52.8 million. We acknowledge the financial support of the Ontario Media Development Corporation for our publishing activities.

For Hasan, Topu and Rubaiyat, the Mansur family of Dhaka, Bangladesh, with love and appreciation. I owe you so much.

AUTHOR'S INTRODUCTION

The events and characters in this story are fictitious. As such, the characters are not intended to resemble any persons, living or dead. However, the background to this story is rooted in fact. In 1994 I was travelling in Bangladesh, searching for tigers, hunting down material for magazine articles, as I had done the previous year and would do for the next few years. After spending a few days in the forest and more cruising the jungle rivers of the Sundarbans with Bangladeshi friends, we were heading home to the boat's base at Mongla. The boat we were on, named *Ma-O-Roba*, was a steel-hulled motorboat with overnight accommodation for a dozen or so people. She was tough and dependable. I have used her as a model for *Fatima* in this book.

Halfway to Mongla we encountered a full-grown Royal Bengal tiger swimming across the river ahead of us. We were able to cut it off, denying it access to the land for a few minutes. The tiger, not surprisingly, objected to this attempt at interrupting its crossing. In anger, it lashed out at us and at *Ma-O-Roba*, its sharp claws slashing at the steel deck, trying to get a purchase so it could climb on board. Unable to hold on, the furious tiger slid back into the river and drifted alongside the boat for a few moments as the current took it astern. Denied its revenge, the tiger roared at us again and again, making the steel hull vibrate with the power of its voice and numbing my ears.

My last image of that big, angry cat was as it clawed its way up the slippery mud bank into the sanctuary of the jungle. It looked back at us on the boat and gave one more powerful roar before disappearing into the forest. We learned later, after we had described the tiger and its markings to a Bangladeshi naturalist, that we had encountered a rogue tiger known as 'the man-eater of Chandpai' to many locals. That surprising event became the catalyst for me to write *Relentless Pursuit*.

Anthony Dalton
Delta, B.C.

PROLOGUE

The Bay of Bengal, 1586

After thirty-one years of life, Dom Diego Jose Bartolomeo Fernando Duarte had less than one hour left to live. He, his ship and his crew, were about to be ravaged by a catastrophic storm. The sea, which had been his provider and his greatest love, was preparing to kill him.

Dom Diego paced the deck restlessly, occasionally casting an anxious glance at the southern sky. The malignant line of black cloud building rapidly on the horizon filled him with fear. "Madre de Dios," he muttered. "Where is my wind?"

Foreward the carrack's square sails hung lifeless. Above Diego the lateen mizzen drooped lethargically: a limp sheet on a washing line. On deck the crew panted with the heat of the Bengal summer as the damp humidity of the Asian monsoon hung around them like a permanently scalded towel. Sweat ran in gleaming rivulets from Diego's head. It dripped in a steady flow from the black curls stuck fast to his forehead, to his ears and to his thick neck. Collecting in his bushy eyebrows it overflowed, rushing in a stream of salt to sting his eyes. Down his nose and his cheeks it swept, through his black wavy beard and trickled onto his silken shirt to merge with the moisture cascading off his massive hairy chest.

The sea, which had been as smooth as his father's shaving glass a short time before, was developing a lazy but ominous swell. And still there was no wind, but it wouldn't be long in coming, and then from the wrong direction.

"We'll have the sails off her, if you please, Paulo," Diego turned to his lieutenant. "All except the mizzen."

Paulo passed the word to furl each of the four square sails. The mizzen he left rigged, sheeted home hard to the outrigger over the stern.

"Check the lashings on the cargo. Make certain all is secure below," Diego's stentorian voice bellowed. "All hands – prepare for heavy weather!"

In a flurry of activity, the crew closed the eight gun ports and secured the rows of cast iron cannons. On the cargo deck the sealed urns of spices and oils, the bales of silks and muslin, had already been packed so carefully and tightly little more could be done to ensure their safety. Below the officer's deck where Diego stood, two ironbound chests of Indian teak remained securely fastened to the wooden floor, and shackled to the walls – one on each side of his cabin. They were packed full with gold ornaments and solid silver plates, as well as diamond-studded necklaces and jewel-encrusted daggers. *Esmerelda*, Diego's ship, was not only a Portuguese merchant vessel – she was also a privateer.

South and west of Diu, on the Gujurat coast, nearly a year past, they had attacked a lone Arab dhow. The dhow and her crew had been despatched to the bottom of the Arabian Sea, but not until the precious cargo had been rescued. Dom Diego hadn't known why the dhow carried such a treasure. He had not bothered to ask. It had been theirs; now it belonged to him and, in some small measure, to his crew.

Esmerelda was two days out of Porto Grande, which some called Chittagong, bound for Goa. From there the Portuguese nobleman planned to set sail directly for his king's

African colonies and beyond to Lisboa with his precious cargo. The approaching weather worried him. Had he been able to, he would have been tempted to come about, to try to flee for the safety of Porto Grande; only, for the moment, there was no wind to fill his sails. To the north there was nowhere to shelter from the coming storm, nothing more than a foetid swamp backed by an impenetrable jungle. A sailor for over half his life, Diego's natural seamanship guided him. He and his ship were safer out at sea.

"Bring her round fifteen-degrees to port," Diego ordered. The rising sea, rolling inexorably towards him from the Indian Ocean to the south, gradually turned the gallant little ship until her bowsprit was aimed directly at the Equator. The swells became steeper. The rigging creaked as the wooden ship rocked monotonously. A puff of wind played with the mizzen sail. And another. The swells rolling towards the ship were developing into sharp waves with creamy white caps. The sky darkened rapidly, the clouds scudding low overhead on a collision course with the forest to the north. The wind, when it arrived in force, was sudden. With it came the first gigantic wave. Together they were violent, their combined strength devastating.

The little Portuguese ship lifted her bow so high she seemed determined to roll over on her back. The helmsman was washed overboard immediately as the wave cleared the decks. Dom Diego, the breath knocked out of him by the force of the initial onslaught, fought his way across the canted deck on his belly, making a grab for the wildly thrashing whipstaff.

"Hold on for your lives," a harsh voice called from the foredeck as two sailors were swept past in the scuppers.

The storm tossed the five hundred ton carrack carelessly aside, crashed over and through her. Diego's left hand shattered as he tried to take hold of the whipstaff. His right arm snapped at the elbow less than a second later as he reached for the blur of a steering pole with his other hand. *Esmerelda* tumbled broadside down the wave, burying herself in the remorseless sea as she went; her crew either swept away or clinging frantically to any handhold within reach.

Dom Diego was hurled from his ship, the wind tearing at his clothes and his mind, a howl of rage and terror ripped from his teeth. *Esmerelda* rolled over him in a maelstrom of foaming white surf, crushing him with her mainmast as she capsized. Cannons broke free of their positions and rammed bulkheads, each other and the thin protection of the ship's hull. Seams burst all along the waterline, the caulking ripped away. The Bay of Bengal poured in through a thousand cracks and holes. Trunnels, the wooden plugs which held the hull planking to the ship's ribs, rocketed from their beds under the pressure. Deadly wooden bullets, they fired viciously in all directions. Decks buckled, snapped, and were swept away by the storm. Less than a minute after the wind and wave hit *Esmerelda*, she was smashed to pieces.

The tropical tempest collected the shattered remains of the once proud carrack and drove them before it. Some of the wreckage was driven to the bottom, to be stirred restlessly by an eternity of oceanic motion. Larger items, mostly chaotic bundles of timber that had once been parts of the master's cabin and the lower decks, were swept before the storm to be pounded against the trees and mudflats of an alien shore.

Three sailors, clinging desperately to the flotsam and even more desperately to life, were swept far inland along an uncharted jungle river – only to be sucked back to the Bay of Bengal again on the outgoing tide as the storm abated. More dead than alive, they fetched up on the southernmost extremity of the forest. In full view of the sea, which they thought they understood, they sprawled on the thick brown ooze of a foreign land with their arms outstretched and tried not to die. Around them countless jagged shards of red pottery clung to the mud, empty of their precious oils. Above them the sundari trees, which gave the forest its name, were topless, their canopies of green shelter sheared off by the brutal force of the screaming wind.

Remnants of the once lovely *Esmerelda*, which had sailed out of Lisboa for the riches of the east, were scattered over a vast area – in the sea, and into rivers and creeks. The solid oak bowsprit rode on the crest of the wind's turmoil, flashing across the wilderness like a shiny wooden missile, to bury itself more than half its length in the fertile soil far inland. It stood amongst the foliage like a silent sentinel, as a highly polished memorial to the ill-fated ship and her dead crew. On the shore, the wreckage that lay about the three exhausted sailors was hardly recognizable as anything more than scrap wood.

Invisible in the thick dark forest, a pair of Royal Bengal tigers – a mother and her half-grown cub – stood up and stretched their cramped limbs. They shook the storm from their coats and their minds. Hungrily they sniffed the air, examining and tasting the messages carried on the breeze, before padding stealthily towards the seashore.

CHAPTER I

Bangladesh, 1990s

The warm air of late afternoon hung over the Sundarbans mangrove jungle. Languid and heavy, it waited for a breeze to trickle up the Passur River from the Bay of Bengal and find its way along the myriad side streams to cool the Ganges delta. Uniform green jungle foliage hung listlessly on both sides of the wide silt-laden brown water. On an orchid branch over the western bank, a kingfisher fluffed the brilliant blue feathers of its wings and preened its pale nut-brown chest. Raising its head, two restless dark eyes flickered over the river. A fisherman working alone in his boat under the palms on the same side offered no threat. Instead the kingfisher focused on a faint ripple on the nearby water. It tensed its red legs and took flight. Swooping low over the slow moving stream, it snatched a small fish in its flattened beak and flew back to its exotic perch. The jungle became still again.

Almost invisible on the same river bank, a full grown tiger stood silent. His magnificently groomed coat of burnished gold decorated with uneven vertical black stripes merged perfectly with the shafts of sunlight and the shadows of the trees. He took a careful, silent step forward, paused for scarcely a second. Without making a sound he took another step. Slowly, gently, silently. One more, then he crouched, lowering his body to the drying mud of low tide, peering through the fronds of the golpatta palms as he did so. He trembled from a volatile mix of tension, anticipation and a painful gnawing hunger. He hadn't eaten for many days, and then it was only a small monitor lizard. He needed this meal badly. As always, his survival depended on another's death.

A few paces away the fisherman sat in his boat with his back to the forest, slowly hauling in the heavy net. Scarcely able to control his need, the tiger wiped saliva from his lips with an impatient flick of a long pink tongue. Instinct and a lifetime of training kept him still. He waited, watching the fisherman pulling in his catch, removing a few fish, and piling the net in the boat. He eased his weight slightly to the right. The bullet still grated against a bone in his left paw, sending sporadic shafts of pain screaming through his nervous system. He had suffered much from his wound on the last few attempts at catching a deer. The pneumataphores, spiky wooden aerial roots of the sundari trees, had attacked him like miniature spears as, intent on his prey, he neglected to watch where he ran. A few days ago, during a chase, one root had probed deep into his wound, jarring a nerve and starting the bleeding all over again. He'd missed the deer that day and been in too much pain to try for any other creature since. Today he had to make a kill.

Nala, the fisherman, grunted intermittently as his sinewy black arms dragged the heavy net into his dingi. He talked to himself softly, muttering in a Hindi dialect, as he picked silvery fish from the net and tossed them on the growing pile of at his feet. He'd been on the river by himself for three days and he was ready to paddle back to Baidyamari on the incoming tide. Down river, others from his village would be taking in their nets. They had agreed to travel home with him in the half-light of early evening.

Under the floorboards, where the bilge water sloshed about in rhythm with the dingi's bobbing motion on the river, there was a good catch of hilsa and a dozen or so giant prawns. He had enough to feed his young wife so her firm dark breasts would produce milk for their baby son and, with this last haul, there would be some left over to sell in the village. Nala was accustomed to being alone. Unlike many fishermen who worked in twos and threes on one boat, or others who preferred to fish from their little wooden dingis in the company of other boats, he enjoyed the solitude of the river and the surrounding forest. He liked to watch the other jungle dwellers. He knew the names of all the creatures, and he knew their habits.

When he saw a mighty white-bellied sea eagle take off from its tree-top roost to hunt over the rivers, Nala watched carefully, well aware that the eagle could lead him to a shoal of feeding hilsa. He avoided the broad muddy riverbanks where the trees were distant from the river. There the powerful saltwater crocodiles liked to wriggle out of the river to warm their cold blood in the afternoon sun. He had no wish to see one close up. One swing of a big crocodile's tail, he knew, could reduce his fragile craft to matchwood. Rarely did he fish under the biggest baien trees. Too often a rowdy troop of monkeys frolicked among the branches shouting abuse at him and destroying the peace of the wilderness. But, they did have their uses. They were always ready to warn of approaching peril, if they saw it in time.

Near enough to the bright green palms to see their reflection in the river, Nala kept a strict watch on the jungle. He knew there were tigers in the Sundarbans but, although he had occasionally seen deep pugmarks, he had never seen the striped terror – alive or dead. Men told stories of man-eating tigers attacking the honey gatherers who invaded the forest in April and May each year. Nala knew a tiger had taken a woman from a village not far from where he sat, only a few weeks before. Although he was instinctively afraid of the big jungle cats, that fear did not keep him from his work. For the last thirteen of his twenty-three years he had fished this part of the river in safety, usually by himself. He remembered his father's words, "The Emperor of the forest is a shy creature; a noble creature. It is to be respected, not feared."

To a casual observer, had there been one, the almost invisible tiger could easily have been asleep, except for a very slight twitching at the end of his tail. As Nala leaned over the side of his dingi to pull in the last of the net, the tiger launched himself with the athletic grace bestowed on all cats. His muscles rippled with the sinuous movements of a serpent gliding across water. Every sinew stretched, taut with anxiety. He touched his right front paw momentarily beside the palms; his two hind paws landed soundlessly astride it. Without breaking his motion, he catapulted himself into the sunlight, over the few metres of mud, over the bow of the dingi and onto Nala's shoulders without making a sound.

A great splash sent waves billowing ashore as the two hit the water together and disappeared. The dingi rocked from side to side, in danger of turning over. The end of the net, where the weights hung, slid slowly over the gunwales, pulling the rest behind it in a jerky motion until the weights sunk into the silt on the riverbed. The fish Nala had freed from the mesh flopped in confusion on the wooden floor of the boat. A few managed to throw themselves into the warm water of the bilge as the dingi stood on its side for a second, in response to the sudden energy around it. From the safety of its orchid, the kingfisher watched waiting for its moment.

The tiger came up first, his proud head breaking the surface some ten metres out in the river. Nala's lifeless body hung limply in the huge jaws, like a flag in the midday heat. The tiger turned and paddled towards shore, his head turned to the right to keep his prey from under his legs. He held Nala by the scruff of the neck, exactly where he had first fastened his powerful jaws. Nala had died instantly, without knowledge of the terrifying teeth, his neck broken by the force of the tiger's charge. Bounding up the slope to the sanctuary of the jungle the tiger winced as he inadvertently put weight on his injured paw.

As quickly as he had appeared, he vanished. The only clues to his aggression were the empty dingi with the net hanging over the side, a few widening ripples on the water, and the trough-like furrow where he had dragged Nala up the muddy river bank beside him.

The kingfisher shook its head twice, launched into flight and skimmed one of the dead fisherman's catch into its beak; then returned to its perch on the orchid.

Less than a minute after the tiger had broken from cover, he finally settled down to a meal. He ate hurriedly, gorging himself on the human flesh. After a while, having eaten his fill, he slept fitfully for a time. Deep in the night he awoke, covered the remains of his kill with leaves, and went in search of water. When he was hungry again he would come back and finish what was left of his feast. Then, once more, part of his never-ending cycle of life, he would have to hunt, no matter how much his paw hurt.

◆ ◆ ◆

Gray Pendennis walked into his office in a Dhaka suburb and turned on an overhead fan.

"Good morning, Rab," he called out.

"Hi, Gray. Didn't expect to see you today. What time's your flight?"

Gray walked next door to his partner's office and dropped into a chair. On the carpet a black and white mongrel looked up at him, smiled and began to wag its tail.

"Hello, Lucifer, you old mutt. How are you this morning?"

The dog's tail thumped harder on the floor as it got up and ambled over to Gray. He reached out and fondled its ears as the dog placed a proprietary paw on his right knee.

"You look after this place while I'm gone, and don't let Rab work too hard. Okay?"

Looking up at Rab, he said, "I have a couple of hours before I need to leave for the airport. Is the coffee ready yet?"

"Almost. Hamid will bring it in soon."

With that a small man came in with two steaming mugs, one with black coffee and one with milk. He handed Gray the black and placed the white on Rab's desk.

"Thanks, Ham. I'll miss your coffee while I'm away."

"Yes, Mr. Gray. You will." Hamid smiled at his two bosses and went out.

Gray Pendennis and Rab Choudhury were both in their mid thirties; both attractive men, slim and athletic. There the physical similarities ended. Gray had a mop of red hair flecked with a few strands of premature silver. He had eyes the colour of a summer sky and a lightly tanned white skin with a lot of freckles. Rab, by contrast, was the colour of dark wood topped by straight black hair. His eyes were so dark as to be almost as black. They were both scientists specializing in zoology and dedicated to the study of Royal Bengal tigers. The two were a good team. Gray preferred being out in the field, while Rab enjoyed the office environment. They had met at university in the States and been friends ever since. For the past five years they had studied the tiger population in the Sundarbans, with particular emphasis on the big cats that enjoyed human meat – the man-eaters. On the door of their small suite of offices was the proud sign, PROJECT MAN-EATER.

"While I'm away for the next three weeks, Hassan and Ali will be in the forest, somewhere near Kotka. Will you send a message to them to keep a watch out for any suspicious activity, please? I am really concerned about the poaching. I'm convinced that that last poor bloody cat I found had been skinned and its carcass left for the scavengers – except for its paws, teeth and tail, they were missing too. There was no sign of any pelt whatsoever. If that tiger had died of natural causes or been killed by another, its teeth would still be intact in the jaw bone and at least patches of its coat would have survived, so would the paws. That skeleton without paws, teeth and tail was clear evidence of a poacher at work. We need to catch the bastard, and soon."

"I've already sent a note to Abdul. He's taking *Fatima* south from Mongla tomorrow with some forestry workers. He will deliver it to the guys by the end of the week."

♦ ♦ ♦

In the southwest corner of the jungle, close to the Indian border where the tropical forest spills over to share its lushness between two nations, a grey-painted military motorboat cruised slowly along another branch of the delta. In the stern, a pair of armed soldiers watched the jungle drift by. Amidships another steered a straight course, his eyes roaming from the river to an officer in the bow. Dressed in jungle green, with only two stars on his lapels to distinguish him from the others, the officer scanned the near bank through binoculars. He was tall with broad shoulders. A pair of brass wings fanning a silver parachute glinted briefly in the sunlight from the brow of his red beret. A high-powered rifle hung ominously from his right shoulder, a sinister dark line against the camouflage jacket. Without changing his stance, he signalled with one hand and the engine beat subsided. The boat wallowed slightly as it adjusted to the lack of forward motion. The officer lowered his binoculars.

"There," he pointed. The helmsman turned the boat to shore.

"Follow me," the officer ordered as he jumped ashore.

While one soldier tied the boat to a tree, the other two shouldered a pair of poles with a coarse net strung between them. Walking in single file the squad trekked inland for a few minutes. The helmsman, a sergeant, took the lead following faint waist-high blazes on trees with the Bangladeshi army general close behind. In a small clearing where dried bones lay scattered, they found a tiger lying on its side. The officer prodded the full-grown beast with the muzzle of his rifle.

"It is dead," he said with a smile. "You men, take the pelt, the paws, claws and the teeth. Put them all in the net. Leave the carcass."

"The poison works well, General," the sergeant grinned at him as the men set to work.

"Yes. The Chinese captain will pay well, too."

CHAPTER 2

Where two rivers join, well to the north of the Bay of Bengal, the tiger lazed on a grassy knoll on the riverbank in full view of the river, three days after he killed the fisherman. The mid-afternoon sun beat down with tropical ferocity. No creatures stirred, other than a Brahmini kite circling over a slight disturbance on the water. The tiger stood up and shook himself, staring down at his reflection in the river for a second or two. He licked at his injured paw, keeping the leg slightly bent to take the weight off it.

Taking its time, the tiger looked both ways, scanning the waters for signs of unnatural movement. The river was wide, a long swim even for powerful muscles, and it was dangerous. Out in the open, away from the muting effect of the forest, his exotic camouflage stood out like a beacon. Much as he enjoyed a swim, the tiger's instincts drove him to be careful. He had no real reason to cross the river that day, and no reason not to. Although, like most adult cats, he had a clearly defined territory of his own, the tiger was still a nomad. He followed scents borne on the wind and his own curiosity. Always he watched for prey.

Leaning forward he slid into the muddy brown water with scarcely a ripple. The current was weak, though the river was part of the mighty Ganges, the Holy Mother Ganga – life-blood of India, which flowed from the distant Himalayan Mountains to cross the northern plains until she exhausted herself in the Bay of Bengal. That afternoon, with the sun halfway to the horizon, the tiger had chosen his moment well. It was that time in the tidal cycle when the moon's influence was changing. The outgoing current and the incoming tide had ceased to clash. The rivers were swollen, much of the low-lying banks hidden, the waters moving hesitantly over and among the tree roots, causing the pneumataphores to keep their seals shut. The water cooled his body after the fierce heat of the day and soothed his burning wound. The tiger paddled steadily, without much effort, enjoying the effect of the moisture on his skin. A few water hyacinth plants drifted aimlessly around him, waiting for the vagaries of the tide to carry them to shore. Their pale blue flowers turned in faithful obeisance towards the sun, the soft green of their leaves licked clean by the gentle flow. Twigs and small branches turned lazily in the eddies, adding their dark brown tones to the natural palette. The slight pressure wave in front of the tiger's chest brushed them carelessly aside.

In the middle of the river he felt, rather than heard, an alien presence. He stopped paddling for a second and searched the river to the south, his eyes alert for danger. A few hundred metres downstream a riverboat nosed out from a side channel and turned in his direction. The throb of a powerful diesel engine trembled through the water to vibrate at his side. Instinctively the tiger struck out with powerful legs for the eastern shore of the Mirgamari River, where the palm fronds beckoned him to sanctuary.

"Daddy, look. There's something in the river!"

Richard Marshall, leaning against the wheelhouse talking to the helmsman, looked down at his daughter on the vee-shaped foredeck.

"Where, Tracy?"

"Over there." She pointed beyond the bow to an indistinct shape outlined against the brightness of the water. Marshall looked ahead. He raised his Nikon and auto-focus telephoto lens. There, in the middle of the river, a head the colour of a golden sunset was clearly visible. A tiger loomed large in his viewfinder. Holding his breath, Marshall pressed the shutter and let off a run of five shots.

"It's a tiger!" he yelled.

Tracy jumped up and down with excitement, her youthful energy and enthusiasm taking charge. Her arm remained extended, her index finger pointing to the tiger. Marshall ran up the metal rungs of the fixed ladder to the upper deck for a better look. His son, Simon, and wife, Jeannette, were already there with most of the other half-dozen passengers.

"Do you see it, Simon?" he asked as he pointed to the swimming tiger, now nearly three quarters of the way across the river. Simon nodded in silence, his mouth wide open in astonishment.

The helmsman steered the boat between the tiger and the shore, cutting off its shortest route to the anonymity of the forest. As the gap between the boat and tiger closed the throb of the engine died and the boat slowed. The tiger opened his mouth, displaying two rows of hideous, sharp teeth. He roared his anger at the boat, trying to increase his speed as he fled the approach of danger. Behind him the river swirled in his wake. On board everyone jumped at the booming voice. It sounded much too loud and much too deep to have come from one animal. The tiger's head with bared teeth, his shoulders, the length of his striped back, his ringed tail, all were visible above the surface. Beneath the murky river, out of sight, the four huge paws ploughed frantically at the water as he struggled to reach the forest. He didn't make it. The boat pushed between him and the shore, trapping him on the river.

The tiger bellowed with rage again; his terrifying voice reverberating its warning off the steel hull. Skimming across the water in shock wave formation it slammed into a barrier of disinterested trees, which threw it back as a series of soft mocking echoes. He turned to meet his tormentors, lashing out with his right front paw, sending sheets of water flying in all directions. On the foredeck, where Tracy stood, a boatman moved a coil of mooring line out of the way to prevent anyone tripping on it and falling overboard in the thrill of the moment. He turned to reach for a long-handled boathook, in case he needed to fend off the furious tiger, which gave every indication of preparing to attack the boat.

"Tracy, Get back! Get BACK!"

Marshall added his warning shouts to the bedlam as everyone on board yelled with excitement and surges of unspoken fear. Simon ran towards his little sister. Before he could jump to the foredeck where she stood, the tiger gave a mighty thrust and reached the boat. His right paw came up and scraped at the smooth metal deck. He could not get a grip. As he began to slide back to the water he forced his hind legs into motion. Thrashing the water, they propelled him up again. With a powerful lunge he reached up with his right paw to where Tracy stood rooted to the spot in sudden fear. The wicked claws hooked into her denim pants, closing on her leg in an unbreakable grip. The crewman with the boathook went into slow motion, mesmerised by the sight of the tiger so close. The motion of the boat and the tiger's own weight caused him to drop back heavily into the river with a noisy splash. With his claws embedded in Tracy's leg, she went with him, catapulting off the deck and striking the metal rail with her head before she flew over the tiger to hit the river behind him. The yells of surprise turned to screams of horror as Tracy disappeared from sight.

Marshall dropped his camera on the deck. Without a thought of the consequences, he hurled himself off the top deck in a near perfect racing dive. He hurtled over the tiger, clearing his head by much less than his own height, and hit the water close to where he had last seen Tracy.

The tiger bumped along the side of the riverboat, roaring with rage and fright, glaring in malevolent fury up at the humans above him. As the riverboat's stern passed he caught the back of his head on the tow rope linking the mother boat with its dingi and suffered a ducking, which did nothing to improve his humour. The rocking dingi smacked into the back of his head as he surfaced. Viciously he lashed out at this latest adversary, ripping long slivers of wood from the dingi's hull. He shook his head to clear his vision, looking around in panic, water dripping off his whiskers, his hair plastered to his head. In front of him, three or four of his own body lengths of open water separated him from the jungle. The tiger took his opportunity and escaped, streaking through the final stretch like a psychedelic torpedo. None saw him leave the river. No one saw him turn as he entered the forest and bared his teeth one last time before he vanished among the palms. No one saw him. They were all looking for Tracy. Marshall surfaced and looked wildly around.

"Can you see her?" He shouted desperately at those on board.

"No!" The answer echoed from a chorus of lips.

Two Bengali deckhands pulled the dingi up close, untied it and jumped aboard. They paddled with deep fast strokes over to Marshall, who was treading water. Together they hauled him over the side.

"Be careful, sir," one of them warned. "There are many crocodiles here."

Behind them the riverboat was turning, heading slowly back downstream to begin a simple search pattern, the decks lined with the crew and the remaining seven passengers. Marshall stood up in the dingi, willing Tracy to surface and to be alive, even as he understood she could not possibly have survived. A shout from the riverboat and an arm pointing straight ahead gave him sudden hope. Fifty metres away a patch of pink showed in contrast to the dirty silt-coloured river. Marshall didn't wait for the boatmen to start paddling. He dived over the side again, throwing himself into a racing crawl, his arms and legs churning the water to milky foam.

Tracy lay face down, her blonde hair spread out on the surface, her pink shirt clinging to her wet back, her denims and bare feet trailing slightly submerged. The left side of her head was a bloody mass of bruised tissue. One leg was badly torn. Marshall took his daughter in his arms, turned on his back and splashed back to the fast approaching dingi. Strong hands took Tracy from his grasp and laid her gently on her back on the bare floorboards. Marshall dragged himself over the gunwales after her.

For a long time – long after it was obvious there was no hope, Marshall fought to bring his child back to life in the dingi. Efficiently, expertly, without obvious emotion, the capable father pinched his daughter's nostrils and blew sharply into her mouth, in an effort to fill her body with life-giving air. He pumped her chest and then rolled her on her side in a vain attempt to force the river from her lungs. There was no sudden cough, no trickle of water from her lips. Tracy was already unconscious, close to death, when she hit the river. The meandering Mirgamari had simply sealed her fate.

Above Marshall and Tracy, lining the riverboat's rails, everyone stood still. Christians and Muslims alike prayed silently. The Christians with their hands clasped tightly together, Muslims fingering their worry beads. All eyes glistened with imminent teardrops as they watched the drama below. Jeannette and Simon clung to each other making no sound. Only the tears coursing down their cheeks expressed their grief. When Marshall finally picked Tracy's lifeless body up in his arms and passed her to the riverboat's captain, the despair on his face was apparent to all. Jeannette let out a long soul-shattering scream that echoed from shore to shore before finally whispering into infinity. Then she sank mercifully to the deck in a faint.

Deep in the jungle, the tiger heard the distraught mother's anguished cry. He stopped cleaning himself; raising his head, he looked in the direction of the river, snarled a reply, listened for a few seconds, then went back to his grooming as if nothing had happened.

In the day cabin, Marshall tenderly wrapped Tracy's body in her bright blue sleeping bag. Before he covered her face, he touched the bruised wound where her skull had fractured when she hit the rail as the tiger swept her off the boat. One leg of her blue jeans had a tear from knee to ankle. Down the beautifully formed slim leg and across her foot, wicked claws had carved three deep furrows. For once in his life Marshall lost control. His chest expanded as he took in a deep breath, his shoulders began to shake as he cradled the cocooned body in his arms. Great gut-racking sobs burst from him. The tears began to flow, staining the sky blue sleeping bag, transforming it into the midnight colour of eternity. For a long time he stood, letting his feelings flow, his arms pressing Tracy tightly to his chest.

♦ ♦ ♦

Marshall, at close to fifty, was a successful businessman. Outside the glass walls of his office a showroom of brand new Land Rovers and Range Rovers gleamed in the artificial light from artfully placed neon tubes. Above the entrance door a sign proudly proclaimed 'Marshall 4 X 4 (Richmond) Ltd'. In pride of place in the display hall, in front of a huge wall map of the world, was one Land Rover fully equipped for expedition use. The tough looking vehicle spelled adventure. From its Michelin XS desert tires to the spare fuel-can racks on both sides; from the custom designed seating to its galvanized steel roof rack, from the sturdy winch on the front bumper to the spare springs shackled to the rear. Beside it, in perfect formation, was set out a complete kit of typical expedition equipment. Marsh jokingly referred to it as his 'go anywhere get-away car'.

Born in Vancouver, but schooled in England, Marshall had journeyed to Kenya in his late teens. Encouraged by his artistic, Nairobi-born English mother and without hindrance from his austere Canadian father, he had become an East African safari guide. Although he had returned to

Vancouver in his early thirties to set himself up in business, he had remained a dedicated conservationist. Using ruthless determination, he had built his company from the start, with Jeannette's undeniable help. Not content with just selling adventure vehicles, he also offered complete expedition planning and support. As a result he had become a favoured consultant to adventure travel companies throughout Canada. Later, as his reputation grew, his expertise took him further afield.

Any visitor to either the Richmond showroom on a weekend, or the Marshall's spacious Steveston home anytime, could not help but be struck by two obvious facts. Each had an abundance of wildlife paintings and photographs, for Marshall was a better than average photographer – and his son, Simon, had inherited his grandmother's artistic talents. Perhaps more important, a little girl, wearing denim bib and brace overalls, was likely to appear from under a vehicle with a greasy wrench, or wander in from the garden and present one of her 'pets.'

Whenever possible, during school holidays, Marshall allowed the family to accompany him on his far-flung business trips. His wife, Jeannette, often fussed about safety, but he always assured her none of them would come to harm. The fortunate children had been within feeding distance of polar bears on Hudson Bay, grizzly bears in the Rocky Mountains, and whales in the Sea of Cortez. Two years earlier the family had spent a Christmas in Kenya, where Marshall had taken great delight in showing them his old haunts, including where he had come unpleasantly close to a rogue lion. On Marshall's current visit to the East, he had assignments as a consultant to adventure companies in Pakistan, India, and Bangladesh. Jeannette and the two children had joined him in Delhi only two weeks before. The jungle river trip had been a natural extension for the family as Marshall enjoyed Simon and Tracy's reactions to wildlife and unusual habitats. Now it had all gone horribly wrong. Marsh hugged his dead daughter to him. In a few weeks she would have celebrated her eleventh birthday.

As quickly as it had begun, Marsh's uncharacteristic display of distress passed. He settled his child's body gently on the leather covered bench seat. Carefully he placed a chair against it, to ensure no unexpected movement could cause her to roll to the floor. He wiped his eyes on his white linen handkerchief, blew his nose hard, took a last look at the pathetic bundle, and opened the door.

The riverboat was turning into another narrow channel, a short cut to avoid a huge U bend in the river, saving an hour's travelling. Almost within reach the mangroves dipped their branches in respect. Ignorant of the tragedy, a troop of monkeys chattered inanely from their perches high in the tree as the boat passed. Marshall saw none of it. He heard nothing. He simply stood at the rail staring directly ahead, his hands by his side, his face filled with restrained fury and overwhelming grief.

"One day, you bastard, I will kill you," he swore.

The tiger, his daughter's death, his futile swim in the jungle river, had combined to wash away more than three decades of committed conservationism. Marshall was at a crossroads. His life could never be the same.

Gray heard the news in Montreal, on the first leg of a fundraising tour across Canada. Rab's message had come in while he was en route from Dhaka. He read it with concern but, far away as he was, there was nothing he could do or say to ease the family's grief.

CHAPTER 3

"Ladies and gentlemen: Professor Graham Pendennis!"

Gray moved his chair back on the smooth stage of the Fairmont Vancouver Hotel, stood up and covered the five paces to the podium in three strides. He pushed his wire-rimmed glasses up to the bridge of his long thin nose, looked at the assembly as if startled to see them there and reached into his inside coat pocket for his notes. He unfolded the sheets of white paper; smoothed them with both hands. His eyes glanced around the ballroom as he began to speak.

"Good evening. It is indeed an honour, Ladies and Gentlemen, to be invited to attend this banquet and to have the opportunity of telling you something of the work we have accomplished so far on Project Man-Eater, and of the work in progress."

He paused. His blue eyes flicked to the top page of his notes and back to the two hundred or so dining tables, each with its eight guests.

"I first became interested in tigers when I was a teenager on a school trip to Europe. In an old cemetery at Malmesbury Abbey, in Gloucestershire, England, I found an unusual gravestone. Faded and worn with age, the stone is still readable. It is a memorial to a lady by the name of Hannah Twynoy who, it says, died in October 1703 at the age of thirty-three. The inscription reads: 'In bloom of life she's snatched from hence. She had not room to make defence; for Tyger fierce took life away. And here she lies in a bed of clay, until the Resurrection Day'. That simple piece of doggerel wandered around my head as I toured the great cities of Europe with my school friends. I could almost see Hannah Twynoy, product of a much gentler era, being ravaged by that tiger. My most vivid memory of that trip, to this day, is not Paris or Venice, nor London. My strongest memory is of that headstone. From the day my next school term started I have studied zoology and associated sciences, with special emphasis on tigers – Royal Bengal tigers. After some twenty years, I believe I know something of their habits."

He smiled for the first time, his eyes lighting up his face. "Panthera tigris tigris, the Royal Bengal tiger, is an exceedingly beautiful creature. It is also an eminently dangerous member of the wild kingdom. That fact aside, it is, sadly, an endangered species. Less than one hundred years ago there were, it is estimated, more than 40,000 tigers roaming the Indian sub-continent. Today, as a result of indiscriminate hunting in the early part of the twentieth century, the more recent population explosion and the resulting deforestation, the number of tigers left in the wild throughout the Indian sub-continent is less than one tenth of that figure. It is quite possible that the total number of wild tigers throughout Asia and, therefore, the world, is far less than four thousand."

"Yes, the Royal Bengal tiger really is an endangered species. Its survival is in our hands, yours and mine. We need to work fast to ensure the work of poachers does not hasten the tiger's journey to extinction. Various projects directed at the study of large cats on the Indian sub-continent are working constantly to ensure, not just the survival of the tiger, but a substantial future increase in population numbers of all large wild cats in that part of Asia. Most of those projects are funded and operated by government agencies. A couple, such as Project Man-Eater, are funded through public and corporate donations."

"Our work at Project Man-Eater runs, in some ways, parallel to the work of the important studies of the Asian government agencies. We certainly work in harmony with their personnel, in the field and in our respective project offices. All information gathered from our project is passed on to a central computer in Calcutta. Any and all information the other project scientists collect relating to man-eaters is relayed immediately to the same computer and on to us. You may be thinking that having rather similar projects working together, or in tandem, is a waste of time, personnel and funds. I'm happy to say you would be wrong. The study of the man-eating tiger is just one aspect of the overall tiger study. It is, however, of great importance if we are to understand, once and for all, what turns a wild animal, such as a tiger, into a killer of Homo sapiens, when it has an abundance of natural prey. It is also, I suspect, quite important to potential victims: those whose work takes them daily into the forests where the few remaining tigers hunt." He smiled shyly at them, not sure if his attempt at humour was appropriate or not."

At a table in the front row, some distance to the left of the speaker's podium, a distinguished looking man with short silver hair scribbled rapidly in a stenographer's notebook. Gray saw him as he paused to accept the audience's polite chuckles.

"The study of man-eating tigers is not new. In an 1891 publication on the fauna of India, W. T. Blanford spoke of the deaths, by tiger attack, of 4,218 people between 1860 and 1866 in the Sundarbans. Since 1965 regular records have been kept of fatalities from tiger attacks in the Indian part of the Sundarbans. Between 1975 and 1989 there were 521 deaths by tigers in that area. Across the border in Bangladesh a similar number of deaths were recorded in that country's half of the Sundarbans. These records show, without doubt, that forestry workers of all kinds are constantly in danger. During the 1960's and early 70's, on average 1,350 honey gatherers entered the forest during the short season in April and May. Most years there have been sixteen or seventeen fatalities directly attributed to tiger attacks. Honey gatherers, for reasons as yet unknown, are most at risk. Fishermen, of whom there are a considerably larger number in the forest at any given time – as many as 25,000 per year, suffer on average only twelve deaths from tiger attacks per annum."

At the back of the room a waiter tripped on a carelessly placed purse strap, causing him to drop a tray of dirty glasses. The thick pile of the carpet absorbed most of the crash, though not enough to completely deaden the sound. Gray peered in the direction of the disturbance, raised his eyebrows and smiled as he continued.

"We formed Project Man-Eater nearly seven years ago on my third visit to Bangladesh. During that extended stay I took the opportunity of seeing as much of the Sundarbans as possible, often alone, although I spent one week in the company of six Bangladeshi officials and an armed tracker. I didn't see a tiger on that occasion; though I did stand on the spot where a tiger had made a kill only a short time before, beside a tiger watchtower. Strangely, that unseen tiger was to have a substantial impact on my professional life. As a result of my jungle adventures and the stories I kept hearing of man-eating tigers – stories which were almost identical to tales I had heard in India – I put together the proposal which became Project Man-Eater. In the first year we amassed a considerable amount of data on the subject and created the link between ourselves and Project Tiger."

Two tables back from the stage, directly in line with the lectern, Melissa Anjuman de Kuyper propped her chin on her right thumb. Her middle finger settled in the hollow between her lower lip and her chin, while her index finger braced the elegant cheekbone on the right side of her face. Her elbow rested on the edge of the table, causing her to lean forward slightly displaying enough cleavage to create interest, without actually showing anything more than a hint of her perfectly formed breasts. Known to her family and friends as Asia, she had been born in Surrey, just outside Vancouver, daughter of a Dutch Canadian father and a Bengali mother.

There were many other beautiful women in the room that evening. None could match the twenty-seven-year-old Asia for her exotic mix of east and west. She was a perfect blend. Skin the colour of creamy coffee, tinted with the luxury of gold, was complimented by the tight white silk sheath reaching to her ankles. Asia's hair, drawn securely back to emphasise her high oriental cheekbones, fell in one long braid of inky black to the seat of her chair. Her eyes held the highlights of both her parents' eyes. She would have said they were blue with dark brown flecks. Others had said they were dark brown with blue flecks. Colourful and fascinating they certainly were. At that moment they were busy studying the speaker intently. She decided he looked like an elegantly designed version of the 1980's rock star Mick Hucknall.

Gray, who had acquired the lecturer's habit of scanning the audience for one face he could talk to while appearing to embrace the complete room, had noticed Asia when he glanced up at the end of his first sentence. She was his focal point, as he had become hers. He struggled to keep his concentration, his mind and body enchanted by the exotic Eurasian woman.

Beside Asia, to her right, her husband of three years was busy flirting with Amanda Hawkins. Amanda, daughter of a Canadian film-maker and his wife, and 'sexily single', as she described herself, had a reputation for being available, especially to her friends' husbands. She loved to be touched and men loved to touch her. Tall, with a slim, but curvy figure and long wavy blonde hair, she was as near to perfect as possible, until she smiled; then one noticed her face was slightly lopsided. The flaw diminished the perfection; made her appear more approachable.

Amanda's sexuality started early in life. As a child she liked to hang on the door handles of her bedroom, with the door clasped between her knees and pressed firmly against her immature body. As she swung back and forth, she moved against the edge of the door. Amanda didn't understand what was happening but the warm tingling sensation between her legs made the exercise a favourite sport. Only later, as she experimented with her own fingers, did Amanda learn, to her delight, that she didn't really need the door at all.

Asia ignored her husband's transparent flirting for the time being, most of her concentration focused on the professor and his message.

Julian slid one hand up Amanda's left thigh. The floor length red skirt, slit to within a fraction of the top of her thighs, posed no barrier. Amanda uncrossed her legs, draping the loose folds of silk over Julian's hand. Enjoying Julian's touch, Amanda stroked her own right thigh with one hand. She shivered involuntarily, anticipating the magic, savouring the wait. She sighed as Julian's fingers danced lightly over her bare upper leg. Opening her eyes, she winked at him. A broad smile spread across his face in return.

"If you keep that up, I'll come right here," she whispered, louder than she intended. Asia turned and looked at her for a second, her face a mask. Julian coughed nervously, guiltily placing his free hand on his wife's thigh. Unfazed, Amanda returned Asia's stare.

Asia picked up her fork and stabbed Julian's conciliatory left hand. The sudden intense pain brought a muffled "Fuck!" from Julian as Asia placed the fork back on the table, still apparently engrossed in Gray Pendennis and man-eating tigers.

"In recent years we have collected volumes of data on a series of tiger-related deaths in the Sundarbans of Bangladesh."

Gray recognized Julian, a wealthy and well-known amateur underwater archaeologist he had met once before, as the handsome man said something sharply to the Asian beauty, stuck his left hand up to his mouth for a second, as if kissing it, clamped a handkerchief over it and left the table hurriedly. The dark, hypnotic eyes on the woman never once left Gray's face.

Gray, who had been in the process of swinging his line of vision quickly around the room, settled on Amanda as, apparently unconcerned by Julian's hurried departure, she crossed her legs ostentatiously. In doing so, her slit skirt fell open revealing each leg's full, gloriously shaped length. For a second his gaze lingered on her thighs, long enough for Asia to look sideways at Amanda and back to Gray again. His eyes met hers and she allowed just the ghost of an amused smile to play briefly on her lips. Gray looked down at his notes, trying to keep the grin off his own face.

"We are convinced that all the deaths in the last three years or so, in one quite large area, can be attributed to one tiger. There is no real pattern, no regularity of aggression. Not even constant sightings near the few villages. There are, however, a few strong clues that point the finger of guilt at just one big male tiger. I believe he has taken up to fifty-seven lives. That's nineteen human kills per year!"

He scanned the audience, looking from face to face without lingering. All eyes were on him, waiting for him to continue. The figure in white watched him with a slight smile, as if willing him to address his remarks to her alone.

"We know this man-eater is lame. I call him Timur, after the fourteenth century Mongol warrior Timur-Leng, who was similarly afflicted. Only a few months ago Timur was accidentally shot in his left front paw, while trying to take an old man from the edge of a fishing camp near a nature reserve close to the coast. Since that time he has been relatively easy to identify as his tracks, with one softly defined pugmark, are not difficult for a skilled tracker to follow. Villagers who saw him attack the old man maintain he has a v-shaped notch in his right ear.

Timur offers us yet another distinctive guide to his identity. Most tiger pugmarks show a triangular shaped main pad positioned behind four toe pads. Normally, on the main pad, the base line is a series of three ellipses. On Timur's right front paw the main pad has four distinct ellipses along the base. That tell-tale pugmark has been seen in the vicinity of all fifty-seven kills in the last three years."

Gray paused and took a sip of water, taking advantage of his simple action to study Asia over the rim of the glass. She was still watching him.

"Contrary to what I have just said about Timur being easy to identify, he is not easy, even for an expert, to follow effectively for long. Timur is a crafty old tiger, estimated to be at least ten years old, possibly more. He likes to swim, regularly. On the few occasions he has been tracked, his spoor either disappears at the edge of a river, or has been washed away by tidal action. It's not unusual for a full-grown tiger to roam forty kilometres in one night. Timur, as far as we can ascertain, is an ardent traveller. He either controls a far larger territory than any tiger I have ever heard of, or he just doesn't give a hoot about other tigers and their domains."

Gray turned his head and shoulders to look at the screen on the wall behind him. A few moments before there had been a magnificent portrait of a lordly male tiger staring at the assembly. In its place a multi-coloured map of a vast river delta spread over the backdrop. Gray picked up a slim black remote control unit and shone a pencil thin laser beam of red on the map, highlighting a village on the east bank of a narrow river.

"Long before he was shot, Timur's tracks were found here, near this village. A woman disappeared about that time. Way down here, close to the Bay of Bengal, beside the government rest house at Kotka, a fisherman's half eaten body was found early one morning. Tiger tracks were clearly marked in the soft earth. The main pad on the right front paw matches Timur's unusual pad exactly. Timur's tracks have been seen here, in Jawtoli field, where there is a tiger watchtower, the same tower I mentioned earlier. They have been seen here on Tinkona Island. And over here where, it seems, Timur likes to take a stroll along a sunny silvery white beach with the sea for company."

Gray turned back to the audience. The map faded and another picture, of a tiger walking on a beach, took its place. Asia smiled and nodded in appreciation at the sudden element of flamboyance, aware that the tiger in the stunning photograph had to be Timur and that Gray had been the photographer.

"Minutes after I took this photograph, from a boat about fifty metres off shore, the tiger changed pace and direction. He looked at our boat for a second, turned and presented his tail, then melted into the long grass in the background. When we went ashore, with an armed guard, all that was left was a wonderful set of autographed prints. Timur, for it was he, had stamped his signature on the sand for hundreds of metres. We took photographs and made plaster casts to compare with others in Timur's file. The pugmarks matched perfectly. I and another member of my staff had been searching for that arrogant old tyrant for over a year, without much success. Never in our wildest dreams did we expect to find him taking a leisurely morning walk on a pristine beach."

Gray half turned again and glanced at Timur on the screen before he continued.

"You see Timur as a healthy adult. I took this photograph last October, four and a half months before he was shot in the paw. When we saw him it was quite apparent he had been scouting the fishing village at the aptly named 'Tiger Point' for an easy meal. We found his tracks led straight back to the village. That same evening, while we were at the rest house at Kotka, a tiger took two young boys from a temporary fishing camp at the other end of this beach within an hour of each other. No other tiger tracks were visible, only Timur's. That camp is within sight of Kotka and no more than one kilometre from the tiger watchtower on Jawtoli Field. When we received the news early that morning we tried to track him but, as so often happened, Timur had vanished."

Gray paused again as Julian returned to his table. This time he sat with both hands visible, one of them covered in a white cloth.

"Timur was not seen again in that area, or anywhere else for that matter, until late February this year. We know his main territory well and we have shown villagers what to look for in his pugmarks. Throughout the winter it was as if Timur did not exist. Not once was he, or his tracks, seen in his usual haunts. There were no tiger related deaths reported from his area, or from adjacent territories. At first I felt he might have fallen victim to a poacher, or to a stronger rival. And yet, deep inside, despite the lack of evidence, I knew he was alive. Not a very scientific attitude, I know." He said the last few words slowly, in almost a whisper.

Gray's face did not change, only his hands, gripping tightly on either side of the lectern betrayed his struggle to control his emotions. He looked through and beyond his audience, his mind back in the jungles of Bangladesh, his feet following a man-eater's trail. Asia could almost feel the tiger's presence: the tension around Gray was so strong.

"In March Timur struck again. As I told you earlier, an old man was attacked at a fishing camp near the coast. It was the same encampment where Timur had killed the two boys. This time the tiger charged in broad daylight, singling out the old man from a small crowd of fishermen. Some fired a few blanks to try to scare him off, without success. Someone fired wildly with a rifle, fortunately missing everybody. A live round, however, ricocheted off a rock striking the tiger in the left front paw. He let go of the old man and escaped into the forest, leaving spots of blood to mark his flight. His victim, not surprisingly, died from his injuries a few minutes after the assault. Thoroughly shaken by the incident, no one had the nerve to track the tiger that day but, the tracks leading into and out of the area told their own tale: the tiger was Timur. One of the men, when questioned a day later, insisted the tiger had a notch in one ear, though he did not remember which ear. Two other fishermen, who claimed they were close enough to touch the tiger, insisted the right ear was notched."

Gray silently counted to ten, taking his time, letting the tiger's image sink in. He studied the people in the balconies before skimming his eyes back to the Asian. He was sure he had seen her somewhere before.

"Project Man-Eater has two experienced trackers searching for that tiger as I speak, although, if the report I received yesterday is accurate, Hassan and Ali are not having much success. The man-eater has disappeared once more. We have to catch Timur before he kills again, or before someone shoots him. Each time there is documented proof of a tiger related death anywhere in the Sundarbans of India or Bangladesh, more pressure is applied on the respective governments to do something concrete about it. If we cannot locate and take Timur out of circulation very soon, we will have a major problem on our hands. We have already been warned by two of our benefactors that they are under considerable duress, from unnamed sources, to withdraw their support for our project. If that happens I think Timur will be ruthlessly hunted and disposed of, even though it is, officially, illegal to kill a tiger. All armed guards and trackers in the forest have a blank cartridge in the rifle's chamber and live ammunition in the magazine. That blank charge's purpose is to scare a tiger away. Some of the braver men have two blanks followed by live rounds. If the authorities place a bounty on Timur's head, those blanks will be removed from the magazines. It follows that, if Timur is hunted, other innocent tigers will die as well. Few hunters will take the trouble to ask a tiger to show its front paws for inspection before opening fire."

Gray took hold of the microphone in his right hand. He lifted it out of its cradle and, flicking the cord behind him, moved to stand in full view in the centre of the stage. Casually he raised one foot and placed the highly polished black shoe on one of the footlights. Leaning forward slightly, he surveyed his silent public, like a politician assessing a group of voters.

"Tigers have roamed this earth of ours for millions of years. We know that from fossils found in a cave in Siberia.

At first it was the sabre-toothed tiger, which, we believe, became extinct as recently as 10,000 years ago. Since then mankind has witnessed the rise and decline of the Siberian tiger, the Caspian tiger – now almost certainly extinct in the wild, the South China tiger, the Indo-Chinese tiger, Sumatran tiger, Javan tiger, Bali tiger – another which is almost certainly extinct – and the Royal Bengal tiger. Those tigers have a right to be here, just as you have a right to be here and just as I have a right to be here. By coming to dinner in this great ballroom tonight, you have pledged to help me, and my staff, delay by a few more days, weeks, months, perhaps years, the possibility of the extinction of the Royal Bengal tiger. A few of you have graciously consented to meet with me later this evening to offer additional support. I thank you all from the bottom of my heart. Far away in Bangladesh, Rabindranath Choudhury, my co-director of Project Man-Eater – a long-time colleague and close friend – thanks you, as do all those who work for the organisation: volunteers and employees."

He took his foot slowly off the black cowl of the footlight and stood up straight, his eyes locked on Asia's. His voice became gentle.

"Sometimes when I'm in the mangrove forest at the top of the Bay of Bengal I sense another presence. Although I can't see him, or her, I know the tiger is there, watching me and waiting. The tiger does not understand time. The Emperor of the jungle doesn't know there is so little time left. No time to lie around in the forest waiting. Time, in this context, belongs to us. We have it, though it is dwindling fast. We must make every second count. For the sake of all endangered species on this planet – for the sake of the Royal Bengal tiger. For the sake of future generations, that they may have the opportunity of seeing nature's most dazzling creation. And for the sake of Timur, who only kills when he is hungry. Your help can and will save human lives in the jungle. Your help can and, I sincerely hope, will assist us in saving the tiger from extinction. Thank you."

Gray gave a slight bow, replaced the microphone and returned to his seat. For a long time, the applause echoed through the ballroom. Gray smiled and nodded his head with pleasure. Twice he got up and waved both his hands above his head in acknowledgement.

"Well done, Professor. I think you've touched more than their wallets tonight," the master of ceremonies said in a stage whisper as he patted Gray on the shoulder before taking his place at the podium. Gray waved once more as the MC began to speak, then slid behind the curtain, going in search of a glass, some ice and a stiff drink. He found them all in the room set aside for the private gathering. As the guests were still in the main hall, and would be for fifteen minutes or so, Gray had the place virtually to himself.

A couple of waiters studied him, without being too obvious, as he sat on a hard chair, stretched his legs out straight in front of him and took a long pull on his drink. He closed his eyes and sighed. He had finally worked out where he had seen the girl before.

"Pendennis!" The voice broke into his reverie. It was harsh. Belligerent. Startled, Gray opened his eyes and looked up. The man he had noticed earlier; the 'journalist' with the silver-grey hair, stood threateningly before him.

CHAPTER 4

Timur waited patiently for the deer to graze closer to his hideout. In the past few weeks he had roamed far and wide across his territory, always returning to the grassy meadow. He was hungry again but his left paw hurt. He wasn't in the mood for a long chase. Selecting the closest fawn as his target, he threaded his way out of the thicket, keeping his profile low. Without warning, the herd of spotted deer scattered. Timur's intended meal vanished in a flurry of white spots as his latest mate, trailed by her cub, exploded into the open. The tigress hit a patch of sand on her second bound. Her ears came up and twitched in alarm as she saw Timur and swivelled abruptly sideways, sending a puff of dusty sand over her cub. As one they fled back to the darkness of the forest. Timur groaned softly, his proud head only partly hidden by the overhanging twigs of his lair. He bared his teeth in annoyance, knowing he was unable to chase and run down a panic-stricken deer.

Two tiger trackers entered Jawtoli meadow from the northeast end together. In the distance, a kilometre or more to the south, the tiger watchtower was barely visible to them. Hassan and Ali, the two trackers, talked in low tones as they searched for tiger tracks. As yet unaware of their presence, Timur ambled over to the tower and squirted his scent on the base. He pushed the rickety gate open with his nose and sniffed. Slowly, with immense caution, he circled the tower inside the fence. Nothing alarmed him. He tentatively placed one paw on the first wooden step. Nothing happened. With his tail fully extended he took another step with renewed confidence. Exercising caution, he climbed higher and higher.

At the top he surveyed his domain, looking at all points of the compass. In the north, almost out of sight, two figures moved in the grass. Timur watched them. He released a low 'Awoom,' not loud enough to reach the humans, but enough to scare all other creatures within hearing. For a few minutes he stood silently on the top platform. Only the conical tin roof rose above the jungle's emperor. A furry chin rested on a wooden rail; two golden eyes switched from side to side. The men were much closer. Timur left his lofty perch. Without leaving any scratches or other indications of his call, he trotted down the squared staircase on three legs and buried himself in the longest grass. From there he crept silently to his thicket.

Hassan and Ali split up. Ali went directly to the tower. Timur's fresh tracks were all around. The damp stain, where Timur had reversed his penis and ejected his scent between his hind legs, was obvious to any tracker. The mixture of urine and anal gland secretion left a pungent odour to warn off competing males. To Ali it smelled of danger. He ran up the tower to warn Hassan that Timur was close.

More than halfway down the field, Hassan knelt on one knee. In the sand he touched a faint imprint where a fully-grown tiger had stepped. Without changing position, Hassan carefully checked the sand all around him. Ten paces to his left, the forest cast a mid-morning shadow on the scrubs of grass. Ahead of him, some hundred and fifty metres away, on the upper level of the tiger watchtower, Ali held up one hand with his fingers splayed to represent a pugmark. He pointed to the base of the tower. Hassan acknowledged with a wave and returned the signal, pointing at the ground around him.

Ali surveyed the extent of Jawtoli through his binoculars, panning left and right until he had covered the field. To his right the long grasses of the field stood vertical beyond Hassan and the large oval patch of sand. For a few moments, he studied the uneven thicket, seeing no sign of danger. He focused on Hassan who was still crouched on the sand. Enlarging his field of vision, Ali took in much of the meadow. Nothing moved. That fact alone kept him vigilant. It was rare for Jawtoli to be so devoid of activity.

Hassan noted where the tiger had smudged its own track as it made a quick direction change to the left. He could see that the tiger had come out of the forest on the run, probably chasing a deer. Something had startled it, sending it bounding back to the forest. Hassan guessed it had been he and Ali as they worked their way up the middle of the field. They had seen deer ahead of them and recorded their flight, assuming they had been the cause. Now he knew differently. There was more than one adult tiger in the vicinity. He looked up towards Ali and fanned his hand over the ground to show there were many tracks around him.

The clearest pugmark was a right front paw. The left was on harder ground and badly distorted by the tiger's tight turn. Close to the right pugmark another indentation caught Hassan's attention. A miniature replica, only a quarter of the size, was just visible. Hassan felt the hair begin to rise on the back of his neck. He hadn't found Timur. What he had found was potentially even more dangerous: a female with a cub no more than three months old. The female was, almost certainly, one of Timur's mates and the cub one of his offspring. This was Timur's prime territory.

Hassan peered at the forest, trying to pick out the highlights of a large cat's unblinking eyes. He sniffed the tracks and he sniffed the wind, scooping invisible smells to his nostrils with one hand. He clicked off the safety catch on his rifle and straightened his legs. He knew exactly where the tigress and her cub were hiding. He couldn't see them, though he was sure they could see him. But he knew. Slowly he walked towards the tower, keeping his eyes on the trees to his left. For thirty heart-thumping paces he paralleled the forest. For the same distance, he knew, the tigress walked with him, hidden by the dense bush. He was sure the tigress would have left the cub in a secluded spot, where she would have ordered it not to move or make a sound. On a slight rise Hassan moved away from the unseen danger and cut through the grass in a straight line for the tower. As he changed direction, the tigress loped back to her cub and moved deep into the forest.

Ali frowned as he watched Hassan from the top of the tower, wondering at his manner. He made another quick sweep of the area with his glasses, seeing nothing important. Hassan detoured around the large thicket to avoid the cloying mud of a drying water hole. For a few seconds only he and Ali were out of each other's sight. Ali let his binoculars hang from the strap round his neck and raised his rifle. Over his perspiration, he felt the chill of fear. As best he could, even though he couldn't see him, he kept Hassan covered.

Timur had watched as the men separated, one following the path directly to the tower, the other cutting across the field to the outer rim. Neither man could possibly see him. Both had crossed his tracks of the previous night, without noticing them in the thick long grass. Both would soon know he was somewhere in or near the meadow.

Hassan, satisfied the tigress would not attack as he left her immediate vicinity, continued his inspection of the terrain. A few steps from the untidy maze of overgrown bushes, he stopped to examine broken stalks of grass. The breaks were clean and dry; no sap bled from the fractures. Hassan reached for a healthy stalk and broke it in half. He watched, no sap there either. He looked closer at the breaks. A tiny bead of moisture formed on the stalk he had just injured. The others remained dry. Deciding the grass had nothing more to tell him he moved on. The field was soft under his feet, the sand replaced by rich dark fertile soil. The expert tracker took his time, stopping every few steps to move the grass aside with his hand. Another cluster of bent stems warned him to be cautious. He pulled them towards him, examining the ground with professional care. Diagonally across his path, where the tough grass entered the black earth, was a big pugmark. Hassan ran the fingers of his right hand over the outline. He counted the depressions formed by the four toes. He traced the triangle of the main pad, feeling a shiver of anticipation up his spine as he recognized the unusual design of four ellipses along the base line. His left thumb checked the safety catch of his rifle to make sure it was off as he called, "Ali, come here!"

Timur, for all his muscular bulk, could slither like a snake when the situation called for it. He came out of the thicket without disturbing a twig, without rustling a leaf, without damaging a blade of grass. His own length from the crouching man, he came to all fours. His leg muscles trembled and bulged as he coiled for his deadly spring. Hassan saw a shadow looming over him.

He looked up, expecting to see Ali. Instead, with his final second of sight, he saw a tiger. Timur bit right through his skull, the cracking of the hard bone lost as Hassan involuntarily pulled the trigger on his rifle. The loud retort from the blank cartridge, so close to his ears, frightened Timur into releasing his deadly grip. The sudden stinging pain of the powder burns on his chest caused him to turn and run. At full speed, with no prey to hinder him and no thought for his old injury, Timur escaped.

Ali heard Hassan's call from the top of the tower. He raced down the steps four at a time and was halfway round the thicket when Hassan's gun went off. Instinctively he ducked his head. He sensed, rather than saw, Timur speeding through the greenery. He whipped his rifle up and took rapid aim. As he pulled the trigger he was aware of the futility of his action. Timur was out of sight before the blank cartridge cracked its benign message.

"Hassan. Hassan. Where are you?" Ali called, his rifle still held high. There was no answer. Ali took a couple of steps forward, his eyes scanning left to right. He turned in a tight circle, his rifle at the ready. There was no sign of the tiger. Ali moved forward a few more steps and found Hassan on his back in a flattened circle of grass, his head bloodied and twisted at an odd angle. In the crook of his arm, the rifle's stock lay impotent. Ali picked up the rifle, flicked the safety on and slung it over his shoulder. He took hold of Hassan's right hand and pulled him to his feet. As the lifeless body slumped against him, Ali stooped and let it fall over his shoulder. Holding one arm to stop his heavy burden dropping to the ground, Ali stumbled back past the tower and along the path to the wooden jetty. Three times he slowed to look behind him. No threat presented itself.

Early that morning the two men had left a borrowed dingi tied to the jetty. It was still there. Ali leaned the two rifles against an upright post and staggered down the uneven steps. As gently as he could he began to lower Hassan, feet first, into the boat.

Ali was never quite sure what happened next. One second he was holding Hassan's body by the upper arms, the next second he was under water. Like an express train Timur had come down the path. He didn't slow. He didn't take note of the jetty. The enraged, hungry tiger flew through the air from the high bank, missing Ali by the thickness of a man's skin. He snatched Hassan in mid-flight and hit the water halfway across the river. Knocked off balance, Ali somersaulted after them. When Ali surfaced, coughing and spluttering, choking on the soupy river, all he could see was the empty boat and the jetty. He spun in the water.

Dragging himself and Hassan up the opposite bank, Timur struggled through a tangle of vines. Ali splashed his way to the steps, having trouble keeping his feet in the thick slimy mud. He ran up the worn planks, spraying muddy water to left and right. In his haste, he knocked one rifle over, almost sending it off the side of the jetty to the river below. Ali seized it with both hands, aimed it at Timur and pulled the trigger. Nothing happened. Cursing loudly he thumbed the safety catch and aimed again. Timur had already extricated himself from the vines, then he and his meal were gone. Ali fired anyway, hearing the bullet whine as it ricocheted off a tree. He listened. No cry of pain followed the shell's murderous passage. The jungle was silent.

Ali tossed both rifles into the dingi, untied it and pushed himself into the stream. Standing with his legs apart at one end of the boat, his chest heaving, he frantically thrashed the water with the one long oar. Coming out of the side stream, to cross the main river, he could see fishermen on the far shore shading their eyes against the sun in an effort to see what the noise was about.

"Tiger! Tiger!" Ali screamed. "He has killed Hassan."

CHAPTER 6

"Pendennis!"

Warned by the man's aggressive tone, Gray got to his feet, casting a quick glance to the door where a security guard stood talking to a waiter.

"Yes? I'm Pendennis. What can I do for you?"

"My name's Marshall. Richard Marshall," he said, without expression on his face. "You didn't mention my daughter in your litany of tiger kills."

For a moment Gray was silent, trying to tidy his thoughts as he looked into Marshall's deep eyes. They made him feel strangely uncomfortable; there was no life in them at all: no sparkle, no apparent highlights – only two empty green pits.

"I'm sorry, I don't know what you are talking about," Gray apologized without knowing why.

"Your man-eating tiger, the one you call Timur, he killed my daughter three weeks ago." The hard voice spat the words through caustic lips. There was still no expression on Marshall's face as he spoke. Gray recovered his composure.

"Are you referring to the young girl who got knocked off a river boat by a tiger in the Sundarbans?" he asked, fairly sure of the answer.

"Yes. That's my daughter, Tracy," Marshall nodded. For the first time, a shadow passed over his eyes. His lips tightened almost imperceptibly.

"I'm sorry, I really am. It was a terrible tragedy, but it was an accident," Gray started to defend the tiger without thinking. "Surely, if anyone is blame it should be the captain of the boat. He forced the tiger into a corner. I'm truly sorry for what happened, but you can hardly claim that as a kill by a man-eater. You don't even know it was Timur. There are many more tigers in that mangrove forest."

"It's your tiger," Marshall told Gray vehemently. "He'd a notch in his right ear."

"Many tigers have battle scars like that. The chance of it being Timur is only a vague possibility. And, as you well know, Timur is not my tiger. He's a wild animal in a jungle." He knew it sounded childish and defensive, but he couldn't stop the words.

"I bloody well know it's the same tiger. I've photographs of it. One day I'll prove it to you." Marshall's voice was getting louder. His eyes glowed with the cold intensity of ice. He pointed one index finger at Gray, the nail hovering right under his nose. He was shaking with barely suppressed pain.

"You're responsible for my daughter's death, Pendennis. You and that useless fucking organization of yours."

"Now just a minute," Gray interrupted, pushing the tightly clenched fist and extended digit away as calmly as he could. "Settle down, Mr. Marshall, let's not have a scene here."

Marshall stabbed his finger hard into Gray's sternum. "Don't you tell me what to do. You call yourself a zoologist? You're useless man. Absolutely fucking well useless. Your incompetence has destroyed my family." His voice got harsher. Spittle flecked his tight lips. He jabbed at

Gray again. "You. You are responsible for my daughter's death, the death of my son and the trauma to my wife's mind."

"What the hell are you talking about?" Gray asked, his brow furrowed, his own anger rising. "I know nothing of your wife and son."

"They were there. They saw it happen. My son walked in front of a truck and killed himself a week later and now my wife has gone out of her mind with grief," Marshall shouted. "You killed my daughter, you bastard!"

With that the finger snapped back, curled up with the others and swung in a full fist at Gray's startled face. He tried to step back to duck under the blow, forgetting the chair was in the way. His feet caught, and he staggered one pace to catch his balance. Marshall's fist, powered by the weight of straight broad shoulders, smacked into Gray's jaw before he could adequately defend himself. Gray toppled backwards over the chair, hitting the floor on his back. The security guard and a nearby waiter, alerted by the loud voices, tackled Marshall before he could attack Gray further.

"Do you want me to call the police, Professor?" the guard asked, holding Marshall in a tight headlock. The waiter stood braced on the other side, pinning Marshall's arms.

Gray used the chair to pull himself to his feet, his head spinning from the blow. "No, no thanks. Just get him out of here," he said quietly.

"You haven't heard the last of me, Pendennis," Marshall snarled as he was ushered out.

"Fuck off, you lunatic," Gray muttered as he wiped blood from his chin.

A waitress, white-faced and wide-eyed, handed him a table napkin soaked in water. "Use this, sir. It will help."

Gray nodded his thanks, pulled off his bow-tie and made his way to the men's room. Stripping off his jacket he washed his face, feeling the tenderness on the right side of his jaw. Already the swelling was obvious.

"You're getting slow, Gray," he told himself. "You should have seen that one coming."

◆ ◆ ◆

Peering into the mirror to inspect his teeth, he thought back to his last fight. He was about fifteen then, working for the summer on his father's ocean-going tug, the year before the sea claimed boat and crew in a winter storm in British Columbia's notorious Hecate Strait.

The half-drunk deckhand who tried to molest him, a seemingly attractive youth, had been surprised to find a hardened street fighter behind the gentle appearance. Being commonly known as a pretty boy at school, Gray had fought off jealous bullies since he was a tot. After his first shiner, his mother had paid for boxing lessons. Gray never suffered a second black eye. The deckhand, who regularly boasted to the rest of the crew he would teach 'tight-ass little Miss Gray' what a real man was one day, knew nothing of his intended victim's skills.

Reaching out for Gray as the boy headed for a companionway, the deckie wrapped one thick hairy forearm round his neck and reached around to undo the boy's belt with the other hand. Gray, taken off guard, struggled for a moment. Suddenly, fighting to control his initial panic, he relaxed his body – letting every muscle go limp. His assailant slackened his grip in surprise. Gray dropped to the floor, spun in a circle and kicked the man's legs out from under him. The would-be rapist fell backwards over the table as another deckhand blocked Gray's escape route. Laughing excitedly as he got to his feet, the deckie reached out with both hands. "Come here, Lover. You're mine. First!"

Gray watched him warily, his fists clenched, his feet apart, his body perfectly balanced. He said nothing. The deckie laughed again. "Ya wanna play rough, do ya, pretty boy? Well okay, let's party. C'mon Joe, help me get this little fucker on a bunk."

Gray let the two rush at him. Side-stepping at the last second, he tripped Joe head first into a cabin doorjamb.

The man collapsed unconscious. The deckie swung a huge fist at Gray's head. The boy was too fast. He swayed back, letting the blow pass harmlessly. Lashing out with his own left, he split his opponent's upper lip. A fraction of a second later his right broke the man's nose.

The bully was not so easily defeated. "I'm gonna fuck you 'til you scream for mercy, my beauty," he roared, "then I'm gonna tear your fuckin' head off."

Gray took two steps backwards, one step sideways. Two gnarled hands reached for him. Keeping clear in the limited room available, he danced lightly on his toes, watching for his chance. The deckhand rushed him again. Gray spun in a tight circle, his right foot arcing up as if to kick a football. It connected with a bulging unprotected groin. The body above it doubled over. Mercilessly Gray took a handful of hair. Wrenching the head down, he brought his knee up into an already bloody face. The audible crack drew a deep groan from the vanquished sailor, who rolled sideways onto his partner. Gray walked away without so much as a backward glance. His father, standing previously unnoticed at the companionway door, said simply, "You'd better get yourself cleaned up, son. We sail in an hour."

Gray had seen the smile of pride his father tried to keep off his face and grinned back. "Aye, aye, Skipper," he replied.

♦ ♦ ♦

Satisfied there was no blood on his tuxedo jacket, Gray tidied himself up. There was nothing he could do about the swollen lip and the bruise discolouring his chin. As he replaced his bow tie, he promised himself, "Next time, Marshall, you'll go down hard."

Outside he called the security guard over.

"Thanks for the help, Sam. Do you have a Richard Marshall on your list?" he asked. "If you have, I want to know where I can reach him and how he got an invitation."

"Okay, Professor, I'll find out for you. I've warned the rest of the staff to keep him out of here."

"Thanks, I appreciate it. That hurt." Gray managed a rueful grin at the guard as he gently rubbed his jaw. "Now I'll finish my drink."

As the waiter handed Gray another glass, his eyes focused over Gray's right shoulder. "You've got more company, sir," he said.

"Professor Pendennis?" The voice rang softly, yet clearly. Gray turned. In front of him stood the blonde in the red dress. She was a pair of high heels taller than he and had eyes the colour of polished steel.

"I'm Amanda Hawkins," she introduced herself. "I hope I'm not disturbing anything."

"No. No, of course not." He accepted her hand, which was soft and smooth yet held a strong grip. "Most people just call me, Gray," he offered with a smile. "Can I get you a drink?"

"Yes, please: a Campari and tonic with lots of ice, in a tall glass. What happened to your face?" Her hand reached up as if to caress the darkening swelling.

Gray stopped her halfway, holding her wrist firmly but gently, preventing her from touching him.

"It's nothing," he told her with a forced smile, "just a slight accident."

Gray signalled to the waiter, who was now ogling Amanda with undisguised admiration. The waiter nodded once as Gray gave the order. Gray took Amanda by the arm and guided her to a comfortable seat, half hoping she would allow her skirt to fall open again. He wasn't disappointed. Amanda, he decided, had a way of sitting and arranging her legs that could give a blind man an erection.

"Well, Miss Hawkins," he began. "It is Miss Hawkins, isn't it?" He emphasized the title without looking at her hands. "What can I do for you?"

"Thank you," she took the drink from the waiter, giving him a warm smile. "It's not what you can do for me so much, as what I can do for you. And yes, it is Miss

Hawkins; although I prefer to be called Amanda." She sipped her drink, holding it in her right hand. With her left she deftly opened her purse and took out a folded slip of paper with a small white card attached to it.

"This is my donation to Project Man-Eater," she handed it to him. "The card has my address and telephone number." As he put the cheque in his wallet and the card in his jacket pocket, Gray made a mental note that, when she spoke, Amanda's tongue constantly teased her lips. He wondered what it tasted like.

"Thank you, Amanda," he said with a formality he didn't feel. "It's considerations like this which keep our staff in the field and, as a result, tigers in the jungle where they belong. Not as memories in a picture book."

"I'll do anything I can to help. Anything at all." Amanda looked Gray boldly in the eye; her smile was as subtle and as suggestive as her offer was blatant.

"You live in Vancouver?" Gray had to talk so he wouldn't stare. "Are you a model?"

"No, I'm a rich bitch, or so the rumours say," Amanda responded with a laugh. "Actually, I work for my father as a talent scout. He owns a film production company, but he divides his time between here, Los Angeles and London. Mother lives in Beverley Hills, but I prefer to be here. So I spend a fair amount of time alone." Amanda covered all possible intrusions in a few sentences. A drone of approaching voices signalled the end of their private conversation as fifty of Vancouver's most privileged invaded the room.

"Ah, there you are, Gray." A loud voice boomed through the gathering. "Come and say hello to Mrs. Whitelocke."

Gray stood up. "Excuse me, Amanda, duty calls." He flashed his blue eyes at her. "Thanks again for the donation — and for the card. I hope we'll talk more before the evening is over." He smiled again, signalling a waiter for a refill before beginning his rounds.

"I'm impressed, Amanda. You're becoming conservation-minded at last," Asia sat down beside her. "I didn't know you were so interested in tigers. I thought you only hunted men."

Amanda ignored the implied insult and held up her empty glass to Julian, "I'd love another drink. I'm sure Asia would like something, too. Look after us please, darling." Amanda dismissed him with a pat on his departing butt.

Across the room they could see the top of Gray's red mop as he listened attentively to a long-winded white-haired friend of the man-eating tiger. His head bobbed as he agreed with something she said. A white hand, stained with the liver spots of advancing years, reached up and touched his cheek. Gray took the hand and held it for a moment. Asia and Amanda strained to hear the conversation over the cocktail party buzz. As one they stood, the better to watch Gray.

"Someone he knows from the look of it," Amanda whispered to Asia.

"What happened to his face?" Asia asked. "He looks as if he's been hit by a truck."

"A slight accident, he said," Amanda answered. "I think he's been in a fight."

Asia looked at her watch. "How on earth could he get into a fight in this hotel in such a short space of time? He was on stage less than half an hour ago."

Amanda shook her head, still watching as Gray smiled warmly at the elderly lady, said something to amuse her, kissed her lightly on the cheek and moved on.

Amanda took her drink from Julian, thanking him with a smile, before drifting to a small group nearby. Julian began to work his way through the crowd. Asia stayed where she was. Gray was staring at her over the rim of his glass again. Asia smiled at him with her head slightly to one side. There was a question in the movement with what looked like an invitation. His eyes glowed at her, sending back an unmistakeable signal. As the glass left his lips, he smiled. His face lit up, only to change abruptly as his thoughts were interrupted.

"Hello, Professor Pendennis. I'm Julian Sinclair. Do you remember me?" The accent was as English as Buckingham Palace.

"Yes. Hello, Julian. I haven't seen you for some years," Gray responded brightly, ignoring his throbbing jaw. The two men shook hands. Julian's grip was confident. He glanced at Gray's injury with a questioning look but said nothing.

"How are you? Still messing about on wrecked boats?" Gray asked.

"I'm fine thanks. Yes, I'm still dabbling in underwater archaeology. Have you found any more evidence of that shipwreck in Bangladesh we talked about last time? I'm thinking of going there to look for it?"

"No, not really. Look, I'll be in Vancouver for the next few days," Gray told him. "How about getting together for a chat about your Bangladesh plans? I'm staying here, in the Fairmont tonight; then I'll be looking after a friend's apartment for a few days. Where can I reach you?"

Julian gave him a card. "Why don't you come for dinner tomorrow night? Say about seven?"

They shook hands again before Julian moved in the direction of the bar. Gray swung his gaze back to where the beauty in white had been. She wasn't there. He felt disappointed for some reason he could not articulate. As he circulated through the crowd, nodding and smiling, stopping to say "hello" here and again over there, he was constantly praised on the work he was doing and his presentation skills.

"Fine speech, Professor." An older man, with a shock of white hair falling almost to his shoulders, patted him on the arm as he moved towards a pair of strangers. "We could do with a few more young fellas like you today. Too many damned poseurs for my liking: happy to get their names in the papers without achieving anything much or taking a risk. Not enough intelligent action these days. Keep up the good work."

Gray thanked him, his eyes sparkling with pleasure. The old man patted him on the arm again. Gray looked around for the Asian woman.

"You look as though you would be more comfortable in the forest." The voice at his elbow was husky, soothing and, for some reason, reminded him of brushed suede. She looked serious, but her eyes said differently.

"Asia de Kuyper," she introduced herself, holding out a slim right hand. "I believe you know my husband, Julian Sinclair."

"Well done, young man," the old man looked appreciatively at Asia. "I'll leave you to your other guests," he said with a smile, bowing slightly in Asia's direction.

"You're Julian's wife?" Gray tried to keep the sudden disappointment from his voice. "I've just been invited to your home for dinner tomorrow night. Is that all right?"

Asia laughed. The sound rippled sensuously through Gray's ears. "Yes, of course it is. Unplanned guests are always welcome. And I already know a lot about you, so you're not exactly a stranger."

"I'm afraid I've been rather rude, staring at you so much," Gray apologized without feeling in the least sorry. "You really are very beautiful. I've seen you on the cover of a magazine, haven't I?"

Asia nodded and laughed, showing gleaming white teeth to match her dress. "Yes, I expect you might have. I've done some part-time modelling and managed to make it on to a couple of front covers."

"You're Canadian – but you're not Canadian. If you know what I mean," Gray managed to sound confused at his own statement.

"Yes, I was born here, but my mother was born in Dacca, in Bengal, well before the spelling was changed to D-H-A-K-A, and it became the capital of Bangladesh," Asia replied. "Do you often advertise your interest so blatantly?" she asked, changing the subject so suddenly and surprisingly that he spilled some of his drink. "I think that's the first time I've ever experienced a telepathic seduction," she continued. "It's an interesting experience."

Gray's face coloured until it almost matched his hair. "Was I that obvious?" He sounded horrified but found the courage to look amused. "I didn't know you were married," he added lamely. "I should have guessed. You really are beautiful."

He was about to dig himself in deeper while trying to extricate himself when he was forcibly removed from her company.

"Sorry, Asia, my darling, we need *him* over here." A photographer, with a reputation for his outstanding portraiture of celebrities, hustled Gray over to meet a pair of Hollywood actors.

Gray spent a few minutes with the Hollywood duo; enjoying the experience and more than satisfied with the promise of a donation to his cause. Gray smiled a farewell to the stars, after being photographed, and turned back to his other guests. An hour later, as they filed out in two's and three's, he shook hands, smiling as he thanked them all for attending and for their financial support. Asia and Julian said their goodbyes to him as he threaded his way with professional aplomb through the crowd.

"See you tomorrow night," Julian reminded him. Gray assured them both he would be there. Asia held Gray's hand a fraction longer than was normal, not that Gray minded. He was pleased at her touch as well as the all but imperceptible pressure of her fingers on his. He watched them leave, wondering about their relationship. Amanda glided towards him on another man's arm, stopping long enough to plant a kiss on Gray's cheek.

"Call me sometime," she said.

Gray smiled and nodded. "I will. Next time I'm in town."

Sam, the security guard walked over and handed him a folded piece of paper.

"Marshall," he explained.

Once the last guest had gone, Gray unfolded the slip of paper and read: Richard Marshall, Managing Director, Marshall Enterprises Inc., Richmond, B.C. Arrived with Mr. and Mrs. Wilkinson. Gray put the paper in his shirt pocket. Before leaving, he thanked Sam and the waiters.

Gray went straight to his room and sent a brief email to Bangladesh. The note was simple. He wrote the details Sam had given him and added one more line, "Rab, find out as much as you can about the young Canadian girl killed by a tiger recently. Get back to me at the Fairmont Hotel in Vancouver asap."

As he closed his laptop the phone rang.

"Gray Pendennis," he answered.

"Hello, Gray. This is Amanda Hawkins. May I come up for a drink?"

CHAPTER 6

Marshall sat in the hotel lobby bar toying with his drink, taking his time, sipping only occasionally. He read his notes from Gray's speech, adding a few more comments of his own. Midnight passed and the fledgling hours of a new day sent most of the drinkers on their way home. Unable to handle the loneliness at home, Marshall stayed at the hotel and arranged for an early wake up call. He slept fitfully, as he had most nights since the tragedies that wrecked his happiness.

Two floors down and as many hours later, Gray woke with a start as a bell jangled beside the bed. Carefully he extricated himself from Amanda's tangle of arms and legs, reaching for the phone at the same time. Amanda moaned and tried to hold him. Gray kissed her forehead, before sitting up.

"Hello."

"Gray. It's Rab. Richard Marshall's daughter, Tracy, was the one killed by the tiger. I have scanned a newspaper clipping and sent it by email. It should be there for you now."

"Thanks, Rab. I'll get back to you."

Gray got out of bed and went to his laptop. He soon had the news-clip on his screen and read it through twice. It confirmed the tragedy and commented on Marshall's heroism in trying to save his daughter. Rab had added a second clipping from a Vancouver paper about a Simon Marshall who had died after being hit by a truck on a downtown street.

"If you come back to bed I'll serve you a special early breakfast." Amanda's voice floated across from the bed.

Gray sent his thanks to Rab, turned off the computer and went back to bed where he allowed the radiant apparition to lead him uncomplainingly to a sensuous start to what would prove to be a long day. Later, as they lay resting, Amanda asked, "Who was the elderly lady you were talking to last night? You seem to know her well."

"I do. Mrs. Whitelocke is one of my favourite people. Her husband was one of my professors at University," Gray replied. "Mrs. Whitelocke sort of adopted me because I was an orphan. Her husband died a couple of years ago; she invited me to go to see her when I get the time."

At five o'clock in the morning Marshall checked out and called for a taxi. He tipped the bellboy a dollar, receiving a sarcastic look in return. Marshall, deep in thought, failed to notice. Outside he settled into the back seat of a yellow cab. The driver made a half-hearted attempt at being friendly; Marshall stuck his nose in a book, ignoring him.

Vancouver International Airport was crowded with early morning business people scurrying like ants through the concourse. Marshall paid off the cab driver, politely side-stepped other pedestrians and checked in at Air Canada. Less than five hours later he stepped out into the humid air of Toronto. He rented a car and drove to the nearby Sheraton Hotel. After a restless night, he drove east along the 401 Highway to bypass the sprawling metropolitan area of greater Toronto. The traffic as usual on the multi-lane highway was dense with undisciplined drivers. Marshall kept to a middle lane, staying out of trouble. Less than an hour later, he left the car in the visitor's car park at the Toronto Zoo.

For the next hour and a half, he sat talking earnestly to one of the resident zoologists. Afterwards, with time on his hands he roamed the open-air zoo for an hour or two, studying the attractive and reasonably liveable setting for the animals. The tiger compound held his attention longest. Marshall noted the nervous pacing of one female, convincing himself it was pent-up up aggression. She walked ten paces left, her muscles rippling under her coat, turned and walked ten paces back. Once again she turned and regarded her audience with no change of expression on her face. Then she repeated her pacing.

Marshall shot a dozen or so photographs of her, then added his comments into a micro-cassette recorder and went on his way. He was back at the airport before the afternoon rush hour blocked most of the highways in and around the city. He checked in with Air Canada and took the overnight flight to London. As most people on the west coast prepared for bed, and those at his destination began to wake up to a new day, Marshall opened his laptop and went back to work.

◆ ◆ ◆

Amanda went home from the Fairmont still looking like a model on a photographic shoot. The cab driver had to be warned seven times in as many blocks to keep his eyes on the road. Gray had a shower and shave as soon as Amanda left. He called room service and ordered a pot of coffee and two slices of whole-wheat toast. The phone rang as soon as he hung up.

"Good morning, Gray," Julian's cultured voice greeted him. "If you're not busy for lunch I'd like to talk to you alone before this evening."

"Sure, okay," Gray answered. "I was planning to go to my favourite eatery for lunch anyway. Why don't you meet me at Pierre's Old Fish Bowl. It's in Yale Town. One o'clock okay with you?"

Gray didn't own a suit: apart from the tuxedo he'd worn the night before, so he settled for a pair of clean faded jeans sporting a broad leather belt with an oversize oval buckle. He fished a dark blue shirt with button down collar out of his bag. Deciding it wasn't wrinkled enough to deserve ironing he tucked it into his pants. His navy blue travelling blazer hung in the closet. He took it off the hanger, replacing it with the tuxedo he had so passionately discarded the night before. On his feet he slipped a pair of long navy blue socks. A pair of dark brown cowboy boots completed his wardrobe.

Gray checked out of the Fairmont in late morning, leaving his bags with the concierge after promising to collect them in two or three hours. The lights were green on the intersection of Georgia and Hornby. Gray ran to the corner and crossed before they changed. A block away, Howe Street was busy, the lights against him. With a crowd of impatient Vancouverites pressing around him, Gray waited as the cabs, cars, trucks and city buses streamed past until he could cross. At the intersection of Georgia and Granville he turned right and sauntered south, surprised at how seedy the avenue had become since he was last there. Three times in one block he was offered drugs by scruffy individuals. The hustlers and the apparent homeless depressed him. He lengthened his stride to get out of the area.

A glance at his watch told Gray he still had plenty of time. He was restless, tiger problems gnawing at his mind. On an impulse he walked to the waterfront and took a water taxi across False Creek to Granville Island Market. After enjoying the bustle; the sights, sounds and smells for an hour he took another water taxi back to Yale Town.

At precisely one o'clock he strode up the three steps beneath the deep blue canopy and through the door of the cavernous brasserie. The Maître D'hôtel showed him to where Julian was already waiting at a corner table by the window. Gray shook Julian's hand as he stood to greet him and seated himself so he could concentrate on Julian without missing a beat of the restaurant's life. He flagged a waiter and ordered a draft beer. Julian already had a martini in front of him. They exchanged pleasantries for a moment or two, while enjoying their drinks.

Their waiter gave them menus, reciting a long list of specials. The two listened politely, impressed by the boy's memory. The menu, which was hand written in French, told Gray all he wanted to know. His favourite was still available. Gray ordered grilled Alaskan black cod. Julian chose poached salmon. They asked not to be served for half an hour and to have a bottle of Pinot Grigio at the same time as the meal.

"As I told you in my letters, sometime towards the end of the sixteenth century, a Portuguese carrack – or merchant vessel – was wrecked in a cyclone in the Bay of Bengal, not far south of the Sundarbans," Julian began. "A lone survivor somehow made his way to civilization and was cared for by Portuguese priests in Dhaka. The sailor wasn't the only survivor, by the way – two others, who got to shore with him, were killed by tigers. That last sailor claimed his ship carried two ironbound teak chests filled with treasure. Legend says he swore on the Holy Bible it was true." Julian stopped and looked squarely at Gray. "Do you know anything more about this story?" he asked.

Gray shook his head. "No. Well, nothing more than we've already discussed. What about the broken pottery I mentioned, scattered on the seashore near Kotka on the Bay of Bengal? Could that really be part of what you're looking for?"

Julian's eyes gleamed at the thought of the pottery. "Yes, it certainly could be. Someone else, an aid worker or something, told me about that a few years ago. From the description he gave, I assumed the shards were quite recent. It wasn't until I got your initial letter that I started to think about the possible significance of the site."

"Well," Gray broke in, "I know little about archaeology and even less about pottery, but I reckon those broken bits are hundreds of years old. They are all smooth and worn; there are no sharp edges anywhere."

"When was the last time you saw them?" Julian demanded, leaning forward.

"Last spring, I suppose. About the end of April," Gray answered. "They're not always visible, you know," he continued. "They seem to be subject to the whims of the tides. Sometimes they stick up in the mud. Sometimes there's no sign of them. I suppose the constant movement of silt covers them and uncovers them."

"The ship, *Esmerelda*, couldn't have been far from the coast when she was wrecked. There has to be other debris on the sea bed."

"Probably, but that area is south of the Ganges delta," Gray reminded him. "The silt could be damn thick down there. When you come to Bangladesh, I can take you to the pottery location easily; it's quite close to our main search area, right by the rest house at Kotka. You have to start somewhere."

Julian nodded. "That's true. When are you going back?" he asked eagerly, "I want to go with you to do a preliminary search of the sea bed near Kotka."

"I should be there in a couple of weeks," Gray replied. "I don't think that's a very good time for you though. It's monsoon time; still wickedly hot and dreadfully humid. If you wait until early next year, February is good; it will be a lot drier and cooler."

"I don't want to wait that long," Julian told him. "February sounds too far away. I'm used to doing reconnaissance trips at short notice, and the heat won't bother me. Sometimes it adds to the excitement." He grinned enthusiastically at Gray. "It won't take me long to get everything organized here."

Lunch arrived as Julian finished. The two men ate in silence for a while as they mulled over the expedition idea.

"If that treasure is really down there somewhere, I'll find it," Julian told Gray with a smile. "Maybe I'll even find that tiger for you at the same time."

The two men laughed, perfectly at ease in each other's company. Gray almost wished he could find something about the man to dislike, but he couldn't – apart from the fact that he had Asia and Gray did not. Julian paid the bill and they left, Gray on foot, Julian in a cab.

Walking to his friends' apartment in the West End, after picking up his bags from the Fairmont, Gray wondered about Julian and his wife. He couldn't deny there was electricity between himself and Asia. He discounted his night with Amanda, knowing that for both of them it had been a pleasurable one-night stand, nothing more.

"But what," he asked himself aloud, "is there between Asia and Julian, apart from a marriage certificate?"

Gray collected the keys from the caretaker and spent the balance of the afternoon alone at the apartment. He read Rab's email again: "Richard Howarth Marshall. Born August 1938 in Vancouver. Former East African safari guide. Respected conservationist – gained some fame in the early sixties for NOT shooting a man-eating lion in Kenya. (He is said to have fired at it but deliberately missed.) Owns Land Rover dealerships in 3 British Columbia cities and another in London, UK. Owns numerous other business interests. Daughter accidentally killed by a tiger in the Sundarbans earlier this year. Son killed by a truck soon after. Wife possibly in mental home. Marshall appears to be amassing information on human fatalities, by tiger attacks. Will advise further."

Rab had signed it, using his full name, with his usual precision.

For a long time Gray sat puzzling over Marshall's interest in tigers and Project Man-Eater. Obviously his daughter's unfortunate death was the catalyst. But what was his intention? Gray looked up the number for Reuters press agency in the telephone directory. He dialed the seven digits and asked if Joe Monterelli still worked there. Thirty seconds later a gruff voice, grating with the accumulated gravel of a lifetime's nicotine stains, answered, "Monterelli!" Gray could almost smell the thick stub of cigar Joe habitually wore in the corner of his mouth.

"Joe, this is Gray Pendennis," was as far as Gray got.

"Hey, Professor, how ya doin?" Joe growled down the line. "What can I do f'ya?"

Gray asked him if he could find a copy of a story about a man-eating lion in Kenya in the early sixties. He told Joe he was particularly interested in anything published about a safari guide named Richard Marshall who, it was rumoured, had intentionally fired over the lion's head. Joe, the consummate researcher, guaranteed Gray an answer within twenty-four hours.

"Gimme ya email address, Professor," he ordered. "I'll send the articles, or links to them, and my bill at the same time." Gray laughed and gave his personal email address and the office address in Dhaka, asking Joe to send copies to each.

"Does that mean ya want two bills as well?" Joe asked, laughing loudly at his own joke.

Gray arrived at the Sinclair's penthouse overlooking English Bay that evening to be greeted by Julian at the door and wonderful smells from the direction of the kitchen. Julian was casually dressed in grey slacks and a black long-sleeved shirt. His feet looked snug in soft black leather slip-on shoes. Gray was thankful he had taken the trouble to partly change – the dark blue replaced by a tan safari shirt. The blazer and jeans were the same he had worn at lunch.

"Come in Gray, Asia's in the kitchen performing miracles," Julian announced. Gray handed him the bottle of Bordeaux he had purchased en route and shrugged out of his jacket. Asia waved from the vicinity of the spice rack.

"You'll have to come in here to say hello," she called, the sensual huskiness of her voice a perfect match for the exotic fragrance of her cooking. Gray did as he was told. Asia accepted his handshake with a smile. Her perfume, with the subtle aroma of sandalwood, made him want to crush her in his arms. Her scent lingered like an omen. He drew back resisting the temptation. Asia took a step back also. She held her arms out, looking down at the same time.

"What do you think?" she asked. She wore a pale pink shawal kameez, covered incongruously by an old plastic apron bearing the simple legend: 'Speciality Of The House'.

"Hi," he said. "You look great: there's nothing like honesty in advertising. And something smells familiar."

Asia's eyes glowed. "That's Chicken Mosamman. Have you tried it in Bangladesh?"

Gray closed his eyes and inhaled. "It's my favourite dish. Well, almost," he answered. Asia laughed and pushed him toward the door.

"Go and get Julian to pour you a drink, I won't be long."

Julian held up a bottle of Glen Morangie and a glass. Gray said, "Sure, that's fine with me. And a couple of ice cubes, please."

Spread across a side table was a map. Gray knew it well. In bold letters spanning the top of the chart was written, 'Map Of Sundarbans Forest'. It was identical to the one Gray used for his own journeys through the region. He had sent it to Julian early on in their correspondence. Julian was obviously keen to make as much use of Gray's knowledge as possible.

"Sundarbans is a Bengali word meaning 'beautiful forest'," Gray began. "It's named after the sundari trees." He stabbed a finger at the lower right corner of the land-mass.

"This is Kotka, the wildlife sanctuary guest house. The tiger watchtower is over here." His finger moved to the right, across a river. He was aware Asia had joined them, standing off to one side.

"The shards of pottery are scattered in this area, a little way to the south west of the guest house. A tiger, iden-tity unknown – although it has to be one of Timur's mates, regularly takes its kills to a spot about here to eat in peace." He indicated a point north of the pottery collection.

"That outdoor dining room is less than fifty metres from the pottery. A female on Timur's land means Timur can walk in at any time. Wandering in that area without a rifle or an armed guard, therefore, is tantamount to suicide."

"The survivor from the *Esmerelda* gave a good description of the first part of his journey to safety, on a raft he built from wreckage and fallen trees. He tied it all together with vines, I imagine," Julian broke in. "He was believed to have been on the Passur River, but I don't understand that, it's far too wide. The sailor's story says he could see each bank of the river clearly."

"Yes, he was definitely east of the Passur," Julian continued his thought. "His description, if the Portuguese priest wrote it down properly, suggests he entered the Passur sometime later, here, near the present village of Chandpai."

"So you think the treasure, if there is one, has to be somewhere along the coast between Dubla, in the west, and Egg Island, here, in the east," Gray asked him.

"Unless it's at the bottom of the Bay of Bengal, far from land," Asia offered, touching a finger to the sea south of the land.

"Don't forget that the pottery somehow found its way to the coast and into an inland channel," Gray reminded them. "Those were heavy items when they were full. The treasure, or some of it, could be there too."

"That's true, but the treasure will almost certainly be scattered over a wide area, I should think," Julian admitted. "Those wooden chests have been down there for over four hundred years. Worms and time will have destroyed them by now. The ebb and flow of the tides could have deposited the individual pieces all along the coast."

He shook his head and pursed his lips. "It's a gamble but the stakes are high enough to make it exciting."

"Can you get the necessary equipment into Bangladesh?" Gray asked.

"No, not at the moment," Julian explained. "The authorities won't let me take in high tech gear. No special dive boat. No robot cameraman. With a robot, we could scan large areas of seabed relatively quickly. As it is, I will have to go alone this time. If I find something of value the rules may change. There's nothing like success to sway a government department, is there?"

"Where do you think that tiger is now, Gray? The one you call Timur?" Asia asked, changing the subject.

"I wish I knew," Gray looked mystified, his right hand caressing the map from top to bottom. "He has a liking for Jawtoli, this meadow here, which is in the southern part of the Sarankhola Forest Range. He also patrols much of the Chandpai Range, over here."

Gray showed them the two large areas. "He probably made one of his earliest human kills up here in the northern part of the Chandpai. He's certainly made a few since then. That's why he's known as the 'man-eater of Chandpai'."

"I know you've seen him, but have you ever come face to face with Timur?" Julian asked.

"Yeah, once last year. I was on Tinkona Island – over here, with Hassan and Ali," Gray pointed to the map, "Hassan showed me fresh tracks: Timur's tracks. While I was inspecting them I heard Hassan's voice hissing: 'Gray, Gray, don't move. Tiger!' I stayed where I was on one knee, almost too scared to look. When I raised my head, I looked straight into a tiger's eyes less than thirty paces away. The tiger growled at us in warning as I ordered the guys not to shoot. As carefully as I could I laid my dart gun on the ground and took one photograph."

"That was risky," Julian interrupted.

"Yes, it was, but I really wanted that photograph, and I knew the others had me covered. One click was enough for me. The tiger flicked an ear at the slight sound, otherwise he didn't move. Slowly I picked up my gun again. I didn't dare fire at him. He was head on to me, you see. I needed a broadside view: the risk of hitting him in an eye head on was too great."

"What happened?" Asia and Julian asked in unison.

"Silently, I begged him to turn away. I was sweating so much the drops were running off my nose onto my rifle barrel. He roared at us again. I swear I felt the ground shake under me. Ali, as frightened as Hassan and myself, instinctively pulled his trigger. The blank exploded loudly causing the tiger to turn. I squeezed off a shot with a dart as he made himself scarce."

"You missed him," Julian guessed. "You missed from close range?"

"Yes. I missed. When we checked his pugmarks, we saw we had met Timur face to face. He was on an island, so I figured we had a fairly good chance of seeing him again. Of course, we didn't. We followed his tracks more than halfway around the island until he went swimming again."

"He seems to live a charmed life. Perhaps you both do," Asia commented.

Gray grinned at her. "Well, in some ways he does." He thought for a moment then, "I prefer to think of him as a professional. Somehow, he always knows what to do, and he gets away with it. Even the monsoon rains don't appear to deter him."

"What's it like there in the monsoon?" Asia spoke up. "I haven't been to Bangladesh since I was a child."

"Well, the monsoon this season has been a harsh one, again. In May forty-one people were reported killed in an early storm. A month later another fifty or so people died. Up in the north three million people were stranded on their own roofs from the excessive flooding."

Gray pointed to the network of waterways in the Sundarbans. "All the water from all the rivers in Bangladesh has to go somewhere. Eventually much of it will flow south through the Sundarbans. When the downstream flow hits an incoming tide it creates further havoc. That sort of weather, combined with the high winds common to tropical storms, could have sent Timur into hiding anywhere in his, or possibly even another male's territory."

"Do you think the monsoon flow on the rivers will affect my reconnaissance if I start later this month?" Julian asked.

"No, by that time the worst of the flooding will be draining. The land soaks up a lot anyway. I don't think you'll have any trouble," Gray assured him. "I'll be there too, in a boat part of the time and on foot most of the time. The heat and humidity will be your problem. The mud, I think, will be mine."

Asia went back to the kitchen while the two adventurers made tentative plans for Julian's expedition. When she called them to the dining room they were still talking about the possibility of finding remnants of the Portuguese boat's precious cargo. Gray stopped in mid-sentence as the subtle spices from the meal reached him.

In the middle of the table, on a heated silver platter, two browned chickens rested on a bed of pilau rice. Sliced almonds, pistachios and raisons decorated the steaming dish. As Asia cut into one of the chickens, to show the vegetables cooked inside, the delicious aromatic smells of ginger, garlic, coriander and cardamom, burst forth. Gray felt his mouth beginning to water. He'd almost forgotten how much he loved and missed well-prepared Bengali food. As Asia poured each of them a tall slim glass of green mango sorbet, Gray started to feel as though he really was back in Bangladesh. He took a bite of chicken and nodded in appreciation.

"I guess your mother taught you how to cook like this? This chicken is delicious."

Asia laughed, delighted at his compliment. "Food was always a big part of life in my family. Mother cooked so well that my Dutch father used to take me ice-skating in winter and hiking in summer so we didn't get fat."

"Where is home, Gray?" Julian asked.

"I'm not sure these days. I was born here in Vancouver. I went to university in Toronto and in the States. Plus I lived in Indonesia for a year to study tigers," he stopped, thinking for a moment. "I suppose Bangladesh is home really. I've spent most of my time there for many years now."

"Where is your family from?" asked Julian.

"From Vancouver. I'm a third generation British Columbian. Both my parents are dead: I've been an orphan for a long time. Mother died of cancer when I was twelve. My dad was a sailor. He had his own tugboat. I used to work for him every summer. He and the boat went down in a storm on Hecate Strait when I was eighteen. They were towing a barge down from the Queen Charlottes to Victoria."

For a few minutes, silence ruled the table. Gray stared at his glass of wine. Asia broke the spell.

"What about marriage, Gray?" she asked brightly. "Have you considered it?"

Gray laughed. "No," he said. "I came close once or twice. But I think I'm too much of a nomad to settle. I don't think my lifestyle would suit a permanent relationship."

"Not even any girlfriends waiting on the horizon?" Asia probed.

"No, not really. I spend most of my time in the forest, so there's not much opportunity for romance. And, of course, most of the ex-pats in Dhaka are married."

"Perhaps you should move back to Vancouver," Julian suggested with a smile.

"I've thought about it occasionally but, my life is really tied up in that beautiful Asian forest as tigers are my true love – for the moment anyway. I think romance will have to wait until I have completed my work."

Asia cleared away the dirty dishes and returned from the kitchen with a tray of diamond-shaped coconut sweets. Gray was impressed and pleased, quite sure the distinctive meal had been painstakingly chosen primarily for his enjoyment.

"Aah!" he breathed in, savouring the latest preparation, "That looks like narikeler..." he stopped, fumbling for the right word, "it's, uh, narikeler borphi, isn't it?"

Asia clapped her hands in delight like a child. "Apni Bangla janen?" she asked Gray.

"Ami ektu Bangla bolte pari," he replied. Telling her he did, indeed, speak a little of her mother's tongue.

It was after eleven when the evening ended. Julian offered to phone for a taxi, but Gray said he preferred to walk for a while. He rubbed his stomach as he spoke and grinned at Asia. "Oh, that was such a good dinner."

Julian patted him on the shoulder. "Okay. Call me sometime tomorrow, please. I will probably have more questions for you."

At the door, Gray took Asia's hands in his and told her, "Apni sundur khoob," complimenting her on her beauty. Then, "Thank you both so much. That was a special evening."

As he walked along the coast road in the darkness, a half moon lit up the bay. Beyond, the black outlines of mountains etched their silhouettes on the sky. Despite the pleasures of the evening with the Sinclairs, all the way home Gray thought about Richard Marshall. Somehow, he felt inside, that man was sure to cause him trouble. He needed to be prepared.

CHAPTER 7

In Toronto, zoologist Allison Butterfield sent an email to Project Man-Eater as soon as her visitor left. She advised Rab of her conversation with a Richard Marshall, recommending he send Marshall up-dated information on the project. She finished by giving Marshall's business and home addresses, plus his email contacts. Like Gray, Rab Choudhury was beginning to sense impending trouble. He immediately sent another email to Gray in Vancouver detailing the latest developments, suggesting a conversation with Allison might be worthwhile.

All day, without a break, Marshall sat in his office and wrote out emails, sending them with electronic efficiency around the world. Conservationists in over a dozen countries read his request: zoological park managers on five continents and as many islands studied his appeal. At a computer terminal in Calcutta, Deepak Voorah called up the desired information and transmitted it straight back to Marshall. As a courtesy, perhaps even as a caution, he sent copies of the original request and a synopsis of his answer to Project Tiger and to Project Man-Eater. In Dhaka, Rab Choudhury scanned the two messages, his mind straying to the email he had received from Gray only the previous day. He sent copies of the latest messages to Vancouver immediately.

A few hours to the southwest of Dhaka, Timur reclined under the shade of a crumbling, overgrown stone wall. Little of the long abandoned fortifications remained intact. The jungle and the climate had allowed the man-made structure to remain only fleetingly. Trees and shrubbery clung to granite and sandstone blocks: embracing them, probing for their weaknesses. Tenacious roots poked through cracks, spreading out like spokes of a fan in their incipient search for a destructive foothold. Directly opposite where Timur lazed, an archway – wide enough for two men side by side – led down steep earthworks to the forest. On all sides the jungle was so thick as to form a virtually impenetrable barrier. It was a perfect shield for a fugitive. Only two paths, almost obscured, led to the building. One originated at a nearby creek. The other roamed south. Both were animal trails. Neither had known the tread of man for decades.

Timur licked his injured paw tenderly, trying to clean it. The infection was worse. Greenish-yellow pus oozed from the pad's side. The constant pain unsettled him, made him bad-tempered. The rifle shots at close range, when he had killed Hassan, had frightened him. The same sound had accompanied the initial agony of his wound. In terror he had dropped Hassan's body when Ali's bullet whistled over his head. He had travelled hard from there to the ruin, where no smell of man intruded. There he could rest without fear of interruption.

In the hour after midnight, Timur stood up and stretched. Following the trail to the creek, he drank deeply before retracing his steps. He was hungry again but rested. Limping slightly he wandered south in search of prey. For hours he roamed the jungle pathways. Nothing came within reach of his killer claws until, shortly before dawn, he caught the scent of deer. Staying downwind he felt his way through the bushes, making almost no noise. There was a rich smell of fresh blood on the air. Timur lowered himself to the ground. Something was wrong. He listened intently. Tortured breathing came from somewhere in front. He could smell deer. He could smell blood. He could almost taste another creature's fear. Timur stealthily moved on. His night vision picked up the glint of another's eyes and he froze. The ragged breathing was louder. Timur walked slowly forward. Under the broken branch of a once live tree a deer gasped, sucking in much-needed oxygen. The deer trembled violently as it fought to control its breathing. Down its back and hindquarters vivid deep scratches, running freely with blood, showed where another predator, a leopard possibly, or a young tiger, had barely missed a meal. The deer had somehow escaped and run until its lungs failed.

It watched Timur approach warily, stamping shaky legs in alarm. Timur took one step at a time. He was a predator. The deer was prey. To him the injured creature was no more than survival. He pounced as the deer found hidden reserves of strength. Such was the instinct for self-preservation that the savaged deer made a ten metre start on the hungry tiger before Timur completed his leap. He landed where the deer had been a second before. The deer bleated in terror as Timur raced after it. Fate, having spared the deer from the jaws of one hunter, now handed it over to another. The chase was short, the struggle shorter. The deer dodged left and right. Without obvious effort Timur stretched his legs, favouring his injured paw, and cut the distance between them. His bulk knocked the weakened deer off its feet. Powerful jaws throttled the doomed animal and devoured it where they fell.

Rab Choudhury got the news of Hassan's death three days after the event, when a distressed Ali disembarked from a forestry launch at Mongla. Only hours after his previous message about Marsh's visit to Toronto, Rab sent another email to Gray reporting Hassan's death and requesting his immediate return to Dhaka. He then advised Calcutta of the most recent fatality.

Because Hassan had been employed by a respected agency, coupled with the gruesome nature of his demise, the news was put out on the wire for any and all newspapers the world over to pick up. A young reporter on a London paper's news desk read the item and, as he had been asked, emailed it immediately to Marshall's home address, confident of receiving a cheque in the mail. Marshall read the long report without emotion. He added it to his computerized file and stared at the screen, lost in thought.

Gray woke up with the taste of fine curry in his mouth and that made him hungry. After a hot shower he toasted a couple of slices of bread and looked for a coffee pot. Unable to find it, or coffee, he chose a packet of English Breakfast tea instead. With a piece of toast in one hand and his mouth full he checked his emails.

Rab's message about Marshall's Toronto detour intrigued him. He phoned Allison to find out more. Years before, when they were both in their freshman year at the University of Toronto, before Gray advanced to Yale, they had studied together. A relationship formed which blossomed into an affair lasting less than one semester. The love, if there had been any, expired. The close friendship remained.

"He just asked a lot of questions about tigers and their habits," she told Gray. "When he mentioned man-eaters I suggested he get in touch with you. That's about it, really."

"Did he tell you why he was so interested in tigers? Or that he had met me a few days ago?" Gray asked.

"No, he didn't, on either count. He seemed genuinely fascinated by tigers though; yet there was something strange about him." Allison sounded thoughtful. "Most people, when they ask questions about animals, have warmth in their voice. Marshall was cold. His voice. His mannerisms. Even his eyes: strange greenish eyes. Everything was cold."

Gray agreed with his long-time friend's professional assessment. He thanked her and put down the phone.

Pouring a mug of black tea, he added one cube of brown sugar and sat down to read a sheaf of other messages relating to the project. Those requiring his immediate attention he answered. In late afternoon, while Gray tapped a series of thoughts into his lap top computer, a new email came in from Rab. Gray read it and went white. He sat back in his chair and read it again with tears in his eyes.

"I deeply regret to inform you Hassan was killed by a tiger three days ago. Almost certainly, according to Ali, Timur was the culprit. Please return to Dhaka immediately. We are in deep trouble now."

"Ah, shit! Shit! Shit!" Gray raged. Hassan had worked with him for seven years, ever since the start of the project. Gray considered him a close friend and a valuable employee. Beyond that, his death would inevitably cause serious additional problems for Project Man-Eater. He agreed with Rab, he must return on the earliest possible flight.

For a moment, he thought he'd lost his ticket. Under stress and extremely upset, Gray went through all the papers in his briefcase three times, without success. He finally located it folded inside his passport, in the inside pocket of his blazer. He booked himself on that evening's flight to Tokyo, with a connection to Dhaka. He then sent Rab a message advising of his arrival time.

A phone call to Amanda got him nowhere. She was out or otherwise engaged. He left a message on her voicemail. "Thanks a million for everything, and I do mean everything. I have to return to Dhaka tonight. A major problem has erupted. I hope we meet again one day. Bye gorgeous." Gray hung up and remembered he was supposed to call Julian. The Sinclair's number was busy. Thirty seconds later his phone rang. It was Julian.

"Ah, Julian, I'm glad you called. Sorry I didn't call earlier," he apologized, "life has been a little hectic today."

He told him about Hassan's death and his plan to fly out that night. Julian offered to drive Gray to the airport and said he would pick him up in two hours. Gray organized all the relevant emails into his laptop's filing cabinet and started to throw his clothes on and around his dinner suit in his faded brown bag.

While he waited for Julian, Gray took a can of beer from the fridge, ripped off the sealing ring to enjoy a long, cold drink. He scribbled a note for the apartment's owners, explaining the situation and promising to write when he got to Dhaka. A final check on his emails proved Joe Monterelli as good as his word. Gray printed out five sheets of paper and put them in his inside pocket to read on the plane.

When Julian pulled up in his sand-coloured Range Rover, Gray was waiting in the building lobby. He put his bags on the back seat and climbed in beside them, sitting close to the middle so he could lean forward to talk to the driver and to Asia. As briefly as possible he told them of his friendship and working relationship with Hassan.

"He and Ali were a damn good team. Those two were distant cousins who had spent most of their lives in and around the Sundarbans. They've been tracking Timur for a long time together. Now, just when we almost had him, he has killed again, and escaped. There will be all hell breaking loose in government circles in Dhaka." Gray paused for a moment. "I guess, even though the trail's stone cold by now, I will have to go after Timur myself. With Ali, of course," he added.

At Vancouver International Airport, Asia's eyes met Gray's briefly. She hugged him and begged. "Be careful, my friend."

"Yeah, I know," said Gray with a wry smile, "it's a jungle out there."

They all laughed, relieved to share a moment of humour.

"I'll send a message to your office and tell you and Rab when I'm arriving," Julian called to Gray as he got back in the car. "That'll probably be in about three weeks from now."

Gray waved in acknowledgement, shouldered his travel bag, picked up camera gear and his briefcase and walked into the terminal. He checked in and got his seat number. As soon as he was through the security procedure he phoned Rab – he had to talk to someone about his problems – someone who understood.

After take-off, Gray put on his own headphones and settled back to listen to his favourite Chris Rea songs. With the rough voice and insistent rhythm playing on his ears he read through Monterelli's messages. They told him what he wanted to know, but, he decided, there was nothing he could do until he got to Dhaka.

Restless and disturbed over Hassan's violent death, he fidgeted in his seat. From the seat pocket in front of him, he pulled out the current issue of the inflight magazine. Although he flicked through the pages, nothing registered. His mind was too full of memories – of trekking through the Sundarbans with Hassan and Ali. He prayed that Hassan had died quickly, without suffering.

For a while he listened to his music, the magazine open on his knees, his eyes closed. It was no good; Hassan and Timur continued to play on his mind. Having exhausted his interest in the reading potential of the magazine, Gray opened one of his recently purchased books. Ken Follett's 'Pillars of the Earth' had been on his list for a couple of years. He finally had the opportunity of curling up and reading the saga without interruption – if he could concentrate.

♦ ♦ ♦

That day Marshall phoned a small zoo in southeast England, one that had been plagued by attacks on its keepers from caged tigers. Two of the attacks had proved fatal. Marshall wanted more details for his research. While he asked questions, probing with the delicacy of a surgeon's scalpel, answers to other questions were speeding through the air waves. In Marshall's office the emails piled up. Once he got off the phone, he read them all, swiftly sorting through the replies. Anything concerning tigers he placed in a new file folder, marked 'TIGER PRIORITY.' As the influx of emailed reports died down Marshall began work on his notes.

He opened a document labelled TIGERS; Human Deaths - 1989 to 1996.

Throughout the night he tapped away at the keyboard, entering locations, dates, times, names of the dead and witnesses, if there were any. He forgot about meals. Only occasionally he sipped on a glass of stale water. If any details of the errant tiger were available he entered those too in a box at the end. He recorded their estimated size, estimated weight, distinguishing marks and pad measurements. Where he had been sent copies of the pugmarks, he scanned those on to the document. If the tiger had been killed at the scene, or within close enough proximity to be absolutely sure it was the culprit, he finished that entry with - KILLER TERMINATED! All other entries concluded with - KILLER AT LARGE!

Once he had the details logged, he saved the information, closed the programme and turned off the PC. Then, many hours since he had last slept, Marshall went home to his London flat. By that time he had collected hundreds of reports on fatal attacks by tigers on humans in the wild. Still to be analyzed were over one thousand more possible fatalities in India, Nepal and Bangladesh, far too many of them attributed to tigers.

Refreshed after a few hours of sleep, Marshall spent the next few days going over each and every entry. Any kill for which Timur could possibly have been responsible, he entered under a separate file headed simply - TIMUR. At the top of that list he typed: 'Tracy Erin Marshall, age 11, British'. Exactly underneath he added: Simon Richard Marshall, age 14, British. Jeannette's name completed the trio. Beside hers, he added an asterisk, as if to remind himself she was a special case. There followed fifty-seven other names, mostly Bangladesh nationals. At Project Man-Eater in Dhaka, there was an almost identical list; but that one listed Bangladeshi names only.

The time was now, Marshall decided. There was more than enough evidence. He had to rid the world of that tiger once and for all. He phoned British Airways reservations.

CHAPTER 8

The monthly meeting of the Forestry Commission in Dhaka became progressively noisier. Usually a fairly sedate and polite gathering, on this occasion it degenerated into a shouting match between opposing factions. Tempers frayed, ties were loosened, sleeves rolled up. Men angrily kicked their chairs over as they stood to emphasize their points of view.

"This man-eating tiger must be exterminated," thundered one voice, to a chorus of approval from one side of the huge, highly polished, round teak table. Overhead a solitary fan whirled quietly, stirring the air, making papers on the table move listlessly.

"I would like to remind the assembly that tigers are an endangered species," an elderly gentleman interrupted, "It is illegal to kill a tiger in our country." The soothing voice went unheeded as the majority called for all-out war on the man-eater.

"Where is Pendennis?" The question echoed through the room from a chorus of angry voices. "He promised us last year he would catch this tiger. He has done nothing."

"More than fifty lives have been lost in Chandpai Range in the last three years. And all of them due to one tiger," the speaker waved a sheaf of paper as he spoke. "It says right here in Pendennis's report that one tiger – just one tiger – has murdered all those innocent people."

Rab Choudhury, called before the meeting to explain Hassan's death, spoke up in Gray's defence. "The report says that we suspect one tiger is responsible. It doesn't say our suspicions have been confirmed. We don't know for sure."

One of the commissioners shouted again, waving a newspaper above his head, but Rab cut him off. "Professor Pendennis has been in Canada raising money to assist in funding the project. At this moment he is on a plane, returning to Dhaka. He will be here tomorrow morning. He is just as upset about Hassan as you are. Hassan was his close friend."

Rab's singsong tones were soft and not strong enough to override the excited department managers, few of whom were interested in hearing anything other than their own voices. In the background an army general leaned against a wall, listening to the exchanges.

"Gentlemen," he interrupted. His deep, strong voice carrying over the tumult. "I am the official military advisor on the Sundarbans. I think we need to hear what Mr. Pendennis himself has to say. Can he be here for sure tomorrow, Mr. Choudhury?"

"Yes. Yes. I want to see Pendennis in my office tomorrow morning," the chairman broke in. "Make sure he is there. The PM's office is now asking questions. This Man-Eater of Chandpai has got to be stopped. If you people can't do it we will hire someone who can."

The news of Timur's latest kill had been plastered all over the local daily papers. Editorials called for immediate action. Most condemned the government for not doing enough to protect forestry workers. One blamed Project Man-Eater for deliberately sheltering Timur. The hastily written article, riddled with inaccuracies, was amplified by a picture of Gray fondling a tiger's ears. The caption read, 'Man-Eater Gets Special Treatment From Foreign Zoologist.'

Unfortunately for Gray, and for the project, there was an element of truth in the line. The tiger in the photograph was an old man-eater Gray had captured a few years before. The somewhat distorted picture had been taken in Mirpur Zoo, while the tiger was still drowsy from the tranquilliser administered so it could be medically examined on arrival. The reporter, of course, neglected to mention that aspect of the story.

Each time one of the commission's senior officers made a point, he picked up a newspaper from the haphazard pile on the table, stabbing his finger at Gray's photograph in emphasis. The others quickly adopted the same routine, except the one voice defending the rights of the tiger, and the general – who murmured his apologies and left. Rab was certain that Gray would have a difficult interview with the chairman on his arrival.

◆ ◆ ◆

Gray was the first passenger through the foreigner's immigration line and quickly through customs. Rab met him outside with a car and driver. On the way home he briefed him on the latest developments, explaining the threat from the chairman had sounded realistic. Gray shared a house in the Gulshan district with two other Canadians whenever he stayed in Dhaka. He stopped long enough for a shower and a change of clothes, then continued to the project's Spartan offices just off New Eskaton Road.

A delaying message from the Forestry Commission relieved Gray of his explanation until mid-afternoon. He wasn't sorry, there were many other items requiring his attention at the office. A delay also meant the chairman probably wasn't as sure of his position as he had tried to sound when shouting at Rab. Either that or he was displaying his position and power to remind Gray who was in charge.

A DHL courier dropped off a thin rectangular packet at Project Man-Eater as Gray started his third mug of morning coffee. His male secretary signed for the delivery and slit it open with a stainless steel paper knife. Inside, in a plain white envelope addressed to Professor Graham Pendennis, was a large colour photograph of a tiger swimming across a river. Fastened to the print with a paper clip was a hand-written note. It said only: 'Timur – child killer.' The note was signed 'Marshall'.

Gray studied the photograph approvingly. It was an excellent picture. He didn't need to look up Timur's portrait in his rogue's gallery. He knew the photograph in his hand was Timur. All tigers are distinguishable from each other by the black markings on their faces and their bodies. The tiger Marshall had photographed, presumably the one that had inadvertently killed his daughter, had a black pattern on its cheek. Gray thought it reminiscent of a child's drawing of the side view of a panda's head, with a unicorn's horn sticking out of the forehead. He knew it well; Timur carried the identical marking.

Gray checked his rogue's gallery anyway, hoping to prove the two tigers were different. He couldn't. The two markings above Timur's eyes, one like a pelican with half its beak missing, the other an inverted tuning fork, were also clearly the same. He examined the body stripes, searching for any possibility that there was a difference. They were identical.

Gray had to admit Timur was partly responsible for an innocent girl's death. He sighed and banged his fist on the table in frustration. The last thing he needed at the moment was Richard Marshall causing him more grief. Somehow he knew trouble would follow anyway.

The meeting with the chairman, General Rahman and half a dozen other committee members was, as Gray and Rab expected, a replay of the previous day's shouting match. Gray suffered in silence for a while, only occasionally speaking in his own defence, rarely on behalf of Timur. After a wasted hour listening to a stream of repeated rhetoric and stern demands for positive action, Gray thanked the chairman politely for his time and his interest.

"I'm leaving for Kotka tomorrow afternoon," he told the official. "I'll stay as long as it takes to put this tiger behind bars."

"Either capture it or kill it. I don't care which," the Chairman said unfeelingly. He picked up an envelope and tapped it importantly on the desk. "Here is a letter of authorization for you to take the most extreme measures if necessary. It is signed by me and by General Rahman."

"You mean shoot the tiger," Gray told him icily. "You don't need me for that. General Rahman could just send the army in. Couldn't you, General? I believe you have a patrol boat on regular duty in the Sundarbans."

Rahman's eyes narrowed, but he remained silent. He studied Gray, his expression betraying nothing. For seconds the two men stood facing each other, the hostility between them vibrating in the air. At last the general spoke.

"Mr. Pendennis. When you have either captured or killed this tiger, bring it to me. I want to see proof."

With that he turned and left the room. Gray picked up the letter and tucked it into the back pocket of his pants. The chairman stood up. "Don't come back to Dhaka without good news for me. Otherwise I will have to look at this matter quite differently." The meeting was over.

Gray returned to his office in a foul mood.

"I don't trust that bastard Rahman. He's up to something. He's never shown any interest in Sundarbans wildlife before," he told Rab.

"I know. He was there yesterday too. Look, why don't you go home and get some sleep. I can look after things here."

Gray stayed in the office anyway. As his temper gradually improved, 'Happy Hour' at the Ex-pat's Club began to tug irresistibly at him as the afternoon wore on. He decided to go home and sleep for an hour after all. Refreshed, he would enjoy the company of his fellow countrymen, and other members, far more.

The habitués of Dhaka's favourite ex-patriot's club, most of whom didn't even know he was in the city, had to enjoy their drinks without the professor's company that night. Gray flung himself on the bed and slept right through until the sun came up. When he woke and discovered it was morning, he was vaguely disappointed at not getting to the club, but felt fit and ready for the chase. When the rest of the staff got to the office, Gray was already hard at work and in a better frame of mind. He phoned a friend in Mongla and asked him to send a message to Ali. The contents were brief: "We are going hunting. See you at Dhangmari tomorrow morning."

Gray caught the afternoon Fokker F-50 flight to Jessore. There he reclaimed his two heavy bags from the baggage cart. Outside the small airport building he boarded the shuttle coach to Khulna. In the anonymity of the Royal International Hotel he ate a solitary dinner. A noisy group of ten British tourists, who came in after Gray had ordered, kept the waiters running between kitchen and table. Gray, at the other end of the room, ate his rice and chicken curry quickly. As soon as he could, he fled the unnecessary din. He ordered tea to be sent up to his room.

While the tourists debated over what to have for dessert, Gray pulled the bedclothes up around his ears and fell asleep. For the next few weeks his bed would be little more than a sleeping bag. On the boat he could look forward to the dubious luxury of a thin mattress on deck, with a light covering of dew by morning. In the jungle the ground would have to suffice. That single bed in the small hotel room was worthy of a full night's sleep. It was not to be.

A pounding on the door interrupted Gray's restless sleep in the early hours of the morning. "Professor Gray! Professor Gray! Wake up please!"

"What? What is it?" Gray called sleepily, dragging himself out of bed. He opened the door and peered into the dim light of the hall.

"Professor Gray," the night clerk repeated, "there is a message for you. A tiger has been seen near Dhangmari. It has attacked someone at the jig jig village."

CHAPTER 9

Asia leaned back against the wooden mast, tilting her head to the light as the make-up artist touched up her eyeliner. Around her an array of lights beamed unnaturally in the afternoon sun. A photographer waited. His assistant checked and re-checked the lights, cameras, and filters, stopping only to snarl at one of the boat's crew to get back behind the rope barrier.

"This deck is off limits to everyone except the photographer and his team," he spat at the watchers.

No stranger to boats, thanks to Julian's archaeological work, Asia looked up at the spider's web of rigging woven between the deck and the masthead. The high gloss finish of new varnish on the woodwork complemented her skin colour.

"That's lovely, Asia," the photographer called as make-up moved out of range. "Hold it there. Great. Now left to right and back again. That's lovely. Thank you, darling."

Responding to compliments and careful instructions in professional style, Asia was relaxed. She felt completely at home on the old windjammer.

"I wonder what Gray Pendennis would look like on this ship?" The unexpected thought startled her and she laughed out loud, seeing Gray as a red headed pirate commanding a privateer.

"Got it! Got it! That's great Asia. Whatever made you think of laughing just then?" the photographer called, breaking into her fantasy. "That's the cover shot I've been looking for. Take a break, everyone."

♦ ♦ ♦

Gray sat tense behind the driver in the early morning darkness as the complaining car rattled south from the Rupsha river crossing. There was little other traffic; only occasional hazards. A stubborn water buffalo slowed them briefly: it stood across the middle of the road ruminating contentedly in the pale light of a half moon. While Gray's driver detoured cautiously around it, the buffalo acted as if the car didn't exist. Across the river from Mongla, Gray woke a snoring boatman and offered him a day's wages to row him downstream to the village. By the time Gray stepped ashore again night was losing its grip on the sky. Red streaks lit up a few high clouds, tendrils of mist drifted in lazy harmony with the river's current. Masts and funnels of freighters anchored in mid-stream broke up the immediate horizon.

Ali was already in the village of 'earthly delights.' He stood talking with a group of agitated prostitutes; there were no other men in sight.

"Are you working or negotiating pre-breakfast pleasures?" Gray called out.

Ali turned at the familiar voice and waved a greeting, a smile baring his tobacco-stained, broken teeth.

"Good morning, Professor Sahib," he replied with deliberate courtesy. "These women heard the tiger. It took away their friend in the night." Ali stuck out his hand and Gray gripped it.

"I'm sorry about Hassan," he said. "Now, what's happened here?"

While the two discussed the attack, the women

– more and more of them – crowded around. Frightened though they were none could forget why they were there. Each time Gray raised his eyes he received a bold smile and a coquettish shake of the head. Most of his audience still wore flowers in their hair. A few displayed garlands around their necks.

"The woman, a girl only I think, was in that hut over there. She was with a man when a tiger came in," Ali related the story as he had heard it a short time before.

"Where is the man now?" Gray asked.

Ali laughed, "He was a sailor off one of those ships out there. He came out with his pants half on and screaming in terror. He's back on board by now."

Gray smiled at the image. "Okay," he turned to the women, "you stay in the village, all of you. Go back to your homes. You'll be safer there. Come on, Ali."

"The tiger is injured I think," Ali offered. "One of the women said she saw things sticking out of its head."

"Porcupine quills," guessed Gray. "It probably has infected wounds; that's why it came to the village. Easier prey here. Let's see if it is our friend."

In spite of the many bare feet which had trampled the ground since the tiger's appearance, Ali picked up the trail quickly. It wasn't Timur. The tiger was a female. Gray traced the pugmarks on to paper before he and Ali tracked the tigress inland, away from the river, through waist high grass. Occasional flecks of dried blood brightened the trail.

"Tiger is going to the forest," Ali announced, pointing towards the distant trees.

In a patch of flattened grass, Ali found the half eaten remains of a teenage girl. The tiger was nowhere in sight. Gray tried not to look at the dismembered body as he threw his light safari jacket over the corpse.

"Here, Gray," Ali called. "She went this way."

They followed the trail to the river. There, where clear pugmarks walked through the silt into the water, they lost her.

"Back to Dhangmari, Ali. We'll get the boat. She can't be too far away."

"She must be sleeping over there somewhere. We will find her," Ali agreed.

An hour later, after organizing two men to recover the girl's remains, Gray and Ali cruised back along the river in their dingi. Clamped to the gunwales, near the stern of the boat, they had a new 20 horsepower outboard motor. Amidships a large wooden crate, scored with multiple wide air holes, took up most of the available space.

Ali soon found where the tiger had taken to the forest. Deep prints showed clearly in the thick brown mud. A few hundred metres away a woodcutters' barge loomed into sight. Mooring the dingi to a tree trunk Gray and Ali went ashore. The tracks led directly away from the river. Gray cleaned around the pugmarks with a soft brush, removing particles of dirt and leaves. Carefully he placed his tracing over the pattern. It was identical. They had found their new man-eater. Both men knew the tiger would not have gone far. If she was indeed injured, she would stay close to an accessible food source, such as the jig jig village.

Keeping alert, with Gray covering him, Ali followed the fresh tracks over a patch of bare ground. Still warm droppings nearby reminded them both of their danger. Instinctively Gray checked his dart gun: a modified shotgun. A low growl rumbled through the trees. Ali stopped and sniffed at the air. He aimed his rifle at a tangled maze of thick vines a stone's throw ahead. With a movement of his eyes he told Gray their quarry was in the middle. Gray peered into the blackness from a respectable distance, without seeing anything unusual. The tiger warned them again, her voice deep as far off thunder rolling heavily over the steaming morning.

Ali looked around him swiftly, checking for obstructions in case he had to defend himself by flight. Gray angled to the left, praying the tiger would offer him a clear shot. He found his palms were sweating. Hurriedly he wiped them on his pants. The red bandanna round his head, under his bush hat, was soaked. He blinked salt from his eyes, hoping his glasses wouldn't fog up at the wrong moment. A constriction in his chest made him want to cough. He stifled the uncomfortable sensation by swallowing hard. He was very frightened.

Tensely the two men sweated it out. Keeping his eyes on where he thought the tiger crouched, Ali bent slowly and picked up a short broken branch. Gray wanted to shout at him to stop. He couldn't; his throat was too dry. Ali tossed the limb at the hide, where it clattered loudly in the silence. Without further sound the injured man-eater came out of hiding, charging straight at Ali. As the tigress started her attack Ali fired a blank, ejected the cartridge and coolly fired a second one without changing his stance, before the tigress had covered twice her own length. Instantly ramming a live round from the magazine into the chamber, he held his aim. If he had to he would fire: his training kept him still.

The sudden explosions so close startled the cat. Twenty metres from Ali she turned away as Gray fired the tranquilliser. The loaded dart tore out of the barrel striking the tiger square in the rump. The impact triggered another small charge inside the dart, driving a plunger down to inject the drug. Stung hard the tigress changed direction a second time, fleeing towards the river. Gray was finally able to cough. He had been holding his breath and the effort, combined with the tickle, made him sneeze as well. He took off his hat and bandanna, wiping his head with his free hand. He was shaking with strain. Ali reloaded his rifle and grinned weakly at him. Gray noticed his partner was sweating as much as he was.

"Got her, Gray. Good shot."

Gray patted Ali on the back and set off to look for his man-eater. Five minutes later they found a tiger asleep on her side under a bush. Four porcupine quills were stuck in her head and two in her neck. Gray's dart was still embedded in her rear.

"Go get those wood cutters," Gray ordered Ali. "We need some help here. And bring the net and water from our boat; we have to keep her cool. This drug can be dangerous; it raises the temperature too high."

Ali reached the river in minutes as the barge was slowly passing. On board four crewmembers stood staring at the forest, having heard the shots. Ali called to them for help.

"We have caught a tiger," he shouted excitedly. "Come and see. We need your help." The wood cutters turned to shore, eager to assist.

Gray had no intention of losing his tigress now. He moistened her open eyes and covered them with a clean handkerchief. Keeping them free of dust and avoiding damage from the strong tropical sunlight was a priority. Tearing large, fresh green leaves from a nearby tree, he rapidly built a cushion and positioned the cat's head so she wouldn't breathe in dust and suffocate. With gentle skills, Gray removed the quills and put them in his backpack. They would become interesting additions to Project Man-Eater's growing museum of artefacts. He cleaned the suppurating wounds, stitching up one on her neck that was torn rather badly. It was obvious she must have been in some pain and, due to the awkward location of the quills, unable to clean the wounds with her own antiseptic saliva. Gray checked her over carefully, looking for other injuries. There were none. Apart from the quills she was a healthy tigress in her prime, about five years old.

Gray took the imprints of her pads for his files. Ali measured her from the tip of her tail to the end of her nose. Then he measured the tail alone. While the hastily gathered helpers prepared to move the sleeping tigress, Gray photographed her from all angles as a permanent record. Quickly the men rolled her onto a net and carried the sleeping burden to the boats. Not until she was safely inside the crate on his dingi did Gray administer a mild antidote. Fearful of the consequences, expecting the dreaded carnivore to wake up instantly and attack, the wood cutters retreated to their barge. Once they were convinced the tigress was no longer a threat, they relaxed. While Gray tended to his drugged charge they stood in silence, watching curiously. Ali watched from shore.

Gray sat alone on the bow of his boat, watching his captive through the open door of her cage while she struggled to revive. She blinked at him uncomprehendingly, trying to wake up. Remembering his own recovery from an appendicitis operation when he was a boy, Gray had an idea how she felt. Freeing one's mind and body from the clutches of an anaesthetic is not a pleasant experience. Gray was so close to the tigress that, had she found the energy, she could have been on him with one lazy bound. She attempted to stand, getting to her knees, breathing heavily. The effort was too much, and she collapsed in a heap. Through half open eyes, she glared at Gray. Once again she tried to stand. This time she got shakily to her feet before crumpling in a heap again. She groaned in frustration, the sound striking renewed fear into the wood cutters. They scrambled high on to their load of logs, chattering in fear. Gray stilled them with a motion of his hand.

The tigress struggled to her feet again, managing to stay upright by leaning against one wall of her still open prison. Holding her trembling legs far apart she fought unsuccessfully to keep her feet. Grumbling in drugged annoyance, she slid to the floor. Her chin rested on her forepaws as she tried to make sense of her predicament. Tucking her right front paw under her, she straightened one leg. With a grunt she straightened the other. Panting, she forced her reluctant muscles to push her rear high enough to get the hind legs locked. Propped against the side of the crate again she looked almost comical, like a drunk with a pleased expression roaming her face.

Satisfied she would suffer no ill effects, Gray closed the front grill, locked her in and made ready to leave. Ali rejoined him as he primed the motor, pulled once on the starting cord and felt a gratifying buzz vibrating the steering arm. With shouts of thanks to the wood cutters for their help, he turned the dingi towards Mongla. For over an hour, as they sped along the stream bordering the jungle, Ali scooped water from the river every few minutes and poured it over the cage to keep it cool until they reached

Mongla. Once the valuable container was safely on shore, Gray sent the dingi back to Dhangmari with his tracker, reminding him to store the engine safely at the forestry office.

"Go home and see your family, Ali. I'll be back in two days, then we'll go after Timur together. Be ready."

At Mongla he ran into trouble. Word of the man-eater spread like a bush fire through the waterfront.

"There's a man-eating tiger! A man-eating tiger!"

Crowds soon gathered on the wharf to see the captured menace. The men and boys called to the bewildered tigress and made faces at her. Gray tried to cordon off the cage with a ring of rope. The excited crowd took it down. Gray felt like a ringmaster trying to keep wild beasts at bay as he fought to protect his dangerous charge. One young man, perhaps to impress his bravery to the rest of the crowd, tried to poke a stick through the cage. Gray lost his temper and kicked him hard on the backside, to roars of approval from the crowd. Before the youth could retaliate he grabbed him by his hair and shook him roughly.

"You try that again and I'll put you in the cage with the tiger," he snarled, his face contorted with anger. The look on Gray's face and his tone of voice left no doubt that he meant what he said. The youth twisted out of his grip and ran. Gray held his unloaded tranquillizer gun in front of him threateningly. The others backed off, a little quieter now, still watchful but not so menacing, unsure of the angry young foreigner with the flaming red hair.

A scarred and grubby old forklift truck clattered through the mob. With long forks extended, it picked up the crate and lowered it onto a wooden pallet. The driver attached slings and the tigress was loaded onto the deck of a freighter, high out of harm's way. The crowd stayed, standing rows deep to see the ship sail, taking the tiger with it. They didn't have to wait for long. Dock workers cast off mooring lines, a whistle shrilled, slowly the ship turned into the Passur River.

On board the captive grumbled a reluctant farewell. Leaving the jungle far behind forever, she was destined for an overnight voyage around the coast to Dhaka. Gray travelled with her. In the early part of the voyage, down the Passur River with the Sundarbans on either side, he sat near her, wondering what she was thinking, knowing she could smell the forest.

Throughout the night he rested beside the crate on a thin mattress in the open air. Sleeping for an hour at a time; then waking to worry about his prize. Through the long night and much of the next day he stayed with her. His meals were brought to him, though Gray ate them indifferently, simply because he was hungry. The tigress was his only concern. Every hour, after the sun came up, he sprayed her with cool water from a hose.

A truck drove them the final stage to Mirpur Zoo, where a veterinarian and a keeper took over. They gave the tigress another sedative and removed all her tics for analysis. The resident vet checked Gray's field surgery and pronounced it would do well enough. As the confused tigress awoke later, she studied the barred and walled enclosure where she was doomed to spend the rest of her life. Outside Gray felt a lump in his throat and the sting of tears in his eyes as he watched. The tigress glared at him with hatred in her eyes. Gray knew he had done the right thing, but he hated to see wild animals in cages. In the back of his mind he pondered the possibility of returning her to the Sundarbans sometime in the future.

"Well," he sighed, "at least that's two I've saved from an early death."

Gray spent two days writing a report for the Forestry Commission, adding the zoo's written clinical observations. He sent identical documents to Project Man-Eater's benefactors. Having this overwhelming success gave the project greater credibility and a promise of much needed government funds.

CHAPTER 10

Happy to have saved another tiger's life, Gray raced back to the Sundarbans with Ali. Together they hunted the length and breadth of Jawtoli meadow. They walked the deserted beach from Tiger Point to an empty seasonal fishing village, where they made their camp. The late monsoon rains beat down on them incessantly. Millions of raindrops lashed the pair, stinging their eyes and tightening the skin on their unprotected faces. Twice they came across Timur's tracks among the trees without seeing him.

"He's been here within the last few hours because his tracks are still visible. Not even these trees can protect trails from this monsoon for long," he said, half to himself, half to Ali.

They searched for the female and cub, but found no sign. Gray had no better luck with the shipwreck. Although there was plenty of broken pottery, nothing else of interest showed in the loose mud. Depressed by the unbearable July heat and the predictable torrential rain, Gray gave up the chase on the morning of the fourth day. At Kotka, where *Fatima* – their boat – waited, they found the rest-house staff and a few fishermen loading meagre possessions on the boat.

"Tropical storm warning," Abdul, the captain, told Gray as he came aboard. "We must go home now."

Gray looked out over the river mouth towards the bay. The sea was calm with only a slight swell. The heavy rain flattened the surface. There was almost no wind, only an ominous feeling in the air.

"We'll be running against the outgoing tide and the current, won't we?"

"Ji, it will be slow," Abdul nodded, "but we have to go."

He signalled the crew to cast off, and the jetty slowly fell away. *Fatima* chugged steadily north, Abdul keeping her to narrower waterways to avoid tidal surges on the main rivers. They made slow progress. At times visibility was zero through the heavy rain. Occasionally they stopped to pick up a fisherman, tying his boat to the others already trailing behind them. One gave them startling news. He had found the carcass of a partly eaten tiger a few days before. Not far away lay two dead monitor lizards.

"Damn. That's the work of poachers, Ali," said Gray. "Someone is using poison to kill tigers. Those scavenging monitors died because they ate tainted meat. Poachers. That's all we need. Find out exactly where. As soon as the weather improves a bit, send a couple of men to bring in what's left of the tiger for analysis."

By mid-afternoon, the rain fell so heavily visibility was limited to the pointed bow. Beyond was simply a confusion of grey and white waves and spray. Overhead the thick clouds moved relentlessly inland, faster than *Fatima* and her passengers on the river. The wind had come up, blowing urgently on shore from the Bay of Bengal, and was increasing. It gusted in vicious eddies up the rivers and creeks, funnelled by the trees on either side. The rivers, struggling to reach the sea on the outgoing tide, built up armies of waves as the wind attempted to hold them back. *Fatima* began to roll fore and aft. Her bow crashed through breaking rollers, sending sheets of dirty brown water over the foredeck and the bridge.

"We'll have to get rid of those fishing boats," Gray shouted to Abdul. "We need to get out of the wind for a while and try to save them."

Abdul didn't reply, he was too busy handling his boat. His eyes and an almost imperceptible nod gave his answer. Taking *Fatima* as close to the west bank as he dared, Abdul searched for a creek to shelter the fishermen's boats. He found what he was looking for and gave rapid orders. As each boat was pulled alongside, its owner and one of Abdul's crew jumped aboard. Frantically they paddled the wild water to the dubious safety of the forest. Gray went with the last dingi. The creek was full, swollen with flood water, though only five metres wide. At least it was calmer than the main river. The fishermen pushed as far as they could, before tying five boats to the most solid tree they found. Water ran in torrents from the land to the river. Obliquely Gray wondered about the phenomenon as he held one dingi back. The soaked and muddy men, ten in total, scrambled aboard Gray's boat. With virtually no freeboard left and in danger of sinking, they paddled back towards *Fatima* as fast as they could.

Abdul held his craft close to the creek opening. The wind howled, becoming stronger by the second, the waves more disturbed. Trees began to whip backwards and forwards as the gusts tore at them. Leaves and small branches were ripped off and carried away. Gray and his human cargo shot out of the creek like a surf boat. Paddling hard they rode the battering storm the last few strokes to crash unceremoniously into *Fatima*'s steel hull. Two men were knocked overboard as the rest scrambled up the sides. Gray grabbed one of the men by the hair as he was washed past by the current, dragging him back on board and pushing him to safety. The other clung to the dingi until Gray could get to him. Together they reached for helping hands and were pulled aboard. The remaining dingi they tied alongside. As the tropical fury worsened, so the situation on the river deteriorated.

"How deep is that creek?" Abdul asked, as a violent gust heeled *Fatima* over.

"Deep enough, I think," Gray answered, "a lot safer than out here, that's for sure."

Abdul spun the wheel abruptly. With the screaming wind battering the hull, he coaxed the big riverboat into the shelter of the channel. Yard by yard Abdul probed *Fatima* into the forest, praying out loud that the creek would be deep enough to keep her afloat, even at low tide.

"We'll stay here tonight," he told Gray, "and go all the way to Khulna in the morning – if we can."

"Good, there's something strange about this creek. Further up, where we left the dingis, the rainwater was flowing rapidly from the forest, almost as if it were running downhill. There are no hills that I know of in the Sundarbans. Where the hell was all that water coming from?"

Neither Abdul nor Ali had any ideas to offer. As a reminder, Gray marked the creek on his jungle map for future reference. No one got much sleep that night. With the hatches closed, to ward off flying debris and predatory intruders, the vessel was wickedly hot inside. The constant noise of the wind, the alarmingly loud crashes as branches were hurled repeatedly at the boat's decks, made it impossible to sleep even if it had been cool. By morning everyone streamed perspiration. The boat, with little in the way of air circulation, smelled like an unwashed armpit. Outside the storm continued to rage, though the wind was down a little. The rain refused to relax. Desperate for fresh air, it was a relief to all when the crew opened side hatches and upper deck windows again.

"We can't go anywhere for a while so I need to look at something," Gray told Abdul. "Ali, let's go for a walk in the woods."

Ali glanced at the rain sheeting down and shook his head in resignation. Looking thoroughly dejected he stepped aboard the dingi, his rifle strapped across one shoulder. Gray picked up a paddle and began to stroke the boat upstream until they reached the other dingis.

"There," he pointed with the paddle. "There's a game trail, and it looks like a little river. We'll follow that."

Ali tied the mooring line to a tree as Gray bent to look at the opening in the undergrowth.

"Here, Ali. Follow me."

Crouching low the two splashed inland along the low tunnel. After ten minutes Gray was sure the water flowed faster. Almost immediately he tripped and fell to his hands and knees. Where there should have been soft mud to cushion his fall there was only unyielding stone.

"What the hell is this?" he asked himself aloud as he felt beneath the ankle deep water. His hands found a regular oblong of masonry. Then another. Gray got to his feet and, treading carefully, followed the pattern of blocks until he broke out into the open. In front of him stood a large earthen mound overgrown with trees and shrubs. A few large pieces of hand-cut stone were just visible along one face. Gray and Ali stood side by side, staring at the unexpected sight. Rainwater ran in wide rivulets from the highest points to collect in a series of streams; the strongest of which ran away along the trail the two had recently walked.

"What is this?" Gray asked Ali in surprise. "It looks like a buried temple, doesn't it?"

Ali didn't answer. He stood, looking in awe at the building, his hair flattened, rain streaming down his body. Gray tugged at his sleeve.

"Over here."

In the lea of the ruin, the two were shielded from much of the wind and some of the rain. High trees further deflected the storm. Close inspection revealed considerably more than a temple. The ruin was in sad shape, the jungle having efficiently reclaimed it and the land it stood on. One thing was sure, whatever had been there, and it appeared to have been a small fort surrounding a place of worship, it was definitely man-made and hundreds of years old. Gray studied the structure from all angles while Ali climbed to the apex, about ten metres above the average ground level.

"There are tiger tracks up there – under that tree. Old ones, many of them," he told Gray when he came down. "There are deer tracks all around too."

Inside the fort, under an overhanging slab of rock protecting a vertical wall, Gray found more tracks on reasonably dry ground. They were recent and they were Timur's.

"So," he smiled, "this is where you come to when you disappear, you old rogue. You have a ruin for a castle."

Gray marked the location on his map, about twelve kilometres north of Kotka and two kilometres east. He made a mental note to tell Julian of his discovery.

"Maybe we'll come back here after this storm is over," he told Ali. "Tigers seem to like man-made objects, especially buildings. At Ranthambore, in India, they roam quite happily through an old palace and the fort. I'll bet Timur will be back here soon."

Ali crouched against the wall and lit a cigarette, cupping his hands around his match and shielding it from the wind and rain with his body.

"We should go back," he said, his words wreathed in blue smoke. "The wind is getting stronger again – and I don't like this place."

Back at the boat Abdul waited impatiently on the foredeck. His clothes were saturated, his thick black hair dripped water. He held a long bamboo pole in his hands.

"Hurry," he shouted, waving one hand furiously, "the tide is dropping. The mud is only just under my keel. We will be stuck soon."

As Gray and Ali swung themselves aboard, Abdul called for reverse and full power. *Fatima's* propeller churned mud from the bottom as she roared backwards down the creek to open water. The waves smashed into her sides as she laboured to turn and present her blunt stern to the wind. With the rain pelting across her decks, Abdul pushed his charge once again towards the north.

Late in the afternoon they finally berthed at Khulna, after dropping the fishermen at Chandpai and the forestry guards at Dhangmari. Exhausted, Gray and Ali spent another night on board, waiting for the storm to subside. Going back to the jungle was pointless for a few days. Gray chose, instead, to return to Dhaka. Before he left, he reminded Ali to send men to bring in the remains of the poisoned tiger.

In central Bangladesh the rivers flooded and burst their banks, creating a shambles of the villages. Houses were swept away. Livestock perished. In places the aged and infirm died. The tropical storm, severe though it was, managed to exhaust much of itself along the coast before it could do too much serious damage. In the Sundarbans the forest dwellers, both man and beast, retreated deeper and deeper into the natural haven where the trees were thickest. Timur found himself a comfortable hide across the river from Jawtoli, a short walk north of Kotka. Deep inside his own territory he was well positioned to hunt and to survive the storm without interference from rivals.

In the towns and cities, the oppressive humidity grew mould on damp walls, inside and out. Simple possessions like books and clothes needed drying every day. Wooden furniture took on the appearance of living trees as fungi found precarious but receptive homes. Those Europeans unable to leave moaned and cursed the dreadful weather. In consolation they drank more to help them sleep through the scorching nights.

Driving into town from the airport, Gray saw the results of the most recent storm in the fields adjacent to the roads. Boats floated far from rivers; a sure sign the monsoon had been troublesome across the country. Gray was not sorry to have missed the worst of it in the city. As soon as possible he planned to get back to the jungle; otherwise he faced another unpleasant session with the Forestry Commission.

In the office, Gray found Rab had taken on a part-time worker. Sandy, an Australian girl Gray knew socially, had volunteered her off duty hours to help the project.

Rab had accepted gratefully, offering to pay when and if the project could afford it. Sandy was a computer operator for a children's aid agency. Her knowledge and computer skills would make her invaluable to Rab and to the project as a unit.

While Sandy showed Rab how to use the computer more effectively, Gray spent the afternoon pacing the office dictating notes to himself on his micro-cassette recorder. Outside the rain created havoc as the overworked drains clogged with refuse swept along by the storm. Bicycle rickshaws struggled against the flow, axles submerged, their pullers forcing down hard on reluctant pedals. Occasional bursts of thunder rent the air. Pedestrians, saturated men and women, splashed on their way: some with umbrellas, others holding an ineffectual book or sodden newspaper over their heads. Gray watched the mess through his window, wondering if the project's old Land Rover could make it through the rapidly deepening water.

"I'm going home, Rab, before this gets any worse. Do you need a ride, Sandy?"

"No thanks, I'm fine here," she replied. "By the way, we're having a monsoon party tomorrow night at the house. Your name is on the guest list."

Gray laughed and thanked her. "I'll be there for sure, weather permitting. Are you going Rab?"

"No, I have a family dinner to attend. I may drop by later though."

♦ ♦ ♦

The party, a loose gathering of ex-pat acquaintances from embassies, consulates and overseas companies, was well under way when Gray arrived. With the monsoon season winding down, those who had fled the oppressive heat at the beginning of summer were beginning to return. Those who had stayed were up for a final fling before they tried to dry out possessions and themselves, in preparation for more bearable weather. People who hadn't seen each other for many weeks found much to talk about. Home, wherever it happened to be, was the main topic of conversation. Gray, having spent much of the summer travelling far and wide, found plenty to talk about, as well as ready listeners.

Sandy, he noticed, made sure he always had a drink in his hand. Any time she passed, or stopped to throw in a few words to his circle, she managed to touch his arm or his hand. Coming home, he thought, accepting that he now considered Bangladesh his home, had certain advantages. He watched Sandy circulating effortlessly, a confident hostess.

She could never be called beautiful, he decided: attractive perhaps, but not beautiful. Her hair was a mousy colour. Worn long but tied back with a plain brown ribbon, the curls reached halfway down her back. She had blue eyes, the colour enhanced by tinted contact lenses, and a permanent tan. Although a little on the heavy side, she was the picture of Australian health. Casually dressed in open sandals with no more than a hint of heel, a thin tan skirt and a white tee shirt advertising the wonders of Australia's Red Centre, she was cool and efficient. There were no tell-tale lines showing under the shirt. Gray studied the image of Ayers Rock spanning her firm well-proportioned chest. The words Red Centre underneath sparked a lewd thought, and he broke into a wicked smile.

"What's tickling you?" Sandy asked, standing with her hands provocatively on her hips.

"I was just thinking about Ayers Rock," he answered, "I've never seen it, let alone climbed it. Does it really have a red centre?"

Sandy burst out laughing, causing those nearby to look up in amusement. She put her hand over her mouth and spluttered into it. She only had to raise her eyes a fraction to look into his.

"If you play your cards right, you might find out one day." She looked him straight in the eye and started to laugh again. "Come and make yourself useful. I need some help with the drinks."

She led him into the kitchen, which was fast becoming the centre of attention, due to proximity to the bar. Sandy ushered everyone out, pleading the need for adequate working space. Gray, she told them, would help her move the drinks into the living room. As soon as they were gone he pulled Ayers Rock against him as she reached for a bottle of wine. She was soft and warm. Gray put his hands on her waist and kissed her. Sandy responded immediately, her full lips all over his and her tongue burrowing in his mouth. Rab burst into the kitchen in time to hear Gray say laughingly to Sandy, "With a promise like that I might have to stay all night."

Rab coughed in embarrassment. "Excuse me, Sandy. Gray, we have a problem."

"What is it Rab?" Gray let go of Sandy, his rising desire momentarily forgotten. If Rab had taken the trouble to call at this time of night it had to be serious.

"The tigress we put into the zoo," he began. "She's mauled a keeper badly. There's talk of putting her down. I have a car outside."

Gray kissed Sandy lightly on the cheek. "Sorry," he grimaced, "gotta go."

Sandy stood in silence for a second, biting her lower lip. As the door closed, she swore softly.

"Not now, damn you. Not now. Couldn't you at least have waited until tomorrow?"

It took Gray and Rab three hours of non-stop argument with the zoo's director to save the tiger's life. The keeper, according to reports, had thought she was locked in the cage when he went to retrieve a football thrown into the compound during the day. She wasn't locked in. She was in the cage, but the lock was open. The keeper was halfway to the exit with the ball in his hands when she attacked. He was lucky. Apart from severe shoulder lacerations, he was alive and would stay that way. The tiger was under sentence of death.

Gray argued that the keeper was at fault. The cage should have been checked before anyone entered the tiger compound. With a thinly veiled threat, he angrily pointed out, "Tigers in captivity are just as much under government protection in this country as those in the wild. If you don't believe me, check with the Forestry Commission, or the PM's office. You can do nothing without approval from the highest level. Nothing, d'you understand?"

The director glared at Gray and interrupted him, "General Rahman has told me we have to put the tiger down..." Gray cut him off.

"Shut up. I haven't finished yet. I shall certainly submit my own report about tonight's events. Forget the general. He has no say in this, so don't you take the law into your own hands. If you try to cross me I'll have your damned head."

Driving back in the early hours of the morning, Rab asked, "Do you think it will work?"

"You're damn right it will. If necessary I'll phone the PM herself. She'll listen, I know she will."

Gray went to his own home where, instead of going to bed, tired though he was, he wrote his report. The tiger, and its plight filled his mind; while Sandy and her implied promise were forgotten. Not far away, Sandy lay awake also, staring in solitary silence at the rotating fan on the ceiling.

That evening, in spite of the appalling weather, Ali went south again in the outboard powered dingi. With him went the fisherman who had reported finding the poisoned tiger's remains and a forestry guard. By keeping to the smallest waterways, Ali made good time and was in the general area within a few hours. The three men spent an uncomfortable night huddled under a plastic tarpaulin which Ali slung between three trees. At daybreak they went inland and found what was left of the tiger. They rolled it up in the tarpaulin and sped back to Dhangmari, fighting the storm all the way. There one of the senior men performed an autopsy and prepared a report for Project Man-Eater.

CHAPTER II

At Kotka, life was miserable for man and beast alike. For two days it rained without stopping. The wind, driving out of the north-west, scattered raindrops as hard as transparent bullets to create turmoil on the ground. Leaves were torn from trees, grass was flattened; the earth was churned to mud. All the creatures of the forest went into hiding, protecting themselves under whatever shelter they could find. The few fishermen who remained at the tiny village by the long wooden jetty huddled under their upturned boats, waiting for the storm to abate.

As suddenly as it had begun, the rain stopped an hour past midday. The clouds, which had darkened the sky day and night for so long, were swept away on the wind. The sun came out to boil the waterlogged ground. The moisture clinging to trees, boats and flimsy buildings simmered. Steam rose everywhere, creating eerie tendrils snaking through the forest. Birds preened their feathers, stretched their wings and sailed into the blazing sky. A kingfisher opened its eyes and watched the river from the shelter of a white orchid. In the fishing villages and camps, men struggled to re-launch their boats and repair damaged roofs. By late afternoon, the heat and humidity were almost unbearable. Throats became parched. Lips dried and began to crack. It was time to drink.

Ismael let the aluminium pot sink into the freshwater hole. He held it down until the water cascading over the rim had slowed and settled. He adjusted his tightly wound cotton donut on top of his head with one hand then lifted the shiny pot with both hands. Holding the neck in a stranglehold, he held the heavy pot above him, before carefully placing it on his head. Steadying the pot with his right hand, Ismael picked up the hem of his tartan cloth lunghi in his left, before starting back along the narrow footpath to his village.

From the shadows of the forest, on the opposite side of the rectangular man-made water-hole, a male rhesus macaque stood to watch his departure. The red-faced monkey grunted, as if in approval. Out of the shade came a female and two young. She passed the watchful male and stopped halfway down the bank, urging her offspring to the water's edge. The young, not much bigger than a pair of month-old kittens, obeyed instantly. Crouching side by side, their bodies low to the water, their front paws clasped together as if praying and shoulders hunched, they stuck out their tiny pink tongues. Thirstily, they lapped the water. Finished, they scampered back past their mother, past the male and into the haven behind. The male grunted again. The female took her turn, looking nervously around as she approached the pool. Exposed as she was, with water in front and open ground at her back, she was at her most defenceless. The skilled watcher by the tree was her only shield. She drank hurriedly before racing back to her babies.

The grey-suited male started down the incline alone, stopping half-way. He stood up on two legs again, like an exceedingly embarrassed and exceptionally hairy little man. Upright he surveyed the pond and the trees. His nervous fingers plucked at the end of a vine. Worried by something beyond the pool, he sunk to the ground, hiding in a clump of long grass. Another water carrier arrived, dropping his metal urn into the pool with a splash. The macaque waited, making no movement. Behind him, hidden in the edge of the jungle, the female and the young were silent. The water carrier filled his urn and left, singing softly to himself. The parched macaque looked around for signs of danger. Sensing no threat, he ran to the water and began to drink.

Above him, a Brahmini kite circled, gliding low over the water to land at the far end. It fluffed its feathers, standing erect like a sentry wearing furry white gaiters. As with the macaque, it stepped to the edge of the pool and dipped its head to sip the water, its extraordinary eyes taking in everything around it. A large spotted deer with a full rack of antlers tip-toed between the two, causing them both to look up sharply. Seeing no danger they drank again.

With a sudden, shrill cry the kite took off, beating its long reddish-brown wings smoothly to gain height and manoeuvrability. The raptor soared over the coconut palms bordering the pool and was quickly out of sight. As the kite launched itself into the air, the macaque raced back up the bank in fright. The buck raised his antlers, as if admiring his beautiful reflection in the pool. He cocked his head, listening intently. There was no recognizable alarm from others in the forest and no obvious cause for immediate concern. He went back to his task, his front legs bent and splayed apart.

Timur lay on his belly watching the scene. He didn't move. Only his eyes roamed from the buck to the trees and back again. He hadn't eaten or even seen a deer for some time. Unlike many other predators, Timur had stayed close to the sea, patrolling the southern reaches of his domain during the storm. After a long wait in one spot, his patience was running thin. The kite and the macaque couldn't possibly have detected his presence. He was downwind and he hadn't moved. Something else had disturbed them.

The buck, normally uneasy and quick to flee, was thirsty enough to delay a second or two longer. Timur gauged the distance from his hide to the deer. There were roughly two strides of forest to clear and about four lengths through water – a few heartbeats only, hardly enough time for the deer to recognize its peril and react.

Silently Timur rose to all fours, keeping low to the ground. He leaned forward with his left forepaw raised. Abruptly he sunk to the ground again as a voice sounded. A man's voice, carried openly across the clearing. The buck snorted and danced out of sight, ducking its head and antlers under the branches as it wove its way through the trees. When its initial fright passed it stopped and listened. Out of sight of possible danger, it lowered its head to browse on a tuft of greenery.

Timur, perfectly still, watched the man. The jungle fell silent, as if all the creatures were holding their breath. Talking to himself, Ismael filled his urn again, hefted it onto his head and turned. Timur, frustrated at the loss of the spotted deer, let Ismael pass. Without a sound he followed him, angling through the undergrowth to get close.

A small stone caught between Ismael's toes and the sole of his sandal. He stopped. Lifting his foot he picked out the offending pebble. With one foot in the air and one hand on his water jug he froze. The hair on the back of his neck stood up and he swivelled his head to look behind him. There was nothing there. He looked to the front again, putting his foot down as he did so. Still nothing, yet his nerves jangled. He was frightened. Again, Ismael turned to look back only to come face to face with a charging tiger.

Ismael looked Timur straight in the eye as, with all four feet off the ground, the tiger hit him squarely in the chest. The collision broke Ismael's back even as Timur's hot breath scorched his face and his fangs crushed his head. Ismael died still trying to get his scream to bubble up his throat. The shiny aluminium pot bounced once, spilled its contents and rolled to a stop against a bush. Timur took hold of Ismael by the chest and carried him without effort into the forest. Man, the creature that walked upright on two legs, was the easiest of jungle prey to catch. A little over four hundred years earlier, his ancestors had learned the same when a Portuguese ship was wrecked on the jungle-clad coast of their Bengal wilderness.

The next water carrier to walk the path found Ismael's topknot lying like a bedraggled chequered snake across the path. A short distance away his empty pot lay inverted in a pool of water. The water carrier saw the two items and the tiger's tracks. At the top of his lungs he screamed to all within hearing that the water hole was no longer safe for man.

Days later and far to the north, Timur killed again while Gray and Rab argued with bureaucracy for another tiger's life. He lay in the darkness; his eyes focused on the hut in the clearing. There was the glow of an oil lamp, a few muffled voices. The smell of cooked fish wafted through the air. Timur licked his nose to taste the scent. Somewhere nearby a dog barked. Timur ignored it. Inside the hut a family settled down for their evening meal. Rezaul was a forestry worker, a guard who accompanied visitors and government officials into the forest. It was a good job. He received regular pay so he could feed his family properly. He had a smart khaki uniform and strong boots. Over in the corner, leaning against the thin wall, his old government-issue Lee Enfield .303 rifle had five live rounds in the magazine and a blank in the chamber. The safety catch was on.

Rezaul and his twelve-year-old son sat cross-legged on a rush mat on the floor. Each rolled the rice and mashed fish into balls between thumb and forefinger. They popped the tasty morsels into their mouths, munching contentedly, enjoying the spicy flavour. Facing them his wife ladled a similar meal on to a plate for her six-year-old daughter. She did the same for herself. They too heard their neighbour's dog bark, without comment. Rezaul scooped the remaining grains of rice from his plate into his mouth with his right hand and burped loudly, reaching for his mug of tea. His son copied him exactly. Mother and daughter continued their dinner.

The night was warm and clammy. Heat from the charcoal cooking fire made the one room building stuffy. Rezaul got up and opened two of the four wooden shutters to let the night air circulate. In the doorway he pulled aside the colourful strips of plastic curtain his wife was so proud of. He slipped his feet into his open sandals and went out onto the wooden walkway.

All the houses in the tiny village were built the same: a framework of straight tree branches, enclosed by tightly woven palm fronds, standing on wooden platforms. Each house was built on stilts, keeping them well above the level of flood tide. Each was connected to the next by a wooden path, like an extended veranda. There was no reason for anyone to touch the ground unless they had to. The walkway branched off in two locations to meet the river, where the boats were moored.

Rezaul walked a few paces to the right of the door. Crouching he unbuttoned his fly and urinated on to the grass a man's height below him. Flattening himself to the ground, Timur slunk towards the figure by the hut. He heard the trickle of water, instinctively wrinkling his nose to get the scent. Rezaul belched again and farted noisily. Doing himself up as he stood, he leaned his back against the rail. Timur could see him clearly, a dark patch against a slightly lighter sky. Rezaul lit a cigarette, drawing deeply on the rich, raw, smoke. He coughed a few times as the smoke filled his lungs, before turning back to his house.

Timur was no more than half a dozen bounds away when Rezaul went inside. He stopped, his body perfectly still. Only the end of his tail moved, slowly, from side to side. Through the doorway a child was held by the light for a second. Rezaul's daughter picked up the empty plates and a jug of water. Out on the walkway she rinsed off the plates, using as little water as she could. Finished, she shook the plates to remove any excess fluid, picked up the water jug and screamed once.

Timur's mighty leap from ground level took him to the walkway in one bound. He landed in front of the child, clamping his jaws on her left shoulder as she screamed. One dagger-like tooth pierced her heart, killing her instantly. Timur's momentum carried him and his prey off the planks to the earth below. He made a sharp turn under the hut, where he paused for a moment. Inside the hut Rezaul heard the scream followed by the clatter of tin plates falling on wood. He lunged for his rifle, clicking the safety catch off as he grabbed it. Within two seconds he was outside. Racing along the walkway in bare feet, he tripped on the water jug, letting off a blank shot as he did so. Timur was still under the hut when the rifle went off, nearly deafening him. He streaked into the sanctity of the night with his prey and was gone.

There was no sign of his daughter and no sign of a tiger, but Rezaul was in no doubt what had happened. Though he and two other men searched the surrounding jungle, rifles at the ready, they found only a scrap of cloth caught on a bush. Torn from the little girl's dress as her life-less body was dragged into the night, it was the only evidence of his daughter.

In the morning, a distraught Rezaul resumed the search. All around the village the tracks of a large tiger mingled with the footprints of the search party. The ground was soft, the pug marks deep and distinct. The right front paw was quite different from the left. Rezaul studied it carefully, confused by the four ellipses on the right pad compared to the three on the left. He knew this tiger was unique. He knew he could identify him if they ever came close again. One day, he swore, somewhere in the forest, he would find him and avenge his baby's death. Rezaul tracked the tiger for days but the cat's aimless wanderings and repeated river crossings confused him. On the fourth day he gave up the unequal chase and returned to his family. If he had known how close the tiger was, he would have kept up the hunt.

Hidden in a broad spread of long grass on the edge of a clearing, not far from Rezaul's village, Timur suddenly came awake. He sniffed the air, his ears listening intently for the sounds of prey. The wind had changed. His olfactory senses told him he was near another village, though his ears could detect no sound from that direction. Timur stayed where he was, all senses alert.

Ahmed stirred in his sleep. He brushed away a fly from his lip and snorted involuntarily, waking himself up. He was hot. He reached out and drew the cloth curtain aside. Sunlight streamed in. The heavy dank air of the hut, polluted with his stale sweat and rank breath, filtered out to mix with the natural odours of the forest. Ahmed sat up, looking at the shadows on the ground. It was late afternoon, time to go fishing. Two metres below him the ground was dry. Ahmed washed his face in a pan of water, drank a little and climbed backwards down his wooden ladder. Alone in the village, he talked to himself as he walked across the clearing to answer nature's call, taking a small pot of water to wash his hands afterwards.

Timur's keen hearing detected the snort as Ahmed awoke. He listened, but there were no other sounds from the village. Silently he walked towards the huts. Ahmed was squatting by a tree when Timur saw him. The man poured water over his left hand and cleansed himself, then cleaned the same hand with more water. He rearranged his lunghi and went back to his hut. Timur began his stealthy approach. Fifty paces separated the two as Ahmed mounted the ladder to collect his few belongings. When he emerged Timur was less than twenty five metres away, still camou-flaged by the shadows of the forest.

Ahmed went behind the hut to the creek where his boat was tethered to a stake driven into the mud. The tide had come up enough while he slept to set the boat afloat. Free of the clinging mud, its stern had swung further up the shallow creek as the tide crept inland. With the added weight of a small man, there was just enough water under the hull to allow the boat to be poled without grounding. Ahmed placed his water, some food and a blanket, under the semi-circular awning that served as a cabin. He picked up his long bamboo pole and stabbed it into the mud; lean-ing heavily on the end, he pushed himself down the creek towards the river.

Timur followed from a distance. Preparing himself for the right moment. He began his charge at the instant the boat caught on an underwater obstruction. Ahmed changed his grip on the pole, swinging it across his body to fend himself off the impediment. Timur sprang from the rear left side, hitting the pole with his head, his claws raking at Ahmed. The pole snapped. Ahmed and Timur hit the shallow water together, Timur landing on all fours a little beyond Ahmed.

The panic-stricken man, with one broken shoulder and multiple deep lacerations on his upper body, lurched to his feet. Screaming at the top of his lungs, he splashed down the middle of the muddy creek. Timur regained his balance and continued his attack. Massive strides, with forelegs extended in front and hind legs almost horizontal behind, sent sheets of spray flying over both banks. Timur caught up with Ahmed within seconds, striking him hard with his uninjured paw to knock the man out of the creek to the dried mud. Ahmed was dead before he bounced the second time. Timur pawed at him roughly a few times, then left his victim in the mud and stalked arrogantly away.

The boat later floated further up the creek with the tide, only to drift back out into the river on the ebb. Two days later another fisherman found it snagged by an overhanging branch about a kilometre away from the creek. He towed it home with him as evidence of another's misfortune.

CHAPTER 12

The British Airways flight from London arrived in Dhaka on time. As the engine whine died a mobile stairway with a metal sun canopy nudged up to the front door. A second stairway was shoved against the middle door, halfway down the fuselage. The doors opened, letting in a rush of hot humid air. Marshall shouldered his hanging valet and camera bag, picked up his briefcase and large duffel. Thanking the flight attendants, he stepped through the First Class door, going down the steps two at a time. A couple of dusty buses waited at the bottom but he, escorted by one of the ground staff, walked the thirty steps to the terminal building. First at the immigration desk on the left side, the one designated for arriving foreigners, Marshall had his visa checked and his passport stamped. Having no other bags to wait for, he followed the green arrows to the exit marked, 'Nothing to Declare'.

Outside, a smartly dressed young man with a clipboard barred Marshall's way.

"Mr. Richard Marshall?" he asked hopefully. Marshall nodded, taking in the name-tag with Salim in bold letters and Dhaka Sheraton Hotel across the top. Marshall was

ushered into an air-conditioned waiting room and offered
a cold drink. He accepted a sparkling mineral water and
waited patiently.

"We must wait for three more passengers, then we
can go," he was told.

Fortunately the three other guests of Dhaka's most
luxurious hotel were also in First Class and soon arrived.
The drive into town, along a wide boulevard with railway
tracks on the left, hardly surprised him. Although he had
been far removed from poverty for a long time, he hadn't
forgotten his previous stay in Dhaka. Marshall's European
mind still found it hard to reconcile the billboards advertising cars and computers with the deformed beggars waiting
at each traffic light.

"One never really gets used to it, you know," a
voice at his elbow broke in. "As time goes by one accepts it
more, but never really gets used to it."

Marshall grunted and continued to study the
streets and the people. The minibus turned right opposite
the Central Malaria Institute and thumped over a railway
level crossing. Traffic increased as they drove through Tej-
gaon, past the rambling red brick offices of the Bangladesh
Parjatan Corporation – the national tourism body. At a traffic roundabout, where untold numbers of bicycle rickshaws
competed for manoeuvring room, they passed a large hotel.
A few minutes later they turned left in front of the Sheraton.
The driver cut sharply across all the incoming traffic, none
of which even slowed, and drove through the open gate.
Marshall instinctively held his breath. He wasn't the only
one. There was a collective sigh as the minibus stopped in
front of the hotel.

A tall, rotund concierge bid the four welcome as
two porters scurried to collect the bags. Marshall, who preferred to carry his own luggage, had a brief tussle with one
who couldn't bear to see a guest so burdened. Marshall was
bigger and stronger. He won the right to bear his own belongings.

Prior to leaving London, Marshall had courteously advised the Canadian Embassy in Dhaka of his visit. He neglected to give his true reasons. A phone call from the hotel that morning put him in touch with an embassy employee, who gave him the name and address of a senior officer in the Bangladesh Forestry Commission.

A second call, to Saddiq Hossein of Bengal River Adventures, arranged for the charter of a large motor launch and crew for up to one month. There would be only two passengers on board and the boat must be available in two days, Marshall insisted. Limited catering would be required, but adequate food and fuel supplies must be carried for the duration of the charter. Next Marshall phoned the Forestry Commission, requesting an appointment for first thing the following morning. After a few moments hesitation from the other end he was told to be there at 09:00.

At one o'clock Marshall and Saddiq had lunch at the hotel. Marshall needed a few items purchased, quickly, without too many questions asked. He didn't beat around the bush. He showed his guest the list as soon as they sat down. Saddiq read the note and turned pale. He shook his head from side to side, his dark brown eyes almost closed. Saddiq was far from happy with the request and said so.

"What you are asking is highly illegal," he whispered across the table, "if you get caught I would be an accomplice. I have my reputation to think of."

"Damn your reputation. I'll pay you cash, in American dollars," Marshall offered, as if that was the ultimate incentive. Saddiq sat up straight and glowered at Marshall, clearly offended and extremely uncomfortable with the conversation. Marshall dropped the subject for the moment. They selected their choices from the buffet and ate as two strangers at the same table. To ease the situation, Marshall went over the boat charter details again. Saddiq responded with enthusiasm, ecstatic to be able to discuss anything other than the visitor's outrageous request. Over coffee Marshall changed his tack.

"Saddiq, do you, perhaps, know someone who could help me – another businessman, maybe?"

A frown crossed Saddiq's forehead. He thought for a moment, then breathed a sigh of relief.

"Yes, Mr. Marshall, I think I have heard of a man who may be able to help you. I don't know him personally, of course. I will see what can be done."

After lunch Marshall catnapped in his room, waiting for Saddiq's envoy to call. Jet lag was beginning to take its effect and he allowed it to lull him to sleep. The telephone rang once. Marshall answered it immediately, waking from a sound sleep at the first click as the bell was activated.

"Mister Marshall?"

"I'm Marshall. What can I do for you?"

"I am told you need to buy some things. Perhaps I can help. Meet me at Sadarghat at half past three, please." The caller hung up.

Marshall looked at his watch, it was nearly three. Quickly he splashed cold water on his face, the back of his neck and his chest. He dried himself as he changed into a pair of grey slacks and a white shirt. On his feet he laced up a pair of old running shoes. A broad-brimmed Panama hat topped the picture. Passing through the lobby he went out the main door, past the airline offices, to the street. There he ignored two beggars and flagged down the first free three-wheel baby taxi.

"Sadarghat," he ordered. "How much?"

The driver held up both hands, palms towards his passenger. Three times he pushed them emphatically at Marshall.

"Thirty taka? That's probably at least twenty taka too much, but I'll pay you anyway."

Marsh bent double and squeezed himself in behind the driver. Before he was even seated, the driver twisted his handlebar gears, revved the motorcycle engine, let in the clutch with his fingers and shot into the passing traffic. Marshall hung on. With his head and shoulders bent, to avoid the plastic awning stretched over the steel frame above him, it was difficult to see much more than the back of the driver's head and the vehicles beside them.

The uncomfortable journey to the passenger and small freight landing stage on the Buriganga River took fifteen and a half minutes. Somehow the driver managed to avoid a dozen accidents as he raced through the congestion of cycle rickshaws, baby taxis and pedestrians. Marshall got there with a stiff neck and time to spare. Having no idea who to look for, he went through the airy passenger terminal building, down the ramp and on to the ghat. There were seven huge river ferries loading at the same time, with passengers and their baggage all over the walkway. On each of the bows and on the dock, ticket collectors shouted out the destinations. Marshall understood none of it. He wandered along to the far end, away from the worst of the noise.

A group of young boys, covered in soap suds, jumped off the end of the ghat into the dirty brown river. Having fun and a wash at the same time, they also managed to splash the occupants of passing boats, laughing and swimming rapidly away from the anger. Dingis and sampans jostled each other for space and passengers, threading their way past the large vessels to cross and re-cross the busy river. Freighters and passenger ships steamed up and down the Buriganga River, sailing from foreign ports to a city dock and away again. At exactly three-thirty a grubby boy tugged at Marshall's shirtsleeve.

"Come, Sahib!" he ordered. Marshall followed the urchin back the way he had come.

Outside the building the boy motioned him into a bicycle rickshaw. Marshall handed the boy one taka and was rewarded with a shy smile. The rickshaw puller said nothing. Once Marshall was seated, the rickshaw moved off along the Bund. Past the Ahsan Manzil, the pink palace of the last Nawab of Dhaka, they turned right crossing Islampur Road almost immediately. A few minutes later the puller took a left on to Yousouf Road. He cut across the oncoming traffic to squeak through into an increasingly narrow street. Pedestrians on either side flattened themselves against the walls of houses to avoid being run over.

Marshall lost count of the turns, keeping sight of his general direction by the shadows on the buildings around him. As the rickshaw creaked through the old city area, Marshall decided he must be somewhere just to the north of Lalbagh Fort. If need be, he was sure he could find his way out of the labyrinth of narrow streets.

Outside a door which had once boasted green paint, the rickshaw puller stopped. Marshall asked him how much and received an apologetic shake of the head in return. Marsh gave him ten taka anyway, which he pocketed without comment or change of expression.

The door opened a little. A child beckoned the stranger enter. He followed the little girl through a curtain into a small rectangular room. On the floor was a thin carpet. Against the wall on one side, a man in his late twenties sat on a tin trunk, his back to the wall. The trunk was covered by a scruffy old tiger skin.

"Welcome. Welcome, Mr. Marshall. You are my guest." Marshall was directed to a simple wooden chair, the only other furniture. The child said something and was answered with the standard, "Atcha."

For a few minutes Marshall was quizzed politely about his health, his journey, and his impressions of Dhaka.

"Isn't this a wonderful city?"

Marshall agreed it had certain charms. The child reappeared, carrying two china cups and saucers, a small bowl of sugar, and a tin of condensed milk on a tray. She set it down and went out, only to return with a teapot. Holding the heavy brown pot in both hands, she poured two cups. With eyes downcast, she left the room. Marshall and his host drank in silence.

"I am told you are shopping." The young man had not moved from his original position.

Marshall nodded, handing him the list without comment. The man pursed his lips and shook his head.

"This is not possible."

"Everything is possible," Marshall argued.

"I can get some things, not everything."

"Just tell me what you can and cannot do."

"I cannot get a machine pistol or ammunition. We are not gangsters in Bangladesh," he sounded quite indignant. "And hand grenades and a high-powered rifle. Huh, the war has been over for a long time, you know. What do you want these things for?"

"That's none of your business. Can you supply me or not?"

"This is very much trouble to arrange, I will need some time."

Marshall sighed and asked, "Please, tell me what you can get immediately."

Marshall's list of weapons was cut and changed to two ex-British Army Lee Enfield .303 rifles and fifty rounds of ammunition, plus a machete. It was far less than he wanted, but he would be able to work with it, providing the guns and ammunition were in working order. The hand grenades had been added as a safety factor for himself, in case of emergency. He could manage without them.

"I need delivery by the day after tomorrow at my hotel in Mongla."

"Atcha!"

"How much?" Marshall asked.

"One thousand dollars. American dollars," answered the young man without changing expression.

Marshall looked sharply at the small-time arms dealer. The man looked him straight in the eye without flinching and shrugged almost imperceptibly. Marshall had no doubt that the simple gesture said, "Take it or leave it." He agreed and counted out five hundred US dollars in twenties.

"I'll give the rest in Mongla, not before. The Al Prince Hotel," he snapped.

Night had fallen by the time Marshall left the house. His host found a rickshaw and sent him back to the Sheraton Hotel. In farewell he offered one word:

"Mongla!"

♦ ♦ ♦

Rab heard about Rezaul's young daughter first. Through a loud phone call from a hot-tempered forestry official, he learned of another death in the Sundarbans.

"Rezaul, the forestry guard, has lived on the edge of the Sundarbans all his life," Rab was told, "he is an expert tracker. He can identify this tiger."

"How can you be sure? The rains will probably have washed away most of the tracks by now."

Rab wrote hurriedly on a pad in front of him as he listened.

"When did this happen?"

"Only two days ago. That's not so long. This tiger has one deformed foot," the voice was getting excited, louder. "Rezaul can describe it for you. Pendennis will have to catch this tiger."

"Where did this attack take place?"

"South of Chandpai," the voice was impatient, snapping the words out. "Rezaul can show Pendennis. He lives there."

"All right, as soon as I can contact Professor Pendennis he will get to work on this. Thank you for telling me."

The phone call to Gray at home produced the expected question. "What does the supposed deformity look like?"

Rab didn't know, of course, any more than the forestry official had known.

"Okay Rab, I'm on my way. There's a flight to Jessore in about an hour. Have someone pick me up there. I'll find out from this guy Rezaul and send a message back to you from Dhangmari tomorrow. And, one more thing -- would you call Sandy and tell her what's happened, please? I'm supposed to have dinner with her tonight. Thanks. See you."

That night, as soon as he arrived at Dhangmari, Gray learned that the tiger brought in by Ali had definitely died as a result of poisoning. He was angry, but knew there was nothing he could do about it unless he was lucky enough to catch the poacher red handed. In the meantime, he had other problems. He and Ali sat outside the forestry office at Dhangmari with a nervous Rezaul and quizzed him about the attack. There were many questions needing answers, but only one of prime importance.

"Can you describe the pugmark for me?"

Rezaul nodded. With the nail of his right index finger, he scratched a rough outline on the wooden veranda at his feet. Gray watched him, feeling a shiver pass up his spine. He stole a glance at Ali.

"Timur," Ali mouthed.

"Are you absolutely sure? Was it left or right?" Gray returned his attention to Rezaul, knowing the answers as he asked.

Rezaul held up his right hand and pointed to the palm. "This one."

"Timur!" Gray got up and looked out at the forest, his mind racing. "What the hell was he doing this far north?"

"Do you know this tiger, sir?" Rezaul stood beside him.

"Yes, I know him. I know him very well. When did this happen?"

Rezaul told him. "A few days."

Gray shook his head in disappointment. "He'll be long gone by now. I doubt that we'll find anything, but nevertheless, we'd better go and look."

He phoned Rab to tell him the latest news about Timur. Like Gray, his first reaction was a sceptical, "Are you sure?"

"I don't think there's any doubt about it, unless Rezaul has got two sets of tiger tracks confused. It's possible I suppose, but unlikely. I'll call you when we get back."

"Okay, but don't forget Julian Sinclair will be here soon," Rab reminded him. "He will need *Fatima* to get to Kotka."

"I know, Rab. We'll come straight back once we've checked out Rezaul's place."

Abdul had *Fatima* up to full speed passing Chandpai when a fisherman signalled them to stop. Recognizing the boat, he shouted at the crew.

"A man has been killed by a tiger at Kotka."

"When?" Ali called back.

"A few days ago," came the reply.

"It's always a few days ago," complained Gray, ignoring Ali's smile. "Why can't anyone around here give me accurate information?"

The fisherman, now holding to the ship's side to keep the current from separating the two boats, said something else to Ali, eliciting a grunt of surprise.

"What's that?" asked Gray.

"He says he heard another man has disappeared. His empty boat was found caught in the roots of a tree, not far from where Rezaul lives."

"What the hell is going on? Three possible killings in so little time," Gray pondered as Abdul brought *Fatima* back up to full speed. "They can't all be the actions of one tiger. They're too far apart. Or are they?"

Gray checked his map, although he knew every imprint on it. His fingers measured the distances between kills.

"It's a hell of a long way from Kotka to your home, Rezaul. I don't think it's the same tiger."

As he expected, picking up Timur's trail was virtually impossible once they arrived at the village. The rain had obliterated all traces in the open. Under Rezaul's hut, however, they found what they were looking for: Timur's pugmark. Protected from the wet, it was the only identifiable mark they had. Gray studied it and shook his head, a worried expression on his face.

"How far away was this other guy's boat found?" He asked.

Ali and Rezaul conferred for a few minutes. Ali pointed to a creek on Gray's map. "Here. It's not far by boat. There's a temporary fishing village with a few huts nearby."

They took the outboard-powered dingi and went to look. The three quartered the village and surrounding area without success at first. Ali found a few indistinct tracks, which Gray photographed, but, washed by rain as they had been, they weren't much help.

"Okay, Ali," Gray finally called a halt. Taking off his glasses he rubbed his eyes. "This is getting us nowhere. We'll go back to *Fatima* and start again."

Ali only half heard him. He was poking at something in the muddy creek. Hesitantly, he shoved his hand and arm up to his shoulder in the water. His fingers touched something soft.

"Gray, there's something here. Help me."

Between them they pulled Ahmed's torn body from the mud. Ali examined the rows of deep claw lacerations.

"Tiger," he said. "He was killed by a tiger."

"Timur!" Gray moaned. "It has to be Timur. Now he's killing for sport, or revenge, or maybe just plain hatred. Who knows?"

With nothing sharp enough to dig a hole for burial, Gray and Ali placed the body in a hut and tied the door closed with a vine. Rezaul looked on in silence.

"We'll take you home and then send people back from your village, Rezaul, to take care of this."

He turned to Ali, "Then we can return to base. We need fuel and supplies before we head south. We'll wait at Dhangmari while Abdul goes on to Mongla."

"We are going for a long time?" Ali asked.

"Yes. You go and see your family. Once we leave, we'll stay in the forest until we find Timur. We'll be gone for a few weeks, I expect."

CHAPTER 13

At three minutes past nine the next morning, Marshall was ushered in to meet the Chairman of the Forestry Commission. General Rahman was there also, sitting with one leg crossed over the other in a leather armchair to the Chairman's right. The general nodded and smiled as introductions were made but did not rise. Marshall politely accepted the offer of tea and controlled his patience through the necessary pleasantries. Fifteen minutes after he arrived, Marshall declined a refill and waited while the empty tea service was removed.

"Now, Mr. Marshall, what can we do for you?"

"I think, perhaps, it's more a question of what I can do for you," Marshall began. "I have achieved some reputation as a conservationist and a wilderness guide. I have a file of references and newspaper clippings with me to justify my claim," he patted his briefcase in emphasis. "I understand you have been plagued by a man-eating tiger in the last few years."

"That tiger, he will cost me my job if he isn't found soon."

"I'm sure Professor Pendennis is doing his best to find *his* tiger," Marshall stressed the possessive and paused for effect, "however, I can't help feeling that he is more interested in keeping the tiger alive for his own purposes, than for the good and safety of the forestry workers."

"That's what I have been telling him myself," the chairman expostulated, warming to Marshall. "I have warned the professor, I will not tolerate another killing. Something must be done."

"If you give me the authority, I will go to the Sundarbans on your behalf. I will not fail. All I need is one tracker who knows how to identify this tiger."

The chairman leaned forward conspiratorially. "There is a man, one of our own forestry guards. His daughter was killed by this tiger. This man knows what to look for. His name is Rezaul."

"Where can I find him?"

Without the chairman saying as much, Marshall knew he now had semi-official backing for his hunt.

"His name is Rezaul. He is based at the village of Dhangmari, near Mongla. We have a forestry station there. I will send a signal to arrange a permit for you and tell him to wait for you there."

The Chairman looked exceptionally pleased at this new opportunity to relieve himself of the responsibility for the removal of the man-eater. He and Marshall discussed the plan of attack. Marshall nodded with approval at the mention of Rezaul's ability with a rifle and his skills as a tracker. He decided against advising the chairman of his own purchases.

"I had already planned to go to the jungle. I have a riverboat on private charter for a few weeks starting on Saturday."

Rahman, who had remained silent throughout the discussion thus far now cleared his throat. After his long silence, it was so unexpected that Marshall started in surprise.

"If you are successful, we cannot take your word for the tiger's death. You must bring the body back to Mongla by boat and advise me immediately. I will then meet you there and inspect the creature. Do you understand?" Rahman stood up as he finished speaking and crossed to the desk. From there he looked down at the seated Marshall.

"Bring me back the body of that tiger, Mr. Marshall. It is the only evidence I will accept."

They agreed that Marshall should leave Dhaka on the early flight the following morning. A car would be waiting to take him from Jessore to Mongla via Khulna. Marsh planned to stay one night at the Al Prince Hotel in Mongla Bazar. In explanation for the delay, he told the chairman he wanted to look at the various forms of river craft in use near the port.

"Oh yes, there are many different types of boats. This is most interesting for you," the chairman stood up as he spoke, signalling the end of the discussion.

♦ ♦ ♦

Julian and Asia landed in Bangladesh at daybreak. Asia's uncle met them on arrival as they walked out of the Customs hall. It was Julian's first visit to the Indian subcontinent and he was looking forward to the experience. They planned to stay a few nights with Asia's relatives in Mirpur, one of the more affluent suburbs of Dhaka. Asia hadn't been to Bangladesh since she was a girl. Her joy at being in her mother's homeland was apparent to all. She was quite content to stay with her aunt and uncle for a few weeks, unless Julian agreed to her joining him at Kotka before that. Julian, anxious as he was to get to the jungle, allowed himself to be pampered for a couple of days and see the sights of Dhaka. With his good looks, his perfect manners and his charm, Julian quickly made himself popular. The women of the house-hold, shy as they were in the presence of any male, became his devoted slaves before he had even unpacked. Asia was delighted. Julian phoned

Project Man-Eater, only to find Gray had been in the jungle for some time on Timur's trail.

"I've heard nothing from him since he left, but that's not unusual. It's not easy sending messages from the far reaches of the forest," Rab explained. "I have an important letter for Gray. Would you mind coming to the office? You could deliver it for me. He can pick it up at Kotka."

"Okay, I'll be there in about an hour," Julian agreed. "I need to discuss getting myself and my equipment to the Sundarbans anyway."

In the office, Rab asked Julian if he could be ready to leave for Mongla on Thursday afternoon. "Our chartered boat, *Fatima*, will be coming in Thursday sometime and going back to Kotka Friday morning with more supplies."

"Okay, that suits me perfectly well." Julian accepted.

They didn't talk long in the office. Julian was tired, and Rab was obviously preoccupied. He handed Julian a sealed envelope, addressed with one word, 'Pendennis.' At the top left hand corner the initials PME surrounded a tiger's head.

"Give this to Gray for me, please, as soon as you meet him. This is most important," urged Rab. "I have been told there is another man come from England who is trying to catch this tiger. I am very worried. I think someone in the government has given him permission to kill Timur."

"I thought tigers were officially protected in Bangladesh."

"They are, but not everyone cares about tigers as much as we do."

When Julian told Asia that Gray was already in the forest and unlikely to be back for a few weeks, and that he was leaving in a few days, she immediately asked to go with him.

"You have too many social commitments already," Julian reminded her. "You can't leave yet. Why not wait for a week or two, and then join me?"

Asia thought for a few minutes, "All right. I'll stay a few days longer, then see what transport I can find."

Mohammed Khan, Asia's uncle, administered a tea plantation at Srimongal, in the north-east of the country. Home for a few days leave and a couple more on business, he took charge of his niece's husband.

"If you are not too tired, we can go to my club this evening," he suggested. "Of course we don't have a bar, but I'm sure we can still arrange to get something resembling a whisky or two."

He gave Julian a fair imitation of a wink as he said it. Julian was certainly not too tired to be sociable over a whisky with this friendly and articulate gentleman. Julian thoroughly enjoyed his stay in the capital. Asia's uncle was interesting and informative. His wife and two daughters, with help from Asia, treated both men like lords. The distinguished tea planter, much to his own sadness, had no son of his own: for a few days Julian served as an excellent substitute.

Mohammed Khan took Julian and Asia, by car, on an exhausting day trip which covered most of the important features of Dhaka and its environs. In a city of over seven hundred mosques, Mohammed thoughtfully imposed only two on Julian, the Ishtar Mosque to see the inlaid mosaics and the Hussain Dolan Mosque from the Mughal period. In between the two they walked among the colourful flowerbeds of the gardens in Lalbagh Fort. The maze of narrow streets in the Old City fascinated Julian. Had he the time he would have been content to get himself lost each day and, probably, each night among the tight pressed dwellings and rows of open-air shops.

The modern buildings left him cold, except the oddly designed grey fortress of the Parliament building. The seat of government was so outlandish in scope, for such a poor nation, that Julian found it ridiculously funny. Mohammed, proud of his country's achievements since independence, was a trifle hurt. Julian made up for his gaff by being particularly impressed with the crumbling ruins at

Old Sonargaon, a long forgotten capital of Bengal. He found the all but deserted streets a peaceful haven after the confusion of Dhaka. By the end of Julian's limited stay, the two vastly different men had forged a bond and were eminently comfortable in each other's company. Mohammed invited Julian and Asia to spend some time at Srimongal with him before they left Bangladesh. They accepted readily.

"As soon as I get back from the Sundarbans," Julian promised.

With the help of Mohammed's contacts, thanks to the evening at the club, Julian was able to rent a dive compressor to refill his scuba tanks over the next couple of weeks. He inspected the unit and tested it, finding it in immaculate working condition. He had it crated with his empty tanks and shipped to the airport to travel with him. Asia and her aunt planned to attend a society fashion show at the Sheraton Hotel the day Julian left: a women only event in an Islamic country.

"After that I want to see the Sundarbans," she informed Julian "We have checked and there is space on a river boat going to Kotka with some German tourists in a few days. I can go with them."

Asia had never been in a jungle. This one drew her to it like a pin to a magnet. She refused to admit, even to herself, that Gray Pendennis had anything to do with her interest. Having no choice but to agree, Julian simply nodded, "Okay, whatever you want."

CHAPTER 14

Through the close set bars of a wooden cage on a small fishing boat, two otters wrinkled their noses. They were hungry and the smell of fish was close by under the floorboards. Beneath the curved roof of woven palms over the middle of the boat, their owners, Sanjay and Kumar, yawned in unison. The two brothers wrapped their thin blankets more tightly around themselves. The mist crept stealthily along the river. Behind the forest the sky was changing colour. Soon the sun would come to rid them of the cool damp of the night. The otters scratched at the inside of the cage, reminding the two men they had a job to do. Kumar kicked one foot lazily at the corner to silence them. Sanjay reached over and opened the cage so the tethered otters could swim if they wished, then pulled his blanket over his head again.

    Across the river, a rufous-tailed hare nibbled on a patch of grass, its whiskers twitching nervously. It hopped to another patch a short distance away. Through the grass it could see the river. Directly in front of the hare, separated by two boat lengths of water, the two fishermen finally roused themselves, stretching and yawning. The hare stopped eating for a moment as human voices filtered across the morning. Satisfied all was well, it continued munching.

One ear was tilted forward. The other leaned back. Both were absorbing sounds and passing them to the hare's brain. None of the incoming messages implied danger. The animal continued its meal.

Hidden by the shade of an old golpatta palm, Timur lay watching the two men on the river. His eyes burned with hatred, his claws itched to kill. He waited. Unless they crossed the river there was little chance of getting to them undetected without a long detour. The hare hopped closer, the movement distracting Timur momentarily. The hare was a tasty morsel and it was within reach. He was ignorant of the proximity of another predator.

Gliding efficiently and silently in its quest for food, an Indian python flicked out its forked tongue tasting the air. Its super sensitive glands detected the presence of a warm-blooded animal close by. The python changed direction a fraction and approached the feeding hare. Drawing its three metres of body close to its head, it made ready to kill. The mottled brown head drew back into the nucleus of a tight coil, almost touching its thick body. The hare, unaware of the reptile's presence, raised its head to look for more grass. The python struck, catching the kicking creature by the back. Within seconds, the harmless herbivore was engulfed and smothered by a mass of writhing tightening coils. Each time it tried to move the big snake squeezed a little more, until the victim mercifully died. When it was still the python unhinged its lower jaw to begin the ponderous task of swallowing it whole, head first.

The two fishermen had heard the commotion and seen a brief glimpse of the tiger. Although he was on the far bank, the tiger was much too close for their nerves. They swept their otters out of the river, untied the mooring line and poled downstream as fast as they could.

Timur slept in the shade. Not far away the python was sleeping, too. A monitor lizard sneaked through the grass without waking either predator. Downstream, far enough away to feel safe, the fishermen urged their sleek helpers over the side. With scarcely a splash, the otters broke the river's surface and submerged. Tethered to the boat by long thin ropes, they sped through the water. They each cornered their quarry, fastening strong jaws and sharp teeth on wriggling heads. The fishermen felt the lines go slack as the skilled marine hunters returned. The two broke the surface together, offering the still squirming hilsa to their masters.

Free of their catches, the otters raced off again. This time the fishermen lowered a net into the river, stretched into a sagging rectangle supported by sticks. The otters, working together like sheep dogs, herded a shoal of fish over and into the net. The fishermen hauled in the catch and emptied it into the boat. The net went over the side again. Once more the otters rounded up as many fish as they could, chasing them to their destiny. There were fewer the second time. The main shoal had passed. The fishermen would have to look elsewhere.

A jerk on their leashes sent the otters streaking down again. They reached the bottom and raced back to the surface, gaining enough momentum to slide their sleek bodies over the gunwales. Landing in a slippery wet heap at the feet of the fishermen, they shook themselves and entered their cage. The lid was closed behind them but not latched.

With a good haul of fish stowed under the floorboards, the two men cast off their mooring and let the boat swing out into the stream. One of them rigged a pole for a mast, with a triangular patch of blue cloth for a sail. Helped by the incoming tide, they let the warm afternoon breeze take them towards home. While one steered, the other sat cross-legged behind the makeshift mast repairing their nets. The tiger, which had alarmed them the previous morning, was far from their thoughts. But Timur was awake and on the hunt again. He roamed the riverbank in search of prey. The hot afternoon and a subconscious instinct sent him into the river at the start of a right angle bend. He was taking his time, his paws paddling in lethargic rhythm when the boat came in view. The fishermen could hardly believe the sight before them. Not fifteen metres away, no more than three boat lengths, a tiger shared their stretch of river.

CHAPTER 15

Julian reached Mongla late at night. He was thankful to have arrived in one piece. For once in his life he had been absolutely terrified. Bangladeshi drivers, he decided, handed Allah far too much responsibility. Either that or they were all doing their utmost to join the Almighty and his prophets at the earliest possible moment. At one point, on the two lane road in the dark, a truck and an overloaded bus raced side by side towards his car. Both vehicles flashed their headlights and blew their horns to announce they were coming through. Julian's driver, in a fit of bravado, did the same and held his course until the last possible moment. Somehow the three speeding vehicles scraped past each other without actually touching. When Julian's driver regained the road, Julian reached forward and took him by the back of the neck.

"If you pull another stupid stunt like that, I'll break your bloody neck," he warned through gritted teeth. "If we are still alive!" His warning rang through the driver's mind for an hour, then gradually receded. Twice Julian had to remind him of his threat.

At Mongla four sturdy men carried his crate and his diving bag to the jetty. *Fatima* was already there, and Abdul welcomed him on board, showing him where to stow his gear and where he could sleep. It wasn't long before Julian found all was not well. The boat had developed a problem on the way up the Passur River from Chandpai, he was told.

"The propeller keeps slipping. Sometimes the engine stalls," Abdul explained. "We will have to haul the boat out, if we can find space over there." He pointed vaguely in the direction of the port.

"Let me go underneath first," Julian asked. "I have diving equipment and can check the propeller underwater."

Not fully understanding the use of scuba equipment, Abdul appeared confused. Julian opened his crate and showed him the tanks, flippers and mask, the better to explain his idea. Eventually he got the message across.

"I'll go down as soon after first light as possible."

That night Julian fired up the compressor and filled his air tanks ready for the dive. In the morning, he tied a long length of rope to the boat's rail and let the free end drop to the water, where it slowly sank into the murk. Not liking the look of the dirty water much, he put on a complete black wet suit, including head cowl and boots, to protect his skin as much as he could. He covered his feet with deep blue flippers. Strapped to the outside of each calf, he wore a long sharp knife with serrated spine. He spat in his face-mask and washed it out with fresh water before pulling it over his head to rest on his chest. On his head he adjusted the rubber strap supporting his NiteRider dual beam scuba lamps. One of the crew helped him on with a tank. As Julian raised his mask to fit over his face, he glanced up. The jetty was packed with silent people, all watching him in amazement. None had seen a scuba diver in full gear before.

Julian jumped off *Fatima* near the stern and checked his dive watch. He clicked on his lights and inverted himself, swimming along the underside of the hull. The people on the dock and on other boats leaned far over, trying to see what the strangely dressed foreigner was doing. All they saw were air bubbles and the ripples from the diver's flippers.

Reaching the propeller Julian found it was almost obscured by an entanglement of ropes and fishing nets. He pulled his own rope to him and wrapped it around the mess, tying it tightly. Drawing a knife he slashed through the thick strands close to the propeller shaft, until much of it fell free, held only by his restraining rope. Getting the final bonds to loosen took him another fifteen minutes. Finally the propeller and shaft were free. Julian checked the bushing as best he could. The prop was tight and the shaft had minimal play on it. It looked fine to him.

As he broke the surface and signalled the crew to pull up his rope, a thunderous round of spontaneous applause greeted him. Julian accepted help getting back on board, stood up and bowed deeply to his fascinated audience. While Julian stripped off his gear, a well-meaning deck hand untied the rope and pushed the tangle of torn nets and cut ropes back over the side. Julian shouted in anger, hopping to the rail with one flipper on and the other off.

"Get me a boathook," he bellowed. The crew looked at him without moving. He found one himself, but he was too late. The sodden weight had already dragged the nets out of reach. Julian turned to the deck hand and tapped his forefinger on his own temple. He accepted that getting mad was a waste of energy. The young sailor still wouldn't understand what he had done wrong.

"Okay, Captain," Julian called, "start her up. She should be okay now."

Abdul rang down to start the engine. At once the deep throaty sound of *Fatima*'s 265 horsepower six cylinder Hino diesel burst into life. The crew hauled mooring lines aboard. When they were free of the dock, Abdul called for half speed astern. The propeller bit into the river as *Fatima* slid her twenty-two metres of hull away from the dock. The gears changed to neutral, then full ahead. Abdul gave the signals, the engineer responded. In mid-stream, with Mongla's distinctive red water tower advertising 'Panther Condoms' dominating the skyline to port, they set course downstream for Dhangmari and the Sundarbans.

◆ ◆ ◆

For a first time visitor the drive along the tree-lined country road running due south from Jessore is a delight. Farmers plough their fields with the help of oxen yoked in pairs. Roadside tea shops become the centre of daily gossip and the dissemination of useful news. Sugar cane grows tall. Rice paddies, with parallel lines of green shoots standing proudly out of the water, reflect the blue of the sky and the white of any passing clouds. Shrimp farms border the road; the interconnected network of miniature lakes and channels kept open by constant attention. Flimsy bamboo scaffolding span parts of some channels where fishermen stand for hours dipping their nets. Boats are built on the roadside and launched by sliding them backwards into canals already choked by the ubiquitous water hyacinth. In the villages women wash their family's clothes on a communal stone beside a freshwater pool.

Some communities, luckier than others, have the marvel of a hand-operated pump to draw water from the bowels of the earth. A rare few even boast electricity. It is a colourful land for those with interested minds. Many who have the opportunity of travelling the route more than once agree, each time they enjoy it more. Marshall, who had taken pleasure in the journey some years before, showed no interest whatsoever. His driver was careful, by the standards of the country, and he kept his own council. Marshall sat in the back seat and kept his eyes closed for most of the journey.

On the short ferry crossing from Khulna to Rupsha, he got out and forced his way through the press of humanity to the upper deck. There he was no longer bothered by the constant tapping of begging fingers on the car windows. Some younger boys followed him from sheer curiosity, intent on asking this tall stranger the obligatory question, "What is your country, please?" The fact that most of them had little or no idea of geography was immaterial. The question was important in itself, just to hear an answer from foreign lips.

Marshall grunted, "Canada," and thereafter ignored them.

Across the river from Mongla, where the road comes to an abrupt end, he haggled for a water taxi. Sitting cramped on a small boat with up to twenty locals was not for him. He had no interest in being sociable. Marshall crossed in typical colonial style: one white man on a boat that could have taken a score more. Of course, he paid for his privacy. Twice as much as a local businessman would pay, if one were so pompous as to journey alone. The fare was still only a pittance.

On the other side, he asked directions to the hotel and was forced to endure a phalanx of guides to show him the way. The Al Prince was a modest tourist hotel. It was by no means luxurious. In fact it was rather shabby, though comfortable. Marshall took little notice of his surroundings, apart from the necessities. The small restaurant, serving the local equivalent of Chinese food, was quite adequate for his present needs. In his room, he had two single beds, only one of which he required. A thin carpet covered the floor. The walls, once painted white, now gave notice of the passing years. He had a tiny night table with a lamp on it. The bulb wasn't bright though the aged pale pink shade was clean. Above the bed was a ceiling fan. Marshall rotated the switch. The fan began its revolutions, without too much noise.

The room had a shower, with a torn plastic curtain to keep the water from spraying too far, and it had a western style toilet. In a primitive metal bracket to the right of the toilet was a full white toilet roll. Another balanced on the cistern behind. To the left, by a tap built low to the floor, was a bucket and what looked like an aluminium teapot. He was aware that for some religions, personal cleanliness required more than paper. There was nothing more he needed for the moment. He was anxious, but forced himself to settle down to wait.

The sun had set. Mosquitoes were becoming active, buzzing into the room in their quest for life-giving bright red blood. Marshall closed the grimy window and turned on the ceiling fan to 'high' to keep the pests away. He was considering going down for dinner when there was a knock on his door. He opened it to see a well-dressed Bengali carrying a tightly rolled bolt of black cloth.

"Good evening, sir. I have the cloth for your new suit," he said. His voice was silky smooth.

Marshall let him in and locked the door. The newcomer unrolled the cloth part way on one of the beds to reveal a long package wrapped in brown paper. Marshall tore it open and held up one of the rifles. It looked old but well cared for. He pulled out the bolt and looked down the barrel. It was clean. He did the same with the other weapon. It too was clean. He checked the magazines. Each was full with six rounds a piece. He replaced the bolts and checked the actions. They were smooth.

"Where's the rest of the ammunition?" he demanded.

The gun merchant unrolled more of the cloth. Stitched into pockets the length and breadth of the cloth were the remaining bullets. Marshall grunted in approval. He selected one shell at random and examined it minutely. It was, as far as his trained eye could see, in perfect condition. A handful of others also passed his inspection. He could only hope all the rest were of the same quality. He checked the bolt action on both rifles again. The live rounds jumped from the magazine clip to the firing chamber smoothly. The spent shell ejection worked. Marshall was satisfied.

The merchant shook all the sewn-in bullets from the cloth to the bed. From the middle, where the cloth was wrapped around a cardboard tube, he drew a machete in a canvas scabbard and placed it on the bed. While Marshall checked more of the bullets, he rewound the black cotton. Marshall handed over five one hundred dollar US bills and ushered the man out of his life without another word. One more night to go.

◆ ◆ ◆

Julian changed into shorts and tee shirt and relaxed in a deck chair on *Fatima*'s top deck. He was the only passenger on board as the river boat left Mongla. Above him a canopy of sky blue silk supported on four bamboo poles, fluttered as the boat's progress created a humid breeze. Gray and Ali joined *Fatima* at Dhangmari. Gray was pleased to see Julian though not so pleased at the contents of Rab's letter. He read it twice, his eyes narrowing with worry. Julian waited, knowing the letter held bad news. Gray swore quietly to himself and handed the letter to Julian.

"Read it, if you like. It seems we can expect some company," he made a grimace of displeasure. Julian finished the letter and handed it back.

"It sounds like trouble all right. Rab was quite upset about it," he told Gray. "Who is this Marshall anyway?"

"That's a long story which I'll tell you as we go. Basically, he's had a rough time and blames Timur for his woes. He's also the cause of the bruise I earned on my jaw in Vancouver."

Julian's face broke into a broad grin. "The mystery is solved at last," he chuckled with delight. "We were all wondering what happened that night."

As the gap between *Fatima* and the dock widened, Rezaul watched from a distance on shore. His orders from the Forestry Commission were to stay at Dhangmari until another foreigner arrived, then to escort him to the Sundarbans.

Fatima's diesel engine chugged her monotonous voice as she cut through the tidal stream. A dozen or so anchored ships lined the middle of the Passur, their bows pointing at Mongla. The helmsman swung the wheel hard to the right, taking *Fatima* past the freighters and into the main waterway.

"We're just over the tide change," Gray advised Julian. "It's on the flood right now, but we have the current with us. Still the journey will take most of the day."

Down the wide Passur River they were escorted by the flashing dorsal fins of river dolphins. Julian and Gray sat on deck chairs on the top deck sipping fresh coconut water. Ali stretched out on a bunk and slept.

"You know, I think I'm beginning to enjoy this," Julian stretched and yawned. "Is there much wildlife here?"

"Yes, far more than most people know. If you keep your eyes open, you'll see plenty."

"Have you ever seen tigers on the river banks?"

"Twice, both times bordering major streams. I love this river trip. No matter how many times I do it, I'm still fascinated by all the birds and the fishermen, even when the tigers stay hidden." Gray pointed to an eagle soaring high above them. "If I had eyes like that beauty, finding tigers would never be a problem."

He reached into his duffel bag and pulled out a file folder. For a few seconds he sat gazing at two photographs. He tapped one thoughtfully, then passed it to Julian. Gray showed him an unusual pugmark.

"See how the main pad is different from this other photograph? This is Timur's signature. I don't suppose you'll ever see it but, if you do, I want to know about it immediately."

Twelve kilometres downstream the captain turned left off the main waterway. On a spit of land a cluster of thatched houses stood close to the river. Upside down on the shore and right way up in the water, the fishing boats were being prepared for work. In the hazy distance behind the village, waiting to unload at Mongla, the upper works of an ocean freighter seemed completely out of place.

"That's Chandpai village," Gray told Julian. "We're at the north end of the Chandpai Range. The Sundarbans is divided into four main regions, each called a range. We'll travel through parts of two of them, the Chandpai and the Sarankhola."

"Where is the best place to see a tiger?"

Gray had been expecting the question and was ready. He unrolled his large, hand drawn map, spreading it out on the deck in front of them. With a pencil, he traced the route he had chosen to take them to Kotka. At five different points along the way, red stars were marked.

"As you can see, there are an infinite number of possible channels to take. I suspect they all have been blessed with a tiger's presence at some time. I chose our route because these stars represent places where we know tigers have been seen from the river, from this boat in fact."

On a sweeping bend, where long grass fronted the jungle, the mud flats were already exposed by the ebbing tide. Gray studied the bank, adjusting his field glasses for maximum effect.

"Professor, Professor," the deck hand sounded excited. Gray followed his pointing arm.

"I see them," he answered. "Here, Julian, take a look. There are two big salties at the far end of those mud flats."

"Two what?"

"Two saltwater crocodiles, halfway up the mud directly ahead." He handed his binoculars to Julian. "Take a look."

Julian focused on the great reptiles sunning themselves well above the water level. When they were only two or three boat lengths away, Abdul let off a blast with an air horn.

"Thanks a lot, Abdul," Gray called in annoyance.

The two scaly crocodiles fled down the mud to the murky depths of the river. A huge smile spread across Julian's face as he leaned over the rail trying to see them as they escaped.

"Things are getting better," Gray told him. "Now all we have to do is find Timur, and then your shipwreck."

CHAPTER 16

Watching the tiger paddling towards them, Sanjay ripped the sail down while Kumar attempted to back water with a makeshift paddle and turn the boat at the same time. With fear trembling across his lined face, Sanjay slammed his long bamboo pole into the water, forcing it deep into the riverbed, desperately trying to stop the boat. A pole and a paddle were no match for the current. The boat's forward motion scarcely slowed, though it swung beam on to the tiger. Timur stopped paddling, letting the current carry him with it. The distance from the boat to the tiger remained the same. Timur faced the oncoming craft. He began paddling again with all four feet, holding himself against the flow. The boat, with two horrified fishermen and two unsuspecting otters on board, drifted closer.

Sanjay threw himself overboard with a cry of fear, his arms and legs flailing the water as he scrambled for the left bank. Kumar, unable to swim and jabbering with terror, made a valiant attempt at fending Timur off with Sanjay's abandoned pole. Twice he stabbed at the tiger as it struck up at him with its right paw. For a moment the doomed man thought he had won as his boat swung lazily around the beast. It was a forlorn hope.

Timur roared at him, the dreadful thundering voice paralyzing the fisherman's terror-stricken muscles. A wicked paw, with claws unsheathed, snatched the pole from his hands. Timur then gripped the boat midway down its length and flipped it on its side. The fisherman screamed as he hit the water and the tiger at the same time. The otter's cage landed behind him, breaking open with the impact. The two otters sprinted for freedom, speeding through the water at full speed, unaware they were hampered by leashes – tied to the collars around their necks and tethered to the boat.

Timur sunk his teeth into his human victim and turned to shore. As he forced the water back with powerful strokes, a hind paw hooked one of the otter's lines. The sudden jerk as the tether reached its end snapped the unlucky creature's neck and the rope where it was tied to the boat. The dead otter was dragged after the tiger as it leaped up the right bank. The boat, with one panicking, swimming otter still attached, nosed into the left bank as the current tried to take it round the corner. The surviving fisherman flung himself aboard, retrieved his remaining otter and poled away as hard as he could, terror adding strength to his muscles.

An hour away *Fatima* pushed against the tide, working her way steadily towards the Bay of Bengal. Progress was slow enough without the water's hindrance. Gray asked Abdul to stop and talk to all fishermen they met. The question was always the same.

"Have you seen any signs of a tiger in the last few days?"

The answer was a uniform, "No."

A long-prowed boat hove into view, travelling towards them in the middle of the river. One man, Sanjay, stood on a narrow platform at the stern forcing the great blade of his sweep through the water. He hailed the familiar steel vessel, shouting and gesticulating wildly with one hand. Often he and his brother had sold fish to the crew and passengers. He was sure of help. A deckhand threw him a line and pulled him close, tying off the end on a cleat. The distraught fisherman was helped aboard, where he promptly went into an animated rush of explanation that Gray missed completely. Abdul translated as best he could, helped by Ali.

Gray asked them to slow down and start again, from the beginning. He smiled to reassure the agitated Hindu, keeping his voice soft. Ali told the man Gray was the tiger hunter who captured man-eaters. That set him off again. He snatched the front of Gray's shirt in both hands. With his face buried in Gray's shoulder, he sobbed out his story once more. Abdul rang down for more speed. Gray had a knot in his gut, a knot which told him Timur was within reach this time. He had no illusions about the man-eater being any other than his main obsession.

"This time, old pal," he breathed. "This time we'll meet, and you will be mine."

"You think it really is Timur?" asked Julian.

"It's Timur all right," Gray answered, "I feel it in my belly."

Timur carried the unlucky fisherman through the undergrowth for fifty or sixty paces, holding him by the waist. The dead otter's leash hooked on a tree and was left behind. To avoid his meal being caught on bushes and trees Timur twisted and turned his head as he went. A sheltered space, mostly hidden by trailing vines and tall thin shrubs, beckoned. He backed into the gap. Changing his grip on the body, he pulled it after him. There was enough room for the two of them, nothing more.

Without haste, the man-eater ate part of his kill. His initial hunger abated, Timur licked his paws and wiped them over his muzzle. Eight times he repeated the action until his facial fur was clean. To complete his toilet, he rasped his sharp tongue over both front paws, removing any last vestiges of blood and cleaning the old bullet wound. With his head on the dead man's chest, he yawned and closed his eyes.

On the river, Sanjay, the grieving fisherman, became *Fatima*'s pilot and guide. He signalled left and Abdul spun the spokes of the wooden wheel, taking a new course. The river wound like a coiled serpent in this part of the Chandpai Range, and many bends appeared the same. Sanjay seemed somewhat confused as to exactly where the attack had taken place. Three times he insisted it was just here. Three times he and Gray had jumped ashore and skidded through the mud only to be disappointed. Gray was thankful he had taken the precaution of exchanging his customary cowboy boots for canvas jungle footwear.

Gray saw the tracks first. From the advantage of the upper deck he noticed more detail. A shadow on the mud alerted him. He ordered Abdul to stop. On the bank, a dead golpatta palm leaf lay with its tip touching the water. Beside it a small depression revealed a potential clue. Abdul put *Fatima*'s bow to the mud. Gray reached down with a boat hook and moved the palm frond aside. A deep smooth furrow lay underneath.

Fate had conspired to assist Timur and trick the hunters by letting the palm fall perfectly on the gouge formed by the fisherman's body. It had almost succeeded. Gray didn't wait for the boarding plank to be run out. Ali covered him with the rifle as he dropped to the mud, sinking to his ankles. Sanjay landed beside him and pulled himself up the remaining stretch with the help of a bent palm. He put out one hand to pull Gray to him. On dry land, Gray was only an arm's length from the 'shadow' he had first seen. It was a deep pugmark. The triangle of the main pad was rounded at the apex and straight along the two diagonals — the base line was broken by four ellipses.

"Timur," Gray sighed. "Can you hold the boat there for a couple of hours, Abdul?"

"Ji," Abdul agreed. One of the crew dropped the end of the plank at Gray's feet, nearly obliterating the pugmark in the process. Ali stepped ashore with unsullied sandals. With a quick action he checked his rifle. Five live rounds nestled one above the other in the magazine and a blank filled the chamber, ready to explode into action. He left the safety catch on, his thumb hard against it. Holding the weapon diagonally across his chest he told Gray he was ready.

"Julian, there's a loaded rifle in my cabin," Gray called. "If you want to join us, go get it."

Not far away Timur had heard the monotonous beat of *Fatima*'s diesel engine. The dull thumping hammered at his mind as he listened, ears alert, his mind awake. The intrusive din grew steadily louder. Timur lifted his head, absorbing the engine's throb. The beat slowed, changing to a quieter tempo. Timur flexed his muscles and came to his feet. Human voices mingled with the untidy mechanical sounds. Timur slunk from the den, making no noise. Once in the open, he loped away with his drunken gait, always favouring the left front paw.

He ran without apparent effort, not fast – but faster than a man could jog, for more than ten minutes. Abruptly he jumped up onto a fallen tree trunk barring his path and trotted along its length. From the complicated maze of dead branches and twigs at the top, he emerged on a different route. Now at forty-five degrees to his original track, he ran for a gully and made another correction, slowing to a walk. He jumped a water-filled ditch and padded off to a grassy knoll. Again he changed direction. Aiming straight for the river now, he quickened his pace. A flat portion of soggy jungle floor, littered with spiky aerial roots blocked his path. Gingerly he threaded his way through, leaving an unblemished trail impossible to miss. At the river he paused, obscured by the palms. The distant riverboat's engine was still vaguely audible. The river in front of him was bare. Confidently he stepped down the muddy bank and into the water. He didn't cross. In the middle he pushed deep and sideways with his right front paw. His tailed curled left as he used it as a rudder. Working hard, Timur swam away from his pursuers. One hundred metres beyond the river turned back on itself. There Timur took to the land again; crossing a short distance to eliminate a horseshoe bend, he entered the river once more. A creek opened up to his left, and he accepted the opportunity. Swimming strongly he stayed with the creek as it narrowed and became shallower. As his paws touched bottom he bounded to dry land and shook himself. Having no further use for concealment, he stalked defiantly south.

Gray cleaned as much mud off his canvas jungle boots as he could with a stick. There wasn't much he could do with the insides so he left them to dry naturally. He had no concern about leeches. In the brackish saline water of the Sundarbans the blood sucking parasitic worms were a problem he had never encountered. Sanjay wiped the mud off his sandals and bare feet with one hand, cleaning it in turn on a clump of grass. Ali waited patiently. Julian ran down the plank, Gray's spare rifle held at the ready.

"Let's do it." Gray nodded to Sanjay and Ali to go ahead. Turned to Julian, "You follow them and keep your safety catch on. I will be rear guard."

Timur's tracks were easy to follow. His pugmarks, indistinct though they were on the hard ground were readable. Parallel to his trail, bordering on both sides, broken grass and bent twigs at the ends of bushes confirmed he still held his prey. They found the dead otter beside the track, its leash tangled in the roots of a tree. Sanjay confirmed it was his otter. They left it for the jungle's scavengers to clean up. Gray and Ali lost Timur's obvious trail near a labyrinth of disorderly greenery. Twice they walked back and picked up the direction only to lose it again. Julian and Sanjay watched them without a word. Where the pugmarks ceased two faint indentations led into a thicket. Kumar's heels, dragging on the ground, had left two indelible lines for the hunters to find. The adjacent terrain had been brushed spotless by his clothes. Gray bent low, trying to see under the branches. There was something there. With one finger, he motioned to Ali, hearing the comforting click as his tracker moved his safety catch to the off position. Heart pounding loudly Gray thrashed at the bushes with a stick. The half-anticipated roar of anger was distinguished by its absence. Gray wiped the sweat from his forehead, letting out his breath. He flailed the bushes with his stick again. Still nothing happened. Feeling confident and satisfied that Timur was gone, Gray turned to Ali and Julian.

"Cover me. I'm going in." With Sanjay's help holding back an armful of branches, he squeezed through. Gray stepped on part of Kumar's hand before he could stop himself. He looked down and felt his stomach heave. Half a man, ghostly pale under his dark skin, lay at his feet. Horrified, Gray fought his way out of the confining den. Sinking to his knees he vomited until his throat hurt.

Knowing the worst, Sanjay crawled into the tiny clearing on his hands and knees, finding his brother's mutilated body under his nose. He let out a bloodcurdling wail of anguish and backed out dragging what was left of Kumar behind him. Gray felt sick again; feeling he was about to pass out. Ali burst into a torrent of prayer, averting his gaze from the sickening half corpse. Julian felt his stomach churn and turned away as he too gagged. Sanjay hugged his brother's upper torso to him, crooning tearfully.

"Ali, stay here with Sanjay. Julian, come with me."

Leaving Ali on guard, Gray and Julian ran back to the boat.

"Abdul. Abdul," Gray shouted, "we've found parts of a body. Send two men with a sheet or a blanket to clean up the mess. Julian, you wait for them and act as their guard. Abdul, wait for us. We'll be back as soon as we can," he issued the stream of orders as he turned to retrace his steps. Sanjay, and what was left of Kumar, was on the ground where he had left him. Ali stood close by, his rifle at the ready.

"Let's go, Ali." Gray slung his tranquilizer gun on his shoulder and scouted around until he picked up Timur's spoor. The tiger had a head start and was moving fast; that was evident from the spread between front and hind paw marks. The two men began to run. They lost the trail momentarily at an old fallen tree. Ali's experienced tracker's eyes and instincts found it again. At the ditch they stopped, thinking Timur might have taken to the water. Ali noticed half a hind pugmark just above the water line and on they went.

By the time they reached the unconcealed tracks among the pneumataphores water had seeped in covering the pad's telltale shape. Ali scooped the water out of one dip to be sure. He said nothing, simply rubbed his wet hand on his pants and kept going. The tracks ended under a huge pandanus, one step from the river. Gray swore under his breath, sure they'd lost him.

"Back to the boat, Ali," he turned away as he spoke.

Once off the mud and on hard ground they ran. In their haste, Ali came close to stepping on a king cobra crossing their path. The deadly snake reared up and truck in self-defence, missing Ali's leg by the thickness of his khaki pants as he sprang into the air to clear the long streamlined banded body. Gray seemed unaware of the near disaster. He kept running. Ali passed him. At the river Sanjay was cutting dry wood for a funeral pyre helped by a crew member. Abdul had refused to have the body on board, insisting it would bring bad luck.

"Shit," Gray let rip. "We don't have time for this. We have to catch that bloody tiger."

He and Ali climbed aboard the boat.

"Let's go, Abdul."

Abdul pointed to Sanjay and raised his hands in an eloquent gesture of concern.

"Leave this guy with my spare rifle to guard him," Gray stabbed his index finger at a stocky middle-aged deck hand. He took the firearm from Julian, put the sling over the surprised sailor's head and pushed him down the gangplank.

"Now, Abdul. Let's go," he insisted.

While Abdul coaxed *Fatima* up to her top speed, Gray studied his map, watched by Julian.

"That's where he hit the river," Gray tapped the point of his pencil roughly where the large pandanus stood.

"He will be somewhere in this area." He drew a circle.

They found the pandanus again with no trouble, but searched the forest on the opposite side of the river in vain. The only tracks were of the dainty hands and feet of a troop of monkeys.

"That sonofabitch has gone swimming to avoid leaving a trail," Gray grumbled, his annoyance overshadowed by his admiration for the creature.

The day was drawing in, the light failing. They could achieve nothing by continuing the search that day. Abdul turned *Fatima* round to pick up the funeral party before it got too dark. It wasn't difficult to find them. A wreath of thick blue smoke fluttered skywards to guide them. Sanjay stood silently on the shore as the fire crackled, consuming the dead and the logs piled around the torn body. The guard squatted on the ground staring into the fire. Gray tried not to breathe as the smell of roasting flesh wafted over the boat. He felt sick again and fought to keep the bile down. Abdul persuaded Sanjay he had done all he could for his brother. Staying with the burning pyre was unnecessary. To make him feel better, Abdul took *Fatima* upwind a short distance and anchored in mid-stream. From there Sanjay could watch Kumar's final hours, while the smoke and fire would keep any predators away from the boat.

Away from the smell, Gray's queasiness soon faded. He and Julian dined together on the top deck illuminated by spluttering oil lamps. Ali, by preference, ate with the crew. Julian produced a bottle of white wine from his cabin locker.

"It's not cold, but I think it should complement these fine looking giant prawns, don't you, Gray?"

"Having a man with your tastes on a jungle cruise is a great pleasure," Gray responded with a smile.

"I forgot to tell you in all the excitement — Asia's in Dhaka. She sends her best. She's coming down next week on another boat with a small party of German adventure tourists. She's never seen a tiger in the wild and reckons you are the best person to find one for her."

"I'm not so sure of that. I can't even find the one I'm looking for."

"Well, I'd certainly like to see one. Not too close though."

"Did you see Amanda before you left?" Gray hadn't intended to ask the question. It slipped out before he could stop it.

"Amanda's fine, as far as I know. Last I heard she was involved with a minor South American diplomat based at a consulate in Vancouver."

They sat in silence for a while, listening to the sounds of the nearby jungle. In the distance a thin plume of smoke trailed slowly towards the stars. A boy removed their empty plates and deposited a thermos of hot coffee in the centre of the table. In front of each man he placed a large china mug, one bearing the image of Donald Duck, the other of Mickey Mouse.

"I hate drinking tea or coffee out of little cups," Gray explained. "I like to wrap my hands around hot drinks."

He held Donald Duck up to the oil lamp. "I found these guys in the New Market in Dhaka last year. I bought a set of six, each with a different Disney character. Figured they were appropriate for the jungle."

Julian appraised his mug with a smile. "They will do for me. I like mugs too."

"I'm sorry I can't run to a brandy," Gray apologized, "but I do have the best part of a bottle of Johnny Walker Black in my cabin. Can I tempt you?"

Julian bowed his head in assent, so Gray rapped out a request to their waiter in Bangla. A few minutes later the cherished bottle appeared. For the next hour or so the two sat talking, sipping strong black coffee laced with amber whiskey. Gray spoke of his concern over Richard Marshall's obsession with Timur.

"I can't shake the feeling he's here for revenge. The death of his daughter was a terrible tragedy, and I understand, his family has been torn apart since then. But, hell – you can't blame a tiger for every misfortune. I hope he stays away from Kotka, but I have a feeling he will show up, and soon."

Gray was silent for a moment, then he added, "And we have another problem. There is at least one poacher at work down here in the forest and he is putting out poison to kill tigers."

"You mean, he's after their pelts?" Julian asked.

"Yes. And their teeth and their paws: all valuable commodities over there in China." He pointed to the northeast for emphasis.

CHAPTER 17

A teenage boy wearing denims and a bright red check shirt came to collect Marshall in the morning as the sun came up. The boy took care of Marshall's clothes bag without argument from its owner. A separate long duffel bag, containing two rifles and ammunition wrapped in a sleeping bag remained in Marshall's hand. The boy led him from the hotel to the dock and onto the deck of a ferry. From there they crossed to a river launch, walked to the stern and jumped down onto the slowly moving bow of a moderately respectable river boat. Marshall recognized it immediately. It was the one he had chartered for his family at the time of Tracy's death. Tears pricked his eyes, and he blinked them away. The captain shook his hand and greeted him like an old friend. When Tracy died, the gentle sailor had allowed his sad dark eyes to weep for her. They were still sad.

Marshall placed his bags on the floor of the day cabin. Shutting the door behind him, he sat alone on the leather bench in silence. There were so many memories floating around the room. Once again he heard Tracy and Simon talking excitedly about the voyage. He saw Jean-nette's smile. He saw the tiger. He saw Tracy die. For a few minutes he buried his face in his hands. Rubbing his eyes he erased the destructive sentiments from his mind. By the time he went up on deck, the boat was in mid-stream, half-way to Dhangmari,

Rezaul came on board at the forestry station with the necessary permits, his rifle, and a black plastic sports bag for his own needs. He was tall for a Bengali, almost as tall as Marshall, but slimmer. Probably no more than forty years old, Marshall thought, though the streaks of grey in his hair made him look ten years older. Marshall introduced himself, and Rezaul shook hands with the light touch common to the east. His hands were small with rough skin. Haltingly, uncertain of his English, Rezaul told Marshall of his daughter's death and his ambition to destroy the tiger. Marshall listened without visible emotion. He related the story of Tracy's death and repeated his own vow. The two bereaved fathers shook hands again. Rezaul's grip was stronger and more determined this time.

"The professor from Canada has gone to find the tiger," Rezaul told Marshall. "He left here yesterday."

"Don't worry about it. Pendennis won't shoot his tiger. But I will."

The boat stopped at Chandpai while Rezaul went ashore to ask a few questions. Being the most northerly of the jungle fishing villages, all news eventually filtered through Chandpai as the boats came home. Marshall remained on board, content to keep to himself. He knew if he went ashore with him there was less chance of Rezaul hearing anything worth calling useful information. An object of curiosity, such as a European, was far more interesting than something that happened in the past, no matter how recent.

Sitting in a tea shop, Rezaul heard a rumour of a Hindu fisherman who had seen his brother killed by a tiger only a few days before. By careful probing, he learned the approximate location of the kill and the actual number of days that had passed. He also heard again that the Canadian professor was on the tiger's trail with the tracker, Ali.

They had passed Chandpai only yesterday, the informant insisted.

◆ ◆ ◆

Day was close to breaking when Sanjay went ashore. Gray went with him, a little embarrassed by his lack of consideration the night before. Between them they scattered the hot ashes from the night-long fire into the river. Kumar was home on the delta of the Holy Mother Ganges and, Gray fervently prayed, at peace. Sanjay untied his boat from *Fatima*'s stern and said goodbye to all on board. Sadly, the lonely figure, with one otter for company, poled his way north. *Fatima* turned her bow in the opposite direction.

Where the big pandanus shaded the water Gray called for the engine to idle. He raked one bank with his binoculars. Ali checked the other. The jungle hung in limp humidity over the river, soaked with the addition of early morning dew. It was impossible to see any tracks without going on shore. Gray guessed that the tiger would have either left the river by the right bank prior to the bend, or he had paddled round the bend and exited to the left. As the river curved, Gray and Ali went ashore on the right bank. Walking back the way they had come, Timur's flight across the promontory showed plainly. Sure of what they would find, they too jogged to the point where Timur had re-entered the water. There was no alternative but to return to *Fatima*. Under way again, Gray and Ali sat in the dingi with the outboard motor attached but silent as *Fatima* towed them along the river.

The creek was more than half hidden by overhanging branches and easy to miss. Fortunately Ali caught a glint of sunlight on water far to his left among the trees. He hissed at Gray, pointing for emphasis. Gray loosened the towline, telling one of the crew to warn Abdul. With rifles across their knees he and Ali paddled hesitantly into the narrow channel. Less than five minutes later, they ran aground surrounded by smooth wet mud.

"I know he came this way." Gray smacked his right fist into the palm of his left hand. He stepped off the boat into the cloying mud and squelched up the middle of the rapidly disappearing creek.

"There." He pointed to Timur's tracks. They advertised his passage like signposts where he too had left the creek.

"He's going to Jawtoli," Ali said quietly. "We can get there first."

Gray thought about it. Timur, if he had travelled all night, could be twenty or thirty kilometres away by now, maybe more. If so, they would never catch him on foot. Alternatively, he might be watching them at that instant. To be sure they followed the well-known tracks for another half an hour. They confirmed it, Timur was heading south. Gray and Ali turned back. Nearly two hours passed before they were able to board *Fatima* again. The tide on the Bay of Bengal was ebbing. All the jungle rivers followed its lead. The creek was drying swiftly. Their wooden boat stuck fast in the drying mud. Ali took the towline and tied it around his shoulders. Gray leaned into the stern. Breaking the powerful vacuum of hull against thick slime meant rocking the boat backwards and forwards, and from side to side. Both men fell face down in the mud more than once before she was at last wrenched free. Caked from head to toe in congealing muck, they paddled into the open until, at last, they could be lifted over the rail onto the mother ship. Gray stripped to his shorts and poured bucket after bucket of river water over his head until he was clean, letting a thin trail of mud run back into the river. Ali did the same. One of the deck boys took their soiled clothes away for washing. Black smoke belched from *Fatima*'s thin funnel as she sped south for Jawtoli and Kotka.

Timur curved his lame paw inward to lick the sole, taking particular care to remove all dirt. He had travelled far south on an erratic course since the men interrupted his meal two days before. He was hungry again. In the heat of mid-afternoon, there was little to stir the tranquillity of the forest. Nature's dependents were mostly at rest. There would be few creatures abroad. Hunger took second place to sleep. Timur completed his grooming, rolled onto his side and closed his eyes. He would hunt by night.

It was dark when he awoke. He scratched his back against the hard earth, all four paws in the air. He wriggled, swinging his head from side to side, his hind quarters imitating the motion. A couple of gorged tics lost their grip on his body and were crushed. He rolled to his feet in one smooth turn and shook himself. He was ready for action. Checking the air for messages, he walked east towards the Supati River. At the water's edge he resumed his southerly journey, keeping the jungle between himself and Jawtoli.

Tiger Point was in darkness when he got there. A few feeble lights showed where oil lamps had been turned down, their wicks barely able to nourish the flames. Otherwise there was not even the moon. Another hour must pass before it brightened the silver beach. Along the sand, well above high tide mark, the fishermen's huts were shut. An occasional drone advertised the sleeping presence of humans.

A woodcutter's boat stood a little way off shore, its crew and guard asleep on their uncomfortable cargo of tree trunks. On Egg Island, a kilometre or more away to the south, already in the Bay of Bengal, two fishermen slept under their half-upturned boat. They had spent the day repairing it after one plank gave way below the water line, almost sinking them. At daybreak they would go back to fishing.

Timur wandered into the village as the first sliver of moon stepped over the highest tree tops. The only sound was a chicken, clucking softly to itself in the dust. Timur whacked the unwary bird across its back, killing it with one blow. He plucked the feathers, leaving a tell-tale pile outside a door. After two large bites only the feathers remained. Timur licked his lips and followed a tantalizing smell to the beach. A dozen fish hung by their tails from a trellis of slender branches. They had been put there to dry. Timur licked at one, pulling it down. Within a few minutes he had eaten the lot. Guardedly, he drank his fill from the fresh water hole in the middle of the village. Then, with uncanny instinct and his feline vision to guide him, he swam the passage to Egg Island.

The smell of the sleeping men greeted him as he padded ashore and shook himself, but he ignored them, his hunger no longer gnawing at his insides. A broad patch of sedge muffled his soft tread as he strode through head-high marsh grass to skirt the potential danger. Day was wakening in the east as he laid his long body under a thick bush and fell asleep.

The transient inhabitants of Tiger Point woke to learn their aptly named village had been invaded by its namesake in the night. Distinctive tracks led twice through the hamlet and along the beach. The loss of the fish was a painful blow, the chicken only slightly less disturbing. The fact that the tiger had been there at all was unnerving. The worried men soon found where Timur had entered the sea. He must have paddled right past the woodcutter's barge and gone ashore on the island where the woodsmen had worked all day. One of the men squatted beside the pugmarks. He kept touching one part, thinking carefully. When he straightened, he went in search of the woodcutters' armed guard. The old soldier, past his prime but wise in the ways of nature, listened to the fisherman. Together they walked back to examine the tracks together. The old one noted the blemish on the right pad and the shallow mark from the left. He told the younger fisherman to go to Kotka by boat and see if the red-haired foreigner was there. He would know what to do.

The ex-soldier then warned the remaining villagers to keep their eyes open: a caution all were eager to obey. Out on the sea the overloaded woodcutters' barge began to move ponderously away towards the mouth of the Haringhata River. The crew, frightened by the knowledge of the tiger's proximity, were anxious to leave the scene – even without their armed guard on board. At least half the villagers took to their boats and went fishing, preferring the sea and all its mysterious moods to a chance encounter with a full-grown tiger.

With his rifle at the ready, the guard crossed the narrow strait with four other men in a borrowed boat. They found the two fishermen taking their time to organize their vessel and their fishing nets. The news that they were sharing a small island with a live tiger immeasurably speeded up their operations. They threw their nets on board and pushed the newly repaired boat into the sea, looking fearfully over their shoulders as the gentle swell took charge. Once afloat they hoisted a patched sail and let the wind carry them away.

The guard and his helpers milled around the deep pugmarks in the sand. Not particularly careful where they put their feet, the helpers scuffed the scene into one of total confusion. Within minutes they had reduced their usefulness to little more than zero by rendering Timur's tracks almost unreadable. It was the grass that bothered them. No one wanted to be the first to walk where a tiger could so easily hide. Instead they walked back and forth on the sand, trying to muster the courage to follow where the tracks led.

Timur lay still, listening to the high-pitched babble rippling in from the beach. There, in the centre of the island, he was relatively safe, until someone worked up the nerve to track him properly. He was still, but agitated – his tail swishing from side to side betrayed that. There were too many voices. Too many men. He smelled extreme danger in the air. It was time to leave. The island, too small to accommodate a host of men and one tiger, had become a trap for him.

Egg Island is shaped roughly like a man's bare right foot with the toes pointing north. The reluctant hunters gathered where the big toe dipped into the sea. Timur left his hide and made for the east. Hidden from view by a large stand of trees, which covered half the island, he glided over the beach to the water's edge. The sea stretched ahead of him; no land to be seen. He turned his gaze to the north where a dark line advertised the mainland. Separated from Tiger Point by the Supati River, it was a longer swim than when he had crossed to the island hours before, but he could do it. He cantered through the shallows until he reached the island's little toe. Without hesitation he struck out for the low-lying land mass, nearly four kilometres away.

No one saw him leave. He entered the sea well to the east of the nervous men. They were busy searching inland, their backs to Timur's escape route. The crew on the cumbersome barge never looked behind them. Had they done so he would have been starkly visible. The fishermen were off the west side of the island, making for the open sea. Those on shore at Tiger Point were too busy staring at the island to see Timur, although he was probably too far away to be recognizable anyway.

Timur swam steadily, his eyes glued to the nearest land. His four wide paws paddled steadfastly, keeping a constant rhythm. Where the sea conflicted with the outflow from the Supati River, he crashed through shoulder high surf and stumbled ashore. He shook his elegant body, sending a spray of fine droplets of water in all directions. As his fur settled, he plunged into the forest without looking back.

CHAPTER 18

Rezaul found a fisherman at Chandpai who claimed to know Sanjay and Kumar. He was sure he could find the surviving brother who, he insisted, was fishing with others near the mouth of the Arauaber River. Rezaul took the fisherman to Marshall and suggested they take him with them. If they could find Sanjay, he explained, he could show them where Kumar had been killed. They could then track Timur from that point. Marshall was sceptical. According to reports Kumar's death had been over a week ago. Tracking Timur now would be no easy task. Eventually he gave in. At least, if they could find the man called Sanjay, they would have somewhere to begin their hunt.

Another day passed before they found Sanjay fishing on a side stream with two otters, plus a new partner and a teenage boy. Rezaul did the talking, trying to persuade Sanjay to lead them to the scene of his brother's death. Sanjay refused. Marshall interrupted with an offer of money. Rezaul translated to no avail. Sanjay was adamant. He was not going anywhere near the place.

"Tell him I'll give him five hundred taka," Marshall ordered. Rezaul looked at him keenly, thinking carefully.

Turning to the poor fisherman, he offered him two hundred and fifty taka. He had to raise it, step by step, to three hundred before Sanjay accepted. Marsh gave Rezaul five one hundred taka notes. He, in turn, counted out three hundred to Sanjay's open hand, out of Marshall's sight, and pocketed the remaining two hundred. The boat's cook purchased three large fresh hilsa to grill for dinner as they left.

It only took an hour to reach the scene of the tragedy by river. The furrow where Timur had dragged Kumar's lifeless body up the muddy bank was still evident. Not as clear were the tiger's tracks. Too many human feet had trampled the area at the time of Kumar's death. For an hour or so, Rezaul studied the area alone without finding any clues to follow. Standing on the mud bank he pleaded with Sanjay to come ashore and show him where his brother's body had been found. Sanjay was scared but, urged on by the two impatient trackers, he finally gave in. On shore he took Rezaul directly to the bush he would never forget. Rezaul found a well-defined pugmark immediately and showed it to Marshall.

Following the trail was easy after that. Even when the tiger's prints faded, Gray's heavy-soled canvas boots left a strong imprint. Where they lost one, they only had to look for the other. As insurance, there was also the faint outline of Ali's sandals. Like Gray and Ali, Marshall and Rezaul lost Timur under the pandanus tree. Together they jogged back to the boat, determined to pick up the trail on the other side of the river. Once again they were in luck, finding the route the tiger and the two men had taken, only to lose Timur's prints again at a river crossing. This time they followed the imprint of Gray's boots to the river bend and hailed their boat. Unlike Gray and Ali, they missed the almost hidden creek because they were higher up on a bigger boat. Marshall recommenced their search some distance down the main stream.

With night fast approaching and no chance of seeing much until morning, they took Sanjay back to his own boat. Anchoring the riverboat out in the current and posting a night-long guard, the trackers and crew enjoyed a dinner of curried fish and rice. They slept at anchor, lulled by the whispering of the river caressing the hull.

In the morning, Marshall and Rezaul went ashore opposite the bank where they had last seen Timur's tracks. It soon became apparent that the tiger had not come out of the river as they expected. Following a hunch, Marshall had the boat back-track along the river. As it cruised slowly up the middle of the stream, he peered through the undergrowth on both sides. He found the creek and took an educated guess. With Rezaul's keen eyes to help, he soon caught up with the three missing tracks. They followed them south until Rezaul pointed out that Gray and Ali's tracks were going in two directions.

"Tiger is going long way south," he told Marshall. "Two men go back to boat."

Marshall squatted on his haunches for a minute or two, thinking over all the possibilities. If Pendennis got ahead of Timur and blocked his southerly path, he could unwittingly drive him north again – to Marshall's rifle.

"Let's go back to the boat, Rezaul. We are going for a long walk. We'll need some supplies."

Once on board Marshall produced two folded lightweight backpacks and shook them out. They loaded up with bread and cooked meat, plus slivers of raw coconut and four bottles of coconut water, with another four of fresh water: enough for roughly four to five days away from the boat. Marshall estimated the coast to be a little less than thirty kilometres away in a straight line. He doubted that Timur had been thoughtful enough to maintain such a direct course. Confident he could reach Kotka in less than two days if he had to, Marshall doubled the figure to compensate for the whims of an unpredictable man-eater.

The two men ate a hearty cooked meal and each downed a mug of hot sweet tea. As soon as they finished they got ready to leave. On top of their packs they rolled a thin blanket each. Both carried a loaded rifle with additional ammunition in the side pockets of their packs. Marshall strapped a machete on his belt.

"Okay, Rezaul. Let's trek. You meet us at Kotka," he told the captain. "We'll be there in three or four days."

The trail was easy to follow at first, until the point where Gray and Ali had turned back. From there Marshall and Rezaul had to make use of all their combined bush skills. Many times they lost the tiger only to pick up his tracks again – often more by luck than judgement. It was obvious to Rezaul the big cat wasn't hunting. He was heading straight for the coast.

"Do you think he's going for the meadow? What's it called, Jawtoli?"

"I think tiger goes to Jawtoli," confirmed Rezaul.

That first night in the jungle they built a small fire in a reasonably dry clearing. For safety they divided the night into four two-hour watches. They were not disturbed. Marshall awoke stiff and sore, groaning softly at the ache in his limbs and back and complaining of getting old. Rezaul remained silent. He made tea and cut a thick slice of bread for each of them. They dipped the bread in their tea and ate hurriedly. Once back on the trail, and moving at a steady pace, Marshall's stiffness soon disappeared.

That day they crossed two creeks, exactly where Timur had crossed. The first one was deep enough to necessitate hitching their packs as high on their shoulders as possible and holding their rifles above their heads. The water came up to the middle of Rezaul's chest and almost as high on Marshall. As they waded past the halfway mark, Rezaul mentioned saltwater crocodiles. Marshall grunted. He had already considered that possibility and was scanning left and right for signs of danger. Crossing the second much shallower creek in the afternoon, Marshall saw a slight movement out of the corner of his eye. The water was only knee high but deep enough for both to run the final few paces to dry land. As they stopped for breath, Rezaul knelt and placed his hand on the earth. Lifting it to his nose he sniffed.

"Look," he said. "Tiger. A female."

Marshall looked back at the spot where he had seen the movement. There was no sign of life. He looked at the new tracks again. Rezaul showed him where they had crossed Timur's tracks almost at right angles. They looked fresher than the man-eater's prints, but he wasn't positive.

"When?"

"Today, I think," Rezaul answered, starting to follow the female's tracks. Marshall called him back.

"Forget her," he ordered. "We have no fight with her, as long as she leaves us alone."

They continued in Timur's wake, keeping watch behind them and on all sides in case the female felt the need to change her diet. Marshall suffered in the oppressive humidity. As his clothes tried to dry from his walk through the river, so they became soaked again with his salty sweat. His skin began to itch. Uncomfortable though he was, he made no comment. He just kept moving. Rezaul showed no sign of discomfort. He seemed to be immune to the heat and the clinging effect of damp clothes. He spoke only when he was spoken to or when he saw something important. Marshall was grateful for the lack of conversation. He needed all his concentration for the task at hand. He sensed that Timur was not far away.

Late that night, as they dozed under their blankets, they heard the far off call of a lonely tigress. Rezaul sat up, listening carefully. Marshall stayed put, his ears straining to hear any answering moans. The same mating cry came to Timur's ears as he scratched his back against a tree. He listened. It was not one of his mates. He answered the distant call anyway, his voice tailing off into a soft moan.

Marshall and Rezaul heard the male's deep solid tones answer. It was followed by a fainter cry immediately after. The calls, varying in strength, echoed back and forth for a long time. There was no more sleep that night. Marshall was convinced that Timur had answered the female and gone to her. He was equally sure it must be the female they had almost encountered hours before. He decided to go back and follow her trail. Rezaul was not so easily swayed.

"I don't think it is him," he told Marshall. "It sounded like three different tigers. The voices came from different places. There. There. And there." He pointed emphatically in three different directions.

"One of them must be the man-eater. There can't be that many tigers loose around here."

"It might be, but we don't know which one," Rezaul argued. "Tracking the female doesn't mean we will find him."

"We'll try anyway," Marshall insisted. "There's nothing else we can do."

While the men argued by the dying embers of their fire, Timur hunted unsuccessfully along the banks of the Betmur River. Far to the east two other tigers greeted each other cautiously as they began their instinctive mating ritual.

As the first rays of a new day stole through the trees, Marshall and Rezaul set off. Picking up the tigress's trail at the creek they went east with it. Marshall found where the cat had stopped for a rest under a bush, no more than one hundred paces from their river crossing. He knew he had seen a movement. She had obviously been surprised by the two men and had gone to ground. Nearly two hours later, with the sun climbing up the trees and warming the forest, they came to a river again. It was too wide and too deep for them to cross and there were no boats in sight. The tracks led straight into the water. The tigress had gone swimming. Marshall swore loudly.

"Okay, Rezaul. We'll go back," he said.

He hefted his pack and turned away. Rezaul followed, retracing their steps to last night's camp. Marshall was bitterly disappointed. They had detoured at least eight kilometres and wasted many hours. The rest of the day was uneventful for both men and the beast they trailed.

While the men followed his meandering tracks, Timur reclined in regal splendour on a grassy knoll overlooking the river. He drifted in and out of sleep as the afternoon sun beat down on the jungle. Around him, keeping their distance, other creatures kept silent – out of fear and respect. The only creature to give voice was a kingfisher. It called out from an orchid branch as it watched the river for fish.

To the north, a herd of spotted deer had a bit of a panic at the sight of two men walking briskly through their feeding grounds. An old wild boar with magnificent curved tusks snorted and galloped off when he heard their low voices. An occasional primate shouted insults from the sanctuary of the tree-tops. Resolutely the men hurried on, moving steadily south as Timur had done. Marshall doggedly placed one foot in front of the other. Rezaul kept to the left of Timur's tracks. Marshall walked right down the middle of them. The prints were his tonic. Hate gave him energy. Throughout the afternoon, the sight of the tiger's pugmarks kept him going. He thought of Tracy and of Simon, occasionally he thought of Jeannette, imprisoned in her own fragile mind. Often he thought of the moment when he would put a bullet through Timur's brain.

Marshall was so busy tramping on Timur's tracks that he didn't notice the change until Rezaul stopped him and pantomimed a semi-circle. Marshall took out his compass and checked. Rezaul was right. The trail was curving southeast. A short time later the tracks ended at a wide river. Marshall studied his map. It could only be the Betmur. Timur had crossed but they could not.

"I told you," Marshall said angrily to Rezaul. "He's gone after that bloody female."

Rezaul shook his head. "They are both over there," he pointed across the river, "but I don't think they are together. The killer is alone."

Without further comment, Rezaul began to make camp. While Marshall stood staring across the river, the Bengali guide collected arm loads of sticks and small dead branches. He lit a fire before dark. If a boat came along, they wanted to be seen. The river remained still.

It was a long, quiet night for both men, broken only by the occasional rustlings of little nocturnal herbivores foraging for food while trying to avoid larger nocturnal predators. Rezaul slept just outside the fire's glow. Marshall hardly slept at all. He sat beside the fire most of the night, keeping it blazing brightly. Staring at the hot coals he began to define images among the flames, images he wanted so much to forget at times, yet strove to remember at others. That night he stirred the embers to find Tracy and Simon. They rode bareback on a tiger behind Durga – the fierce Hindu god. Marshall covered the scene with burning brands, wiping his streaming eyes with the back of one hand. At daybreak, after a sleepless night, he was still in the same position.

All morning Marshall and Rezaul waited on the riverbank. They could have gone south, or north to find a boat but Marshall was determined to cross where Timur had crossed. He couldn't lose him now, not after all he had been through. As the sun reached and passed its zenith, Rezaul shaded his eyes with his hand, looking to the far shore. North of where they waited, and close to the opposite bank of the river, two small fishing boats drifted slowly into view. For another half an hour they waited until the boats were close enough to hail. Rezaul cupped his hands and shouted to get their attention. Abruptly one boat cut across to their side, stopping one length away from the bank. The boatman held his craft stationary against the feeble current with a pole dug into the river bottom. He kept his distance from the strangers while Rezaul told him of their need to cross the river.

"He says it will cost one hundred taka," he told Marshall after a brief shouted conversation.

"Pay him from the two hundred taka you kept from Sanjay," Marshall replied without change of expression.

Rezaul started to protest, saw the stern look on Marshall's face and shut his mouth. He said something to the boatman who shook his head. Rezaul tried again. The same result. Finally he held up a one hundred taka note and the boat moved closer in. As soon as they were both aboard, Marshall pointed to the opposite bank and urged the fisherman to get moving. Rezaul pointed to a particularly tall tree.

"There," he said. "Go there."

As they crossed Marshall had a morbid thought about the river Styx. He shook his head angrily to clear his mind. The second boat met them as they poled in, the occupants asking Rezaul about the white man, and why they were in the forest without a boat. Rezaul was quite content to take his time and be sociable. In the company of his own kind the usually taciturn forestry guard became a voluble conversationalist. Marshall silenced him and stepped ashore. He didn't thank the fisherman or acknowledge his presence. He simply strode into the forest looking for Timur's spoor, leaving Rezaul to pay the ferry fare. The guard quickly caught up and cast around for signs. Together it took them over an hour to re-establish the tenuous contact with the tiger.

Timur had drifted lazily with the current and crossed the river at forty-five degrees, coming to land among a cluster of golpatta palms. He had slipped getting out of the water, carving a distinct gouge in the muddy bank. Wide as a tiger's paw and more than twice as long, the hollow could have been made by any large animal. To the uninitiated, it wasn't obviously a tiger print. No pugmarks were visible – just a deep furrow. The clue was enough for Rezaul; he located Timur's tracks seconds later.

Timur was travelling south. The ground was hard, the pugmarks indistinct. Already far too many hours old, it was not an easy trail to follow and Marshall was well aware Timur could be almost anywhere in the Sundarbans by now. The faint tracks were all they had to go by, so they stuck with them. There was no sign of the female. By nightfall Marshall estimated he and Rezaul had only covered about five kilometres. Timur was as far ahead as ever.

The two hunters spent most of their fourth night in the jungle soaked as a heavy rain shower blew across the

Sundarbans from the Bay of Bengal in the early hours – a final wet reminder of the recent monsoon.

Timur was on the move again when the rain started. He could smell the acrid scent of man in the air and on the ground. He was hungry again and man was a meal. Since killing Kumar, Timur had roamed to the southernmost extent of his vast territory. He had returned north along the eastern boundary. He had crossed part way to the west and back to the east again. The downpour drove him under the shelter of a large pandanus, where he slumbered through the squall.

Awake as the rain stopped, Timur crawled into the open. The night was nearly over. He took the scent again. Man had definitely passed through this part of his land. He turned due south, away from the river. When the sun came up the ground began to steam and the humidity soared sky high. Both Rezaul and Marshall were extremely uncomfortable. Marshall was beginning to show the strain and Rezaul finally in some distress. To make life more complicated, the tracks were harder to read after the rain. With Kotka less than a day's walk away and the terrain getting softer by the hour, Marshall told Rezaul to take the lead. He was more experienced in the jungle. He could read the signs faster.

The creeks were full, partly from the rain and partly from the incoming tide. Crossing them meant getting soaked to the waist each time. Rezaul cut himself a long sturdy hiking pole with a vee-shaped notch at the top. His hand fitted neatly around the top of the staff while his thumb rested comfortably in the notch. He tested it and found it helped him walk more efficiently on the slippery ground and in the creeks. He offered it to Marshall who shook his head.

They lost Timur again near a deep, narrow creek. Keeping to the north side, they walked far in each direction without success. Back where the tiger's trail had petered out Rezaul suggested, "Tiger has made big jump." He described a broad arc with his hands. Marshall thought about it. Either the tiger had deliberately paddled along the creek to lose his pursuers or he had made a mighty leap – landing well

beyond the creek's south bank. Rezaul unslung his rifle and
took off his pack. He tested the water with his staff. It was
more than chest deep.

"I can jump," he told Marshall.

Still holding his staff he walked back twenty paces.
Turning, he broke into a run. He dug the thick end of his
staff into the bank and projected himself over the creek like
a pole-vaulter. Rezaul landed heavily on his left foot. His
right foot skidded on the mud and he went down hard.
Rezaul roared with pain and clasped his ankle. Marshall
swore in frustration. Then, with no choice, he picked up the
additional burden of Rezaul's pack and rifle. Securing them
on top of his own pack he lowered himself gingerly into the
water. The extra weight made him sink in the loose mud on
the bottom and he almost fell. Struggling angrily he fought
his way across and up the steep slope to Rezaul.

"Let me look," he ordered, running his hands over
the rapidly swelling ankle. He was sure it was broken.
Wrapping it up as best he could with a spare dirty shirt,
he helped Rezaul to stand. But Rezaul could not put any
weight on the foot. Still furious at the accident, Marshall
found a reasonably straight branch that could double as a
crutch. He cut it to fit under Rezaul's armpit and secured
a short piece of wood across it halfway down for him to
grip with one hand. It wouldn't be comfortable but it would
work.

"Now, Rezaul," he rasped, "try to walk."

Looking a bit like an Asian Long John Silver, Rezaul
hobbled up and down testing his ability.

"It hurts, but I think I can walk slowly."

"I'll leave you here, with a rifle for protection, and
go on to Kotka alone," Marshall suggested.

"No," Rezaul disagreed, looking at him in horror.
"It is too much danger for both of us if we separate. We
must stay together."

Marshall insisted on scouring the area to pick up
Timur's trail. "I'll be back in a couple of hours," he promised. "You stay here and rest that ankle."

Leaving Rezaul propped against a tree, the packs at his feet, Marshall quartered the area trying to find the spoor. He was unsuccessful. Once again the man-eater had vanished. There was no alternative but to collect Rezaul and take the shortest possible route to Kotka. Marshall calculated it was about a day's walk for a fit man – more for a cripple. It would be a demanding trek for Rezaul, with many more creeks to cross.

Marshall stripped the two packs. Stowing essentials, such as food and water, plus ten extra rounds of ammunition, in one pack, he discarded the other. Both rifles held full clips of ammunition. Marshall also had the machete on his belt. He left the rest of their supplies beside the creek. They were of no further use to them. Marshall weighed his camera in his hand, debating whether to take it or leave it behind. Habit was, in this case, stronger than need. He placed the strap around his neck, letting the camera hang against his chest.

Rezaul slung his rifle diagonally across his back and, with a grimace of pain, took a tentative step, supported by the crutch. His ankle hurt, but he took another – and another. Slowly the pair made their way south. Every half an hour they had to stop to let Rezaul rest. The skin under his arm was rubbed raw from the crutch. The palm of his hand blistered from the moving pressure of his grip. Marshall took off his own shirt and bound it round the top of the crutch to alleviate some of the suffering. It helped for a while. There was nothing he could do about the blisters. Rezaul bit them to release the fluid and tore a strip off the tail of his shirt to bind them. As the day advanced Rezaul's pace slowed to a crawl. Marshall knew he had to find help. The map showed a river not far ahead, which flowed from the Supati River to meet the Bay of Bengal at Kotka. Surely there would be fishermen on the Supati to help them.

"It's less than two kilometres from here to the river, I'm sure. I will go on ahead. You can either wait here or follow at your own speed."

Marshall wasn't asking a question this time or making a suggestion. He was stating the only way to progress. Rezaul didn't like it, but Marshall gave him no choice.

"I'm not staying here alone," Rezaul complained. "I will walk behind you and rest when I get tired. All the time I will stay with your shoes."

"You mean in my footprints," Marshall muttered. "Do what you will. If I find a boat, I will come back for you."

Marshall tucked a bottle of coconut water inside Rezaul's shirt and left him. Without the injured man to hold him back, he moved quickly. Soon his bare chest and back glistened with sweat. His camera became a burden, bumping incessantly against his ribs. He took it off and wrapped the strap tightly around his waist so he could still get at it quickly if need be. The warm sweat ran down his spine, staining his pack and seeping through it. His pants had more wet patches than dry. Relentlessly he pushed through the forest, thankful he didn't have to hack his way through creepers and vines.

After twelve minutes he came to a narrow stream. It was too small for his purposes; there would be no fishermen working there. Studying the map, he saw that he was further from the main river than he had thought – too far to the west. Turning east he began to jog, keeping up a steady pace for a full hour until the trees cleared and the river lay before him. It looked to be about one hundred metres from shore to shore. Not two boat lengths away, a fisherman slowly hauled in his net. In the shade of a thatched cabin on the same boat, another man was cooking fish.

Alone and far behind, Rezaul stumped heavily along. To keep his nerve, and to warn any jungle dwellers of his presence, he talked loudly to himself. Where the narrow stream sent Marshall's big footprints to the east, he lowered himself to the ground by a tree and took a few sips from his bottle. For a few minutes he sat there, massaging his legs, feeling the tightening of the calf muscle on his healthy limb. His injured ankle throbbed, the pain constant.

Carefully he rewound the binding to keep the bones from moving. Taking the rifle off his back he cradled it across his lap and lit a cigarette, drawing the smoke deep into his lungs. He exhaled with a deep sigh, worrying about his predicament. Rather than move on immediately, he dozed against the tree to regain some strength, the cigarette burning itself to ash.

Marshall and Rezaul had not gone far in front when Timur came upon the deep creek for the second time in a few days. Unsure of their route he followed the strong scent in Marshall's tracks back and forth along the channel, ending up back at his starting point. He looked around, bunched his muscles and sprang, clearing the water with ease. As the trackers followed the vestiges of his old spoor, so he trailed their fresher path. Still uneasy near mankind, in spite of the years he had hunted them, Timur followed but kept well to their rear.

Rezaul was alone, half-asleep against the tree when Timur caught up with him. The tiger flattened his body to the ground and watched, his tail whisking back and forth. Rezaul sat still, his chin resting on his chest, his eyes closed. Timur crouched behind and off to one side. He looked straight at the right side of Rezaul's face. The rifle's muzzle was pointed away from the tiger.

CHAPTER 19

Gray heard about Timur's visit to Tiger Point as soon as *Fatima* tied up at the Kotka jetty. He and Ali paddled the dingi to the opposite shore and hurried overland to the village immediately, leaving Julian on board to prepare for his dives.

Tiger Point was almost deserted when they arrived. One man waited on the beach to ferry them across to Egg Island where the old guard and his men were still trying to pluck up courage to beat their way across the small island. As soon as he stepped ashore, Gray could see that the tracks on the beach had been all but destroyed by the many feet, yet no one had ventured beyond the shoreline. Ali moved cautiously into the grass and found Timur's trail a few paces in. With Gray off to his left, he worked carefully to the centre of the island.

"Tiger stopped here," he indicated the faint outline of a body. If Timur was still on the island, he had to be dangerously close. Ali released the safety catch on his rifle. Gray did the same with his dart gun. Together they stepped where Timur had stepped not long before. They lost the tracks briefly on the beach when it looked as though he had paddled straight out to sea. Knowing it was impossible, Gray went south while Ali looked north. Ali found the tracks again and called Gray to him. They followed together until the trail walked into the sea. Gray looked at the mainland to his left and, much further away, in front of him. For a second or two he stood there, staring at the distant mainland and nodding in understanding.

"Son of a bitch," he said. "Ali, we'll have to organize a line of beaters and sweep this island to make sure, but I'll bet my boots he's gone over there."

Ali rounded up a gang of fourteen men and boys and ordered them to cut long sticks. He lined them up as if on parade and explained what they had to do.

"We must make a lot of noise to flush out this tiger, if he is here."

One boy was sent back to Tiger Point in a boat to collect as many pots and pans as he could. While the parade waited, mutterings of unrest rippled along the line. Ali confidently calmed the men.

"We have three rifles here to protect us," he reminded them. "No one will come to any harm."

He placed himself in the middle of the line, the old guard at one end and Gray at the other. Banging their sticks on metal pots the jittery line advanced, chattering nervously to each other. Most expected a tiger to spring at them at any moment. The rabble, noisy and hesitant as the advance guard of a mini-revolution, tramped rowdily from one end of the island to the other. A few dozen birds took fright and squawked their displeasure at the intrusion. Nothing else was disturbed as far as Gray could see. There was no tiger on Egg Island.

He and Ali went back to Kotka, taking a scenic route along the deserted silver-sand beach for as far as they could. Opposite the watchtower, they cut inland through the forest and came out onto the meadow, following a well-trodden path back to their dingi. The one place where Timur could be relied on to visit regularly was Jawtoli meadow. It wouldn't be too many days before he returned. When he did, Gray and Ali would be waiting.

◆ ◆ ◆

Rezaul stirred, lifting his head to look around him. Not fifty paces away a tiger crouched on all fours. As if in a dream Rezaul clicked off his safety catch. He rolled sideways onto his chest, swinging his rifle to bear on the cat. Forgetting his injury momentarily, he straightened his legs, gritting his teeth with pain as he knocked his broken ankle with his other foot. Timur charged as Rezaul pulled the trigger.

Rezaul had been trained to always keep a blank round in the chamber. Hunting with Marshall had not changed that habit. He squeezed the trigger and the loud bang deflected Timur from his path, as it was intended to do. He passed Rezaul by a wide margin, spraying water to both sides as he splashed across the stream. Before Rezaul could change position and get him in his sights, Timur was a disappearing blur. Rezaul fired a live round after him anyway, knowing he had missed. Shuddering with aftershock, he struggled to his feet, his rifle pointed in the direction the tiger had taken. He was too late. Timur had fled.

Marshall heard the shots as he stood at the river's edge, watched warily by the two fishermen. He spun round at the first crack and swore loudly. Releasing his safety catch he raced back the way he had come. Far along the trail, he met Rezaul hobbling towards him as fast as he could on one leg and a crutch. He babbled out his story, tripping over his words, getting English and Bangla muddled together. Marshall got the gist of it and sent him on to the river.

"Tell the fishermen we need to cross," he ordered.

Positive the tiger would still be running after its fright, but hoping it was still in the area, he went back alone. To an experienced tracker, the scene was painted in bright colours: the scuffs where Rezaul had rolled to take his first shot and the indentations where his elbows had dug in to support the rifle. The roll on to his back for the second shot was less clear, but visible nonetheless, as was the deep mark where he had pushed his crutch hard into the ground to help him stand. The tiger's signs were strong. Marshall soon found where he had stopped and settled his belly on the ground, and where he had risen to begin his charge. Rezaul had fired when the tiger was halfway to him, the location marked by an abrupt change of direction. Where the tiger had leapt across the river the prints were clearest. Marshall knelt beside them, tracing their patterns with his index finger. It was Timur.

"Bloody hell," Marshall exploded. "That sod's been tracking us while we were tracking him."

Knowing it was futile to try and follow Timur that day, but determined to catch up with him eventually, Marshall hurried to meet Rezaul at the river.

Timur ran hard until he was well out of range. The explosive noise from Rezaul's rifle still echoed in his ears. Limping awkwardly, he slowed and forced his way through thick undergrowth until he felt safe. With his chest heaving from his exertions he lay down. Within minutes he was asleep. For one whole day he rested. When the shadows lengthened, he groomed himself, taking particular care with his injured paw. Tidy and clean again, he stretched all his muscles and left the hide. Stiffly at first. he walked silently into the night, his nose testing the air for prey.

There was little game. Towards dawn he almost caught a tufted duck, just managing to get his right paw up to it before urgently beating wings gave it altitude. Close to the northern reaches of the Betmur River, which vaguely mimics the Supati's serpentine course, though further west, Timur turned his steps south again. High in a gewa tree, a monkey saw the tiger padding through a grove of thorny paludosa palms and hooted the alarm. The call was echoed from tree to tree. A small herd of spotted deer stopped browsing to raise their heads and listen, turning as one to face the direction of the warning. A sea eagle whistled shrilly from its high perch, though unconcerned by the tiger's presence. Timur heard the calls without changing his shambling gait.

The small herd of deer trotted through the trees and stopped to browse again a few minutes later. Timur gradually caught up with them, keeping downwind. A doe and a fawn stood closest to him, grazing side by side. Timur bunched his muscles. Two deliberately controlled steps put him in position for a charge. His hind legs catapulted him out of the undergrowth landing him face to face with the deer. Mother and offspring spun as one, leaping into the air with fright. Timur's weight and speed carried him through. He knocked the fawn to the ground as the doe fled. Skidding to a halt, sending a fine spray of dust and dirt after the doe, Timur turned.

The fawn got unsteadily to its feet facing Timur. It bleated nervously, crying for its mother. From a discreet distance the doe answered, calling her baby to her. The fawn stayed put, mesmerised by the sight of the great cat. Timur stared at the half-grown fawn, only a foreleg's reach away. The fawn bleated again. Timur tapped it on the head with his good paw, his claws sheathed. The fawn fell over. Surprised at the blow, it struggled on weakened legs back to its feet. Timur tapped it again, hitting the fawn on the side of the jaw. The fawn rolled over and again fought groggily to its feet, more than a little stunned. The doe continued to call from a distance.

Timur sniffed at the pretty little creature, raising his right paw again. The fawn flinched, ducking its head, it's legs braced wide apart. Timur put his paw on the fawn's head and held it there for a few seconds. The fawn struggled, bleating its terror to the world. Timur let go. The fawn looked at its tormenter helplessly. Timur raised his paw again. His victim trembled and danced sideways, almost getting out of reach. Timur's claws hooked into its skin and drew the kicking fawn to him. The tiger's jaws fastened around the fawn's throat killing it instantly. Timur settled down to eat his meal while the doe called again in despair before dancing away to the shelter of the herd.

CHAPTER 20

Gray and Julian sat talking on *Fatima*'s top deck late in the afternoon. The Kotka rest house was just visible through the Sundari trees. The tide was on the ebb. Aerial roots, like a vast bed of long nails, cast elongated shadows across the glistening mud. Beside them the old wooden jetty welcomed the first shade to block the sun and cool its hot, tired and cracked planks.

"That fort you told me about," Julian asked, "do you think Marshall knows about it?"

"I shouldn't think so. I only found it by accident. I'll bet it hasn't been seen by a visitor for over a hundred years."

"Is it worth looking at?"

Gray thought for a moment. "Yes, it is. But it's quite a way from here and doesn't have any bearing on your search. I might go back if we can't find Timur down here and wait for him to show up there."

"I suppose I'll have to wait until I read your article about it in National Geographic."

Gray laughed, "Yeah, I should write it up. It's definitely worth a story."

He stood up. "If we're going to spend the night on the tower, we'd better get a move on. It will be dark soon. Ali, let's get going."

Leaving *Fatima* at her mooring, he had one of the crew paddle the three of them across the river in a dingi. Up a side creek they came to another untidy jetty with steps leading up from the low tide level.

"You go back now," Gray ordered the paddler. "Come for us in the morning at first light."

Ali said something quietly to Gray and Julian was surprised to see him shudder. "What's the problem?" He asked. "You don't look happy."

"No, I'm fine. Ali just reminded me that this where Timur stole Hassan's body from him."

Shouldering a blanket each, the trio wandered along the well-worn path to the watchtower, two hundred metres distant. Ali carried his rifle. Gray had a rifle slung over his shoulder and his dart gun at the ready. Julian brought up the rear with an aluminium pot in each hand – the evening meal. Julian, suddenly nervous, kept close behind his companions. At the tower, Gray checked all four heavy duty guy wires for tension before closing the gate behind them. As a precaution, he tied it shut with a piece of wire. Julian watched him with a quizzical smile.

"What's to stop a tiger knocking the gate down and coming up the tower?" he asked.

"Nothing," answered Gray with an amused smile. "If a tiger wants to come up and join us there's not a lot we can do about it – apart from this." He patted his rifle. "It's highly unlikely one will try anyway."

"It's nice to know you are so confident." Julian smiled back at him. "I guess I'll have to take your word for it."

"That will do for me," Gray continued. "Now, some advice. If you need to answer a call of nature in the night, you stay inside the gate. We'll clean up in the morning if we have to."

On the top level, twenty metres above the ground, they had a panoramic view encompassing the rapidly darkening meadow and parts of the surrounding jungle. The sun had dropped behind the trees. Night was imminent. Ali's acute hearing soon separated one sound from the bird calls and occasional monkey chatter.

"There's a boar under that big gewa tree to our right," he whispered.

Gray pointed the wild pig out to Julian. The indistinct shape snuffled among the leaves and roots around the base of the tree, but kept to the darkest patches. Gray willed the boar to step out into the open, without success. It gradually moved into the forest until it was gone from sight.

"This is Timur's prime hunting ground, as far as we know," Gray told Julian quietly. "There is a herd of deer and often boar like that one feeding on or beside the meadow."

A sharp barking reached them from the direction of the south coast. They listened carefully, waiting for a repeat. Another sharp bark sounded once.

"That sounds like a dog over there," Julian whispered. "Is there a village? Or would it be wild?"

"There's no village and that's not a dog. That's a warning signal from a deer. No sudden noises now," Gray warned. "Maybe, just maybe there's a predator on the prowl out there. If there is it's almost certain to be a tiger – a female: or, one chance in many, it is Timur. I doubt there would be another adult male in the vicinity."

"What's your guess, Gray?"

"No guesses. If it's a tiger it is either Timur, or it is not. Time will tell."

"With all that chest-high grass and the surrounding jungle, there could be thousands of creatures out there and we wouldn't know it," mused Julian.

"You're right. We, Ali and I, have roamed all over Jawtoli. It's littered with tracks of many animal species."

Gray uncovered the pots. "Let's eat now, before the food gets cold."

Sitting cross-legged on the wooden platform, the trio hurriedly ate a meal of boiled rice and hot curried chicken. Julian used a fork while Gray and Ali rolled the food into bite-sized balls with the fingers of their right hands. Expertly they flicked the morsels into their mouths. Once finished they washed their hands with fresh water, letting it trickle down the side of the tower to the ground far below. Contented, they sat back against the uprights in silence, listening to the sounds of the Sundarbans as the diurnal creatures adjusted to the night and the nocturnal foragers came awake. Ali had a powerful lamp with him to illuminate the field near the tower if they heard anything interesting. He tied one end of a long piece of string to the handle and secured the other end to the rail for safety. Twice prior to midnight they heard warning barks from deer, but the tiger, if there was one out there, remained hidden.

On a broad spreading tree, whose branches came within reach of the top of the tower, a troop of rhesus monkeys slept fitfully. In the early hours of the morning, one of them shivered violently in its dream and started to fall off its perch. Frightened, it screamed in alarm as it grabbed hold of another. The ensuing disturbance, of one frightened primate shrieking at the others, woke all creatures within hearing.

"That may bring us some results," Gray whispered, reaching for the lamp. He shone the beam over the tree's top branches, down the trunk and in a wide arc round the tower. Julian's eyes travelled with the light, trying to see through the long grass. Gray stopped the beam abruptly and changed direction.

"There's a deer," he whispered.

The deer twitched an ear, its eyes staring at the light. Gray held it transfixed for a few moments then cast the glow further out into the field. He held the lamp steady. The grass settled. There was no other movement. Gray slowly fanned the beam over the meadow. A few bright spots showed in and around the light: fireflies and the eyes of small creatures caught for a fraction of time. None of the tiny glows suggested the presence of a tiger.

"Sleep if you want to," Gray suggested. "I'll wake you if anything happens."

Within a few minutes both Ali and Julian were snoring lightly. Gray was almost asleep himself, standing propped against a corner post, when he felt a subtle change come over the meadow. No new sound broke the humid stillness of the night. No unexpected smells reached him. The change was almost imperceptible, but somehow menacing. It urged his mind to full alert in a second. He touched Ali's shoulder, then reached down and placed a hand over Julian's mouth, whispering tautly, "We have a tiger. No noise, please."

Ali sat up as Julian rose stealthily to his feet. Motioning the two to maintain silence, Gray pointed into the darkness.

"There's another deer, but it's not alone and I think it knows it. There is a tiger here, somewhere close by. I'm sure of it."

Gray switched on the lamp and slowly played the beam over the grass until he located a dark mass. The three men held their breath as two bright amber lights stared back at them.

"There it is. That's its eyes. It's worried about the light. It doesn't understand it or trust it," Gray kept his voice low.

As they stood shoulder to shoulder, their eyes fixed on the slowly moving twin pinpoints of light, a striped head broke into the beam for a few seconds, then it was gone. They saw the dark lines running down the body clearly, followed by a glimpse of the tail as the tiger turned away from the potential danger and vanished. Gray played the light all over the meadow but their elusive quarry had apparently forsaken the chance of a meal. Julian let out a softly explosive, "Wow!" as he slapped Gray on the back.

"Sssh. Keep it down. Whispers only," Gray warned. "I'm not sure it's gone yet."

The deer that Gray had inadvertently saved trotted to the base of the tower and stopped suddenly. Its ears twitched, searching for the danger it still sensed. Gray placed a cautionary hand on Julian's shoulder. He pointed to a lighter patch in the darkness.

"At the end of that guy wire there's a large sand patch. Something is moving on the other side of it," he breathed.

Gray shifted his gaze momentarily to the deer, now directly below him. There was no breeze to carry its scent to a hunter. No slight wind to foil a predator's approach. Still the deer turned nervously to face the unknown. As if kick-started into action, it sprang sideways, bounding into the protection of long grass. Gray stabbed his thumb on the lamp button again, sending its dazzling beam to the sand.

"There it is. There it is," he hissed with excitement. A tiger streaked across the open space after the deer. Gray held the lamp steady, tracking the two as the deer dodged left and right. The tiger was too strong, too experienced. The young deer feinted left and swung right. A wicked paw smacked it to the ground at the furthest extremity of the light. A flurry of activity, with deer and tiger locked in a terminal embrace, signalled the end. Julian gripped the tower rail tightly and took a few deep breaths. When he was sufficiently composed, he nodded a couple of times in the darkness, trying to clear his dry throat.

"Fantastic, Gray," he croaked. "Absolutely fantastic. It was worth coming here just for that."

"It wasn't Timur," Ali said suddenly, the first sound he had made since he stood up.

"No, I don't think it was either," Gray agreed. "It was too fast and too agile for a wounded cat. It must have been that female. We'll see for sure in the morning."

They talked softly for the remainder of the night. The dawn announced its arrival with pink tremors in the sky. A silvery mist crept over the purple meadow. The occasional trees stood out as badly conceived dark blobs on a child's first painting. Gray leaned on the rail watching as the light steadily improved. Trees took on their natural shape and colour. Grass showed through the gossamer threads of mist drifting away from the sun's imminent warmth. Gray estimated where they had last seen the tiger and the deer. There was nothing unusual visible from a distance.

"Let's take a look." Gray picked up his gear and ran lightly down the steps followed by Julian and Ali. On the ground Ali automatically assumed the lead, unerringly picking up the deer's panicky trail. Ali knelt at the first tiger print. Clean and deep. The pugmarks were not made by Timur.

"As I suspected, it was a healthy female," Gray noted. Ali nodded his agreement as Gray photographed the prints, then scribbled something in his notebook.

"How can you be sure it was a female?" Julian asked. "Surely you can't tell its gender from four prints?"

Gray crouched, showing him which tracks were made by the front paws and which came from the hind feet.

"Yes, we can. See how the hind pugmarks have pointed toes? That's the sign of a female. I'm sure she's only a young one, probably only recently left her mother because her pads are relatively unscarred."

"Only a young one," Julian exclaimed. "She looked huge to me last night."

Oh, she's fully grown. That's two known females in this area, don't you agree Ali?"

Ali nodded thoughtfully. Motioning Gray and Julian to stand still, he walked the tiger's trail to an irregular circle of flattened grass. The deer's tracks stopped abruptly, the tiger's continued alone. Ali signalled Gray and Julian to join him. Gray read the signs and pursed his lips.

"That's why we didn't hear her crunching bones last night. She carried the deer away. I'll bet she's sleeping not far from here right now."

Ali began to follow the tracks, but Gray stopped him. "We don't need her. I'm hungry. Breakfast must be ready by now I should think."

Nearing the jetty, Gray stopped to show Julian a tan tree-climbing frog. Carefully he plucked it from the bark.

"These little guys are quite common in the Sundarbans, both here and in India. Look at his tiny translucent pads."

He held the frog tenderly between his thumb and index finger as he let the sun shine through the delicate hands. Gently he put the frog back on the tree exactly where he found it. In the distance the howl of a powerful motor made them all look in the direction of the river.

"What the hell's that?" Gray asked. "That's not our boat."

In single file, they trotted to the river bank, arriving just as a military boat raced past with four armed men and a large wooden container on board. Standing in the bows was the distinctive figure of General Rahman.

"Now what the hell is he doing down here?" Gray wondered aloud. "I really don't trust that bastard."

Gray's dingi rolled in the boat's wake as it approached the jetty.

"Come, Mister Professor," the boatman greeted them. "Breakfast is being ready."

Gray ignored him for the moment. His eyes were focussed on the fast disappearing military boat. There was something strange about its presence at Kotka. It was not part of the normal patrol route he knew. Shaking his head, he joined the others. Breakfast was a quick and quiet meal of cereal, followed by spicy omelettes. All three men were hungry and anxious to get on with the day. As he ate, Gray mulled over the general's sudden appearance earlier, wondering what he was doing so far from his base.

◆ ◆ ◆

General Rahman's boat raced along the coast, leaving Kotka behind. After a few kilometres, it turned into the broad Passur River. Rahman stood like a sentry in the bow, his crew of soldiers behind him. Coming towards them was a nondescript freighter with Chinese Markings. Rahman's boat circled and came alongside where a boarding ladder had been lowered. As he climbed to the deck, a crane lowered slings to the container on his boat. The soldiers placed them around the container and signalled the crane operator to hoist it onto the freighter's deck. Rahman stood there with the Chinese boat's captain. He motioned to the crew to open the lid. The captain looked inside and smiled.

"How many in here?" he asked.

"Four tigers and eleven cured crocodile skins. Now, my payment, please."

The captain handed Rahman a large envelope, bowed to him and returned to his duties. Rahman ran down the boarding ladder and jumped into his boat. "Let's go," he told the helmsman, pointing to the north.

◆ ◆ ◆

As soon as breakfast was over Gray drained the last of his tea and walked to the rail. Ali picked up the rifles, handing the dart gun to Gray.

"Okay, Julian. We'll take you to the pottery shards," Gray announced as he stepped ashore. "The site is just beyond that promontory." He nodded his head towards the southwest.

Together, with Ali bringing up the rear, they circled in front of the rest house to follow the shoreline for about one hundred metres. Gray showed Julian old tiger pug-marks and more recent tracks from shore-birds.

"How many species of birds are there in this forest?" Julian asked.

"There are over three hundred which either make their homes here or visit regularly," Gray answered.

"That's a hoopoe," he pointed to a sand-coloured, long-beaked bird above them. "See its striking feather crest, and the zebra stripes on its wings? He looks a bit like a scrawny cockerel wearing someone else's clothes, doesn't he? There are lots of them here. They range far and wide, from Europe through Africa and much of Asia."

By a bottle-brush tree, they stood silently for a few minutes watching a pair of colourful gold-fronted leaf birds picking insects off a branch.

"Those pretty little creatures always remind me of Christmas," Gray smiled at the thought. "Perhaps because they enjoy mistletoe berries so much."

Julian reached down to touch a vertical wooden spear sticking ankle height out of the mud.

"These are pneumataphores, right?"

"That's right. It's the aerial root of the sundari tree. As the tide goes out the tip is uncovered, it then opens and exchanges gases with the outside air. When the tide comes in, the root closes again. It's nature's way of allowing trees in the mangrove forest to breathe."

The tips of the pneumataphores were well above water, so the sea had receded enough for much of the pottery to be seen. In the shallows, a school of mudskippers whipped up the surface as they fled in alarm from the perceived danger of the three men. Julian took photographs of the broken pottery and collected two of the larger shards to examine more closely back on board. From where they stood they had a clear view south over the Bay of Bengal.

"I'd like to have a good look at this part of the bay with the radar. If it works properly," Julian said. "How far offshore can we go in *Fatima*?"

Not more than eight or nine kilometres I should think," Gray told him. "And then it depends on the weather. Remember, she's a top heavy riverboat, not an ocean cruiser. The radar's quite new, though, so it should work – unless the crew have been messing about with it."

They walked back to the boat on a different route. Gray showed Julian an area where a cyclone had roared ashore ripping the tops off trees and snapping thick trunks like matchsticks.

"This region has suffered through numerous cyclones over the centuries. Those Portuguese sailors from the old shipwreck probably were swept ashore near here, while trees of this size were being snapped like twigs in the wind. It's a miracle that three of them survived to get this far."

As is common with that part of the southwest coast, there were many signs of the tigers' existence. Old pugmarks and relatively new pugmarks littered the edge of the forest. Tracks of deer and birds crossed and re-crossed from forest to seashore.

"Why are there so many tracks here?" asked Julian. "There can't be that many tigers in this vicinity, surely?"

"Most of these come from one female. She's one of Timur's mates. Perhaps the one we saw last night. There are plenty of deer around Kotka for her to eat and, I think, not much competition from other predators, apart from Timur. Come on, I'll show you where she dines in private. Ali, you keep watch."

Gray followed a narrow path through a grove of saplings. In the middle he stopped in a small clearing, hardly bigger than the two men standing side by side. One man might have been able to lay down, but not stretch out. One tiger could do the same. A few bones littered the ground.

"She likes to carry her kills here and eat in peace. Timur has been here too. I've found his tracks." Gray picked up one of the bones, studying the shattered ends. He handed it to Julian. "Imagine the power of the jaws that could crush that with little or no effort."

"Have you thought about setting a trap in this clearing to catch Timur? It would be easy to set up."

"I've thought about it. Trouble is we are more likely to catch his mate than him and I don't have the reserves to handle it. We could catch her and put a radio collar on her; we have one Rab brought back from Nepal. We've never been able to use it successfully because we don't have the manpower to monitor the signals. If we collar her, I have to have at least three skilled technicians available for round the clock surveillance. They would need specialized transport. A small helicopter is ideal in many ways, but too noisy for me – far too expensive as well. In India they use elephants. We don't have that luxury here in Bangladesh. Keeping up with a tiger on foot is physically impossible. Dangerous, too." Gray was silent for a while. Then he started again, a thoughtful expression on his face.

"Some years ago, when we were getting started, I tried to find a tiger down here to collar. That was during the monsoons and we were unlucky. Perhaps if I had caught one then I would have been tempted to monitor it myself and follow it on foot with Hassan and Ali. I'm a bit smarter than that now." He smiled and turned away.

"Come on, let's get back."

Behind the rest house a group of fishermen filled their urns from the freshwater hole. Gray took Julian to watch, but his mind was elsewhere as he looked beyond the water to the jungle on his right.

"Come with me," he said suddenly, setting off down the narrow path the water carriers used: the shortest route from their ramshackle village to the pool. He stopped halfway between the water hole and the village.

"This is where a young Timur killed a man, as far as we know. That was a few years ago. The man was returning from collecting water, just like these guys do. One minute he was alive; the next he was dead. All they ever found of him was his empty urn and the cloth donut they use on their heads to support it."

"Do you know for sure it was Timur?"

Oh yeah. We know. His tracks were quite clear and impossible to mistake. That one paw will always give him away. Another local was killed here only recently. Timur got blamed for that death too."

Back at the boat Julian cleaned and examined the pottery, while Gray watched.

"I would say it's at least two or three hundred years old, maybe more. I'll have to have an expert check it for sure when I get back to Dhaka. However, there's every possibility it could have come from that Portuguese ship." He tagged the pottery and stowed it safely away.

"If you are ready to start, we'll patrol the shore beyond the rest house while you check out the bay with the radar," Gray told Julian. "If you see any signs of a tiger from out there, I want to know about it as soon as possible."

With Julian on board, *Fatima* eased away from the jetty as Gray and Ali walked ashore. Retracing their steps of the morning, they picked up their search beyond the pottery site.

"You keep to the shore, Ali. Follow the coast to the first creek and wait for me there. I'll take the inland route."

The forest close to the Bay of Bengal lacks under-growth. For much of his walk, Gray could clearly see Ali silhouetted against the skyline as he passed from tree to tree. Hundreds of deer tracks crossed and re-crossed the trail. No new tiger tracks followed them. At the creek, waiting for Ali to catch up, Gray sat on a stump and tried to imagine where Timur might have gone.

"Any luck?" he asked as Ali joined him.

"No. Nothing new along the shore."

Gray stood up, planning to angle back to Kotka through a thicker part of the forest. Instinctively he swept his eyes over the immediate area. Something was out of place.

"Look over there, Ali," he pointed with his rifle at a symmetrical pipe sticking out of the mud among the aerial roots where the creek flowed into the bay. Together the two splashed through slimy grey mud to the pipe. About half a metre projected almost vertically into the air. Gray handed his rifle to Ali. Kneeling in the mud, he started digging with his hands.

"It's metal," he grunted. "Help me dig it out."

"What is it?"

"I'm not sure, Ali, but I think it might be a very old cannon."

Ali laid the rifles down on a dry patch of ground, where he could reach them quickly in an emergency. Settling on his knees he scrabbled at the mud opposite Gray. Digging, they soon learned, was futile. The more mud they removed the more water poured in to refill the hole. Gray, lying almost face down beside the thick pipe, managed to get his right hand and arm down its length. He looked up at Ali, one side of his face muddy, the other relatively clean.

"I'm sure it's a cannon. Go back along the shore and see if Abdul is in sight. We need *Fatima* to pull this out for us."

Gray sat uncomfortably on the cannon's muzzle with his rifle across his knees and waited as the tide crept slowly in. Idly he scraped at the metal with his sheath knife until a dull brown emerged through the mud and verdigris of time.

"Aha," he exclaimed to himself, "it's bronze."

By the time the boat hove into view Gray was standing thigh deep in water and the cannon was submerged. On deck Julian watched him through binoculars.

"Send me a steel hawser in the dingi," Gray called.

With Ali's help, Gray wrapped the hawser tightly around the cannon's barrel and waved to Abdul. On deck the crew had already made the hawser off around the capstan. Abdul signalled for reverse engines and shouted a warning to the crew on the foredeck. They scattered immediately. The hawser tightened. Gray and Ali moved clear in case the cable snapped. For a few minutes nothing happened. Then the strong steel cable began moving slowly through the water. Behind it, the seabed churned as the cannon was dragged upside down through the mud.

Gray and Ali climbed aboard *Fatima* as the cannon, minus its original wooden firing cradle, was hauled out of the sea. The crew attached shackles and chains before removing the hawser. Using a small crane they winched the cannon aboard.

"I'll bet it's Portuguese," Gray said as he rinsed the mud off with a hose. "What do you think, Julian?"

"It could be. Early cannons were made of bronze like this one. We'll take it to Kotka and leave it there until we have time to clean it properly."

"Yeah, okay, we'll put it in the garden at the rest house. I'll get someone to start polishing it, once the mud's been washed off."

CHAPTER 21

Marshall returned to the river to find Rezaul alone. The fishing boat was gone.

"There was a boat here with two men on board," he shouted in frustration. "Where the hell is it?"

"Gone," Rezaul shrugged his shoulders. "I think you frightened them with your rifle."

"Ah, shit. Okay, we'll follow the tiger's tracks and see where he went. Maybe we'll find another boat somewhere. Come on, let's get moving."

With that, Marshall strode angrily back along the path to where he had last seen Timur's tracks. Rezaul hobbled along behind, fear of the tiger helping him forget the nagging pain in his ankle. Estimating they were at least one day's walk north of Kotka, with one – maybe two –more rivers to cross, Marshall examined his options as he walked.

"We'll stop here for the rest of the day," he announced after an hour, dropping his backpack in a substantial clearing. "You make some tea and take the weight off your leg while I look around for a bit. And for God's sake, Rezaul, if you see a tiger, shoot the bloody thing this time."

Trailing Timur was easy. The ground was soft underfoot, his pugmarks distinct. Marshall moved forward cautiously, but with determination. Constantly alert for a sudden confrontation, he turned through a complete circle every twenty paces. The tracks led to a river and disappeared at the water's edge.

"Fuck it. He's gone again," Marshall swore loudly.

Once again there were no boats in sight. Across the river, well hidden, Timur watched the distant man from the cover of a shady tree. Marking his trail back with occasional blazes on the sundari trees with his machete, an angry Marshall set off to return to Rezaul.

Once Marshall was out of sight, Timur relaxed. He slept until the sun reached the western treetops. The tide was low, the damp mud shining in the sun's final rays from riverbank to the water. Frogs and mudskippers fed on flies flitting aimlessly over the silt. Out in the stream, two black dorsal fins marked the passage of a pair of Gangetic dolphins. A rush of wind heralded the arrival of large adjutant stork. It flew in gracefully, braking with a strong flapping of enormous grey wings. Once on land, it staggered ungainly on the mud for a few paces in an effort to stop without crashing. Timur opened one eye to watch. The stork hunched its white-feathered shoulders, its bare yellow head only partly visible. A large yellowish-brown beak gaped open as the huge bird decided which delicacy to select for its hors d'oeuvres. A dirty green frog caught its attention. Stiff as a soldier on a parade ground, the great bird marched across the slippery muck. The frog saw the advancing peril, took one startled leap, flexed for another. The stork stabbed at it as the frog started its second take-off, catching it by the neck. With a flick of its head, the stork swallowed the live frog. Timur watched, without moving.

In the river, a pair of nostrils broke the surface. Some distance behind, two eyes surveyed the scene. Without disturbing the water, the crocodile glided closer. With its nose almost touching the mud, it sunk until out of sight. The stork continued to parade on the mud in the half light, midway between Timur and the river. The young crocodile, no longer than Timur's body, burst out of the murky depths and fastened its dreadful teeth on the stork's legs.

Timur hit the mud and grabbed the stork's body at the same time. The inexperienced crocodile tried to turn. It was no match for the tiger's adult muscles. With all his strength, Timur struck at the crocodile's flank while still holding the stork. His wicked blow, with claws unsheathed, caught the crocodile under the left shoulder and rolled him on his back. Timur let go of the stork, changing position to rip the saltwater reptile's throat from its body.

With two victims in as many seconds, Timur chose the crocodile first. He dragged it up the mud to dry ground and ate his fill. Before the incoming tide could carry the mutilated stork away, Timur rescued it. His hunger satisfied for the moment, he buried the remnants of the unlucky crocodile under a pile of leaves and earth. He left the limp carcass of the once military looking stork with it. A few paces away, he crawled under a bush and went to sleep.

◆ ◆ ◆

Marshall shot a small duck on the way back to Rezaul. They shared a simple meal of boiled rice and duck roasted over an open fire. Marshall was almost as exhausted as Rezaul, the heat and constant activity beginning to wear him down. Convinced the fire would keep any predators at bay, he catnapped for an hour after dinner while Rezaul snored loudly. In the middle of the night the rains returned with a vengeance. Unable to sleep, Marshall and Rezaul sat hunched together by the spluttering fire under a square of plastic sheet Rezaul carried in his bag.

On the other side of the river Timur too was awake. He ate again, crocodile and stork, the rain washing feathers and dried blood from his mouth. The rain fell heavier, the trees bowing under the weight of water on branches, twigs and leaves. Thoroughly soaked, Timur went in search of shelter. Near the stump of a long dead baien tree he found what he was looking for; a long thick tree trunk resting just off the ground on decaying branches. He shook himself hard to rid his fur of rainwater before crawling under the protective layer.

◆ ◆ ◆

Not far away, to the south, Gray and Julian sat on the guest house veranda at Kotka watching the rain stripping the last of the mud of centuries off the cannon. Between them stood the dregs of Gray's bottle of Scotch and a fresh one donated by Julian.

"That old cannon will be spotlessly clean and ready for polishing by morning, then we can have a really good look at it," Gray said.

"Yes. It looks as though we are off to a good start."

The two men were silent for a while, until Julian spoke again. "Don't you ever get lonely, Gray? I mean, lonely for female company?"

Gray sipped at his drink, staring into the night. After a few moments he looked at Julian. "Yes, I do. I am often lonely, but I'm usually too busy or too far away from civilization to do anything about it." He grinned, nodding his head, then added, "And, as you have seen, there aren't any women out here."

"I don't know what I would do without Asia. We have our ups and downs, of course, just like any married couple, but she has been the best partner for me."

"You're a lucky man, Julian. You really are. From what I've seen, Asia is a special lady – and she puts up with you, somehow." Gray laughed and gave Julian a light pat on the shoulder. "Maybe one day, when the jungle lets me go, maybe then I'll go hunting in a different way. Right now, I have a tiger to keep my mind and body occupied." He stood up. "I'm ready for bed. Tomorrow will be another long day."

"Is it safe to sleep out here on the veranda?" Julian asked.

"Sure, nothing much can get through that steel mesh, although we have occasionally been visited by unwanted guests. Last time I was here there was a hell of a ruckus in the night. One of the villagers nearly stepped on a cobra in the dark. He was walking down the middle of the path from the jetty when the snake crossed in front of him. He had a stick in his hand so he tried to beat the cobra to death. Of course, the cobra wasn't too thrilled at the attack and retaliated. The man was lucky not get bitten. The snake though was not so fortunate. One of the guards shot it in the head." Gray related the incident with a mixture of amusement and annoyance. "If only we could teach people to leave things alone," he continued. "A snake, like most wild creatures, is only dangerous when provoked. If the man had simply stood still, the cobra would have gone on its way without any trouble."

Julian nodded his assent, though his eyes registered surprise in the glow of the oil lamps. He recognized the fisherman's panicky reactions only too well. Sleeping on the open veranda did not seem like such a good idea after all.

CHAPTER 22

Off the seven kilometre wide estuary, where three rivers discharge their lives, Julian commenced his exploration of the sea bed next morning. First he laid out a simple grid pattern on the chart and coached Abdul into following it. Gray stood beside them in the wheelhouse to watch. Early on the depth sounder picked up a hump on the sea bed that Abdul asked about.

"That's a sand bar," Julian explained. "The currents build them and tear them down again. They are constantly moving at the mouths of great rivers like this one."

"Yes," Gray nodded. "I remember that from my youth, when I worked at sea with my father."

All morning they cruised back and forth, hoping for a spectacular find. Julian made two notes on his chart where the radar offered hope. One showed a large metal object, the other a smaller one. They dropped anchored marker buoys at both locations.

"I'll take a look at those two tomorrow morning at low tide," he said. "The first one will only be ten metres down then. The small one even less."

That afternoon they traced the coast west as far as Dubla Island without result. Abdul turned his boat east and they repeated the exercise, keeping a short distance off shore until Tiger Point. Gray suggested a circumnavigation of Egg Island and its smaller neighbour to the south. Once again they found nothing to arouse their interest. To satisfy his own curiosity Gray asked Abdul to enter the mouth of the Supati River and put him ashore on the right bank.

"Feel like going hunting for an hour?" he asked Julian as he handed him an old Lee Enfield rifle.

"Yes, of course," answered Julian, checking the magazine and the chamber.

"The first round is a blank," Gray told him. "Don't use anything unless you absolutely have to. I want that tiger alive – if I can find him."

Gray turned to Abdul. "We'll be back in an hour or so. Wait here for us."

With his dart gun slung over his shoulder, Gray led the way along the shoreline. Less than a kilometre along the coast Gray found indistinct pugmarks in the sand, where Timur had come ashore after his long swim. As they traced the tracks inland, Gray told Julian the story of the tiger's audacious break for freedom from the confines of Egg Island, just visible through the haze to the south. Once under the shelter of the trees, the tracks became clearer. Gray showed Julian how easy it was for an experienced tracker to identify Timur from his unique right pad and the softer than normal print from his injured left paw. Once it became obvious that Timur had kept firmly to a northerly route, Gray turned back for the boat.

"He will be back. He's too fond of the deer at Jawtoli to be gone for long," Gray explained. "Even a man-eater has to consider normal game at times. Man may be tasty and quite slow on his feet, but he's a dangerous target all the same. Timur knows that by now."

With *Fatima*'s sharp bow aimed directly at the setting sun, they cruised back to Kotka. Julian stood in the doorway of the wheelhouse watching the radar and the depth sounder. A sudden ill-defined shape etched itself in pale green on the radar's dark screen.

"Hold it," Julian called. Abdul rang down for neutral while Julian kept his eyes on the screen. "There's something down there. Can we go back over it, please?"

Abdul turned the wheel and *Fatima* circled back while Julian prepared another buoy. This time the boat cut across a corner of the submerged object. It was much clearer. For Julian it was enough. He dropped the marker and pencilled a cross on his chart. The orange buoy bobbed astern more than half a kilometre from shore.

"That's another one, Gray. I'll get a few dives in tomorrow for sure."

"You'll have to be careful," Gray warned. "Apart from the obvious dangers of diving alone, there are poisonous sea snakes in this area – at least seven different species. Last time I was here a fisherman caught a viper in his net and got bitten. He lived, but he was very sick for a few days."

"Don't worry about the snakes," Julian laughed. They may be poisonous but they are rarely dangerous to divers. I've dived with them off the Philippines. They come up close and have a look, but I'm too big to eat and no real threat. As for diving alone, I'll use a long tether attached to the boat and have someone watch out for me on deck."

Another boat stood at the end of the jetty when they got back to Kotka. Considerably older and scruffier than *Fatima*, her faded paint and the streaks of rust down her sides, made her look menacing. *Fatima*'s deckhands lowered old car tires over the side to act as fenders as Abdul came alongside. Gray looked the boat over apprehensively. He asked Abdul to find out where her passengers were.

"Do you think it's Marshall?" Julian asked, handing Gray a mug of tea. Gray nodded once without taking his eyes off the boat.

Abdul came back on board to tell them the newcomer had been chartered by an Englishman.

"He is hunting a tiger for the Forestry Commission. The captain put him and a tracker ashore well to the north some days ago. They are to meet him here."

"Ask him where he's been until now." Gray was curious about the time lapse. Abdul spoke with his counterpart for a moment.

"They went to Hiron Point to drop off supplies for the forestry base. They stayed there until this morning."

Gray bent over his map, trying to put himself into Marshall's mind. On foot the journey from the northern reaches of the jungle would be a hard slog and extremely dangerous. Marshall was either desperate or deranged, he concluded.

♦ ♦ ♦

Marshall and Rezaul sat dejectedly on a low bank. To the east and to the south, the only trails were blocked by rivers. The west offered only a long arduous trek to yet another river. Sweating heavily in the high humidity and oppressed by the dank smell of wet vegetation, Marshall had little choice but to wait at the confluence of the two streams until a fishing boat happened along. He deeply regretted sending his chartered boat to Kotka.

"If there's no sign of a boat by tomorrow, I'll swim across," he sighed.

"Crocodiles will eat you," Rezaul reminded him.

"Dammit, then we'll cut down a few trees and make a raft." Marshall jumped up, his weariness forgotten. "That's it," he said, suddenly excited. "We'll build a raft."

♦ ♦ ♦

Julian chose the first buoy in the estuary as his initial dive. The boat's depth-sounder read a little over nine metres under the keel. Ten metres in all. The ever present silt darkened the water. From above it was muddy brown. As he prepared for his dive Julian wondered at the potential for diamond and gold panning in the rivers of the Sundarbans. He knew there was gold in the Irrawaddy, not far away in Myanmar. Both river systems began their long journeys in the Himalaya Mountains. If one had gold there was every possibility that the other carried the precious ore as well. Once he'd finished his dives, he decided, he would spend a week or two putting his theory into practice.

While an armed deckhand kept watch for croco-diles, Julian slid beneath the surface. At first, sunlight filtered through high-lighting individual grains of silt. As he went deeper, down to the sea bed, it was like swimming through thin brown gravy. Without his lights Julian would have been virtually blind. Directly under the buoy, Julian dug through the surface layer of accumulated river residue until he touched metal. Digging raised a few million more silt particles to interfere with his vision. He kept at it. The gloom was restricting but he was well versed in identifying underwater objects with his hands. This one was a far cry from what he had hoped for. Quite unexpected, in fact. Taking his time to re-adjust, Julian returned to the surface. Pulling off his flippers he tossed them on the deck before clambering up the rope ladder, gratefully accepting an arm at the top to gain the deck himself. He removed his lights and face mask, then shook his head at Abdul.

"There's nothing down there for us, unless you want an old army jeep," he told him. "Let's take a look at the other one."

There was considerably more light at the second location. Not that it really helped all that much. The metal the radar had fastened on was more military rubbish. A collection of large gun shells, used of course, were scattered over a wide area. Julian took his time exploring the shallow site, making sure that's all there was. He was about to give up when a different shape caught his attention. It was half buried and heavy. He tugged it free and hooked it on his belt. Slowly he rose to the surface. Holding on to the rope ladder with one hand he looked at his find in daylight. He held up a rectangle, made of a flattened iron bar, with one side exhibiting a distinct curve and the other three sides straight.

On deck he stood it upright, the curve to the top. He measured the metal from all angles. The flattened band of iron was five centimetres wide and half a centimetre thick.

A line of holes, drilled dead centre, marked its length. Worn with the accumulated rust of time, the band had the look of something which had once been much thicker. Julian put it in the cabin.

Leaving the marker buoy in place, he persuaded Abdul to make a few more passes over the bay in case they had missed anything the day before. There was nothing. Abdul turned *Fatima* towards the jetty.

Gray and Ali were coming out of an inlet on the opposite side of the river when *Fatima* tied up at Kotka. The other boat was still there. Gray opened up the outboard as much as he dared and the heavy dingi trundled through the water to pull alongside the mother vessel.

"Any luck," Gray called, as he climbed aboard. Julian told him about the jeep and the big shells.

"They must be relics from the war of independence," Gray suggested. "The Pakistani forces probably had some naval activity going, even down here."

Julian then showed him the band of iron. "It's just possible, nothing more, that this could have been one of the iron bands holding a treasure trunk together. It's certainly big enough and it's the right shape."

Gray rubbed his chin with the tips of his fingers thoughtfully, "If it really is a part of a chest, that means there is a possibility that some, or all of the treasure from one chest is there too."

"There's no sign of anything else down there," Julian said, with the practicality borne of experience, "anything the sea deposits in this estuary will be covered in layers of silt very quickly. I'll need a powerful suction pump, or a miniature dredger, to check it thoroughly."

At least the iron band was an incentive. Having spent little time at any depth Julian decided he could safely take a look at the third buoy in the afternoon. There was a huge sea bed to cover and he was anxious to explore as much as possible.

Gray and Ali returned to Jawtoli as *Fatima* took Julian back to sea. From the top of the tower they raked the meadow with their binoculars. A herd of deer grazed placidly in the open. A pair of Brahmini kites circled lazily overhead. A few flies buzzed around the tower.

"Let's walk," Gray lowered his field glasses and went down. Exercising the utmost vigilance, they scrutinized the thicket where Timur had killed Hassan. While Gray probed among the branches, Ali kept him covered. The occasional resident was absent. There were no recent tracks. It didn't matter much which direction they took. The tiger they were bound to find could be anywhere in an area of up to eighty or more square kilometres.

With memories of Hassan for company, Ali led the way along the perimeter of the field. Under the shade of a large tree with spreading branches, a small waterhole had been visited by a boar and deer. They hadn't stayed long. The waterhole's only occupant that afternoon was a brilliant red darter dragonfly, practising figures of eight and sudden stops over the green lily pads.

Where the forest thins out and the meadow meets the sand dunes, they stood to watch *Fatima*. She was stationary near the orange marker buoy. As they watched, a black figure broke the surface and heaved himself up the rope ladder. He carried nothing that they could see. The beach where they stood held no new surprises. Their own footprints were still there, above the high tide mark. The usual dirty mark of wood chips and assorted rubbish, which every sea deposits on its shores, lined the upper reach of the tide's advance. Clumps of water hyacinth, trying to stay alive long enough for the next tide to rescue them, wilted in the sunlight.

Gray waved to those on *Fatima* and went back to the meadow. Taking their time he and Ali sifted through the grass. Tracks there were in abundance. A young female tiger had been there within the last twenty four hours. The spotted deer left their droppings in clusters and their prints in the thousands. Ali found where a long-legged jungle cat had pounced on a bandicoot. The struggle, according to the signs, had been brief. A porcupine waddled across their path, showing no interest in their presence. The tiger trackers halted to let it go by. A purple sunbird hopped up and down on a branch, rudely raising its tail and relieving itself on Gray's bare arm as he passed under the tree. Common mynahs screeched their harsh crow-like calls – whether in alarm or for effect – was not clear. The jungle on all sides sounded normal. Gray and Ali went to see if Timur had been anywhere near the abandoned fishing village on the promontory across the estuary from Kotka. The day was too quiet.

Out in the bay, Julian soared slowly over the sea bed. The foreign object the radar had showed so vividly from above a few minutes before was a disappointment. It was just an empty tin crate, perhaps an ammunition box, with its lid open lying face down on the bottom. He felt around on the sand for clues to its former contents. There was nothing else there. He surfaced and re-boarded *Fatima*. They retrieved the marker buoy and motored back to the estuary. Julian thought he'd try snorkelling close to the shore line where the pottery shards stood. There was always a slim chance that there was more than pottery waiting for the right hands to pluck them from the sea.

Gray and Ali saw *Fatima* cruise past as they came out of the woods behind what was left of the village. The boat came into the shelter of land and dropped anchor in the mouth of the Betmur River. Gray found few signs to stir him. Timur hadn't been there, unless his tracks had been washed away by rain or tide. A few vertical poles, with twine stretched between them, still remained in place. One hut, better secured than the others, had retained its covering of woven palm fronds. The rest were mere shells, destroyed by the latest monsoon storms. There was no reason for them to linger. Rather than detour back round the watchtower they chose to wade the creek, where the fishermen used to moor their boats, and follow the coast back to their dingi.

Julian put his hand over his face mask to stop it being ripped off and jumped into the sea. He blew through his snorkel. With a quick glance at the land to verify his bearing he put his face in the water and let his flippers carry him forward. On board *Fatima* the crew lined the rail to watch him, wondering what he would find this time. They all knew by now of his quest for treasure. They also knew, if he were successful, they would be well rewarded. Nobody wanted to miss it if he found something.

Over at the jetty, crew untied Marshall's chartered boat. Black smoke burst out of the slim exhaust funnel and she soon disappeared up the river. Gray saw her leave and guessed she was going to pick up Marshall. He wondered where he might be.

Ali found an old dried print where Timur had plunged through a patch of long-drained mud. They agreed he must have been chasing something to have left such a deep mark. No other prints had lasted to complete the tale. In silence, their eyes alternating from the ground to the forest and the shore, Gray and Ali continued their walk.

"Sssh! Tiger!" Ali whispered urgently, his left hand grasping at Gray's arm. Ahead of them, clearly visible, a young tiger, probably not more than a few months old, pounced across the mud chasing a frog.

"Oh, shit," Gray breathed, "Mummy, where are you? I hope you're not behind us."

They both shot rapid glances over their shoulders and in a semi-circle back to the cub. With hearts pounding, they stood motionless. Ali flicked his safety catch off. Gray armed his dart gun. The cub, still playfully terrorizing frogs, was unaware of their proximity.

"That's one of Timur's young, I should think," Gray whispered. Ali agreed.

"When Hassan was killed, there was a female and a young cub by the field. This must be the same one," he told Gray.

"Where the hell is that mother?" Gray kept peering through the trees, "She can't be far away, unless this little guy has forgotten his instructions and strayed too far."

"She'll find him anyway," Ali stated the obvious.

The tiger cub finally caught the frog with one paw. To hold it he pressed it into the mud. Slowly he released the pressure and lifted his paw. With a start the cub jumped back as the frog made an almighty leap for freedom. Gray almost laughed out loud, having to stifle the sound with his hand over his mouth. Ali's eyes twinkled, but he didn't move a muscle. The cub pounced again, getting it right this time. It swallowed the frog in one gulp. Having won the mismatched contest the cub tired of the game. It turned away from the sea, as if to go back to the woods. In doing so it looked straight at the two men. Ali raised his rifle and aimed over the cub's head. Gray held his dart gun ready. The young tiger was not prepared to tackle one human, let alone two full grown men. It coughed a warning and bounded away from them towards Jawtoli.

Gray and Ali slowly lowered their guns, both letting their breath out in a long "pheeew!" Gray photographed the pugmarks and noted the encounter in his diary, adding the possibility that it was the same cub which had been present at Hassan's death. For the rest of the way back to their dingi, they turned in circles occasionally to prevent a surprise attack from an unexpected quarter.

Julian knew nothing of the cub playing on the mud flats across the bay behind him. With his powerful lights illuminating the sea bed, he swam to the nearest piece of land. When his hands and feet touched bottom together he changed course. For two hours he swam back and forth in the warm water. If he was impatient, an observer would not have noticed. Julian's mind was concentrated on the job at hand. There was a lot of shoreline to explore and he intended to cover every part of it.

From *Fatima*'s decks all that was visible was Julian's snorkel, the back of his head, sometimes his flippers and, occasionally, when he dived for a closer look at something, his bottom. The crew watched anyway.

Julian heard an engine, the throb and beat of the propeller much louder underwater. He surfaced and trod water, removing his mask to look around. On *Fatima*, Abdul heard it too. Marsh's boat had gone up river, past Kotka. This boat was coming down the Betmur. On the far shore Ali saw the boat first as its bow poked past the trees the other side of *Fatima.*

"Another boat," he said to Gray.

As the boat came abreast of *Fatima,* on the seaward side, a party of tourists on the upper deck waved at the anchored boat. Only Abdul waved back. The others were too busy watching Julian. He in turn, put his face down and lengthened his body into a smooth racing crawl. He was pulling off his flippers on *Fatima's* deck before the newcomer had shown her stern. Asia must be on board, he knew. Over on land, Gray was thinking the same thoughts as he and Ali pushed their dingi off the mud.

With expert precision, which even Abdul admired, the helmsman on the new arrival nosed between the thick vertical marker poles and rang for reverse. The propeller thrashed the water and the boat stopped, its bow touching the jetty. The engine was put into neutral as mooring lines snaked over wooden bollards. Abdul moved *Fatima* slowly towards the jetty, holding her out in the river until he was sure the other boat was secured. Before he could bring his own vessel alongside the other captain signalled he wasn't staying.

One passenger got off with two bags. Clad in a traditional brown sharwal kameez she stood on the jetty and waved at the other passengers as the boat backed away, turned in a circle and left. Abdul brought *Fatima* neatly to rest, port side to the dock, as Gray and Ali tied off to her starboard side. Still in his dripping wet suit, Julian stepped ashore and embraced his wife. Gray came on deck in time to see Asia wrap her arms round her husband's neck, squeeze briefly and let go again. She's a true Bengali, Gray thought, no overt public displays of passion for her. Over Julian's shoulder, she saw Gray and smiled at him.

"Hello, Professor. I made it," she called huskily.

Gray dined with Asia and Julian on *Fatima* that evening. Asia told them of her travelling companions: a sextet of Germans, all in their seventies, who go on one adventure holiday together each year.

"They weren't interested in going ashore anywhere. All they wanted was adventure in a modicum of comfort. On this trip they only wanted to cruise the jungle rivers for a few days in the hope of seeing wildlife."

"Where are they going now?" asked Gray, "it'll be dark soon and there's nothing to see at night."

"Oh, the captain said he would overnight off Tiger Point once he saw your boat here," Asia replied, "and that intrepid old group are convinced they will see a tiger somewhere. Is there any chance for them Gray?"

"Not much," Gray laughed, "though only a short time before you arrived Ali and I watched a young cub playing with a frog over there." He pointed behind him at the barely discernible line of trees. "We didn't see the mother, but she couldn't have been far away."

"So there really are tigers here," Julian offered, laughing to show he was teasing, "not only tiger tracks."

"Oh yes, they are here. All except the one I'm after, I think. There could be as many as four or five hundred tigers in this jungle, spread across both sides of the border, but they are rarely seen. We were just lucky today."

"And the one you call Timur?" Asia asked. "Have you seen any sign of him? Do you have any idea where he might be?"

"We've seen signs, plenty of them," Gray told her. "He was over at Tiger Point recently doing a bit of scavenging. But he left before we arrived."

"Gray thinks he went north again, but that doesn't mean he'll stay there," Julian added, "but he also thinks Marshall is up there somewhere with another tracker."

Asia looked at him curiously, then at Gray. She opened her mouth to ask a question.

"Sorry, you don't know about him yet," Gray explained, "Richard Marshall is an Englishman. He has come here to kill Timur if he can. I'll tell you that long story later. Anyway, I think Marshall and his tracker will turn Timur back to the south, whether they are aware of it or not. I'm sure he will come. If he doesn't – if he kills again and I don't find him, I may as well stay in the Sundarbans forever."

"Should I stay at the rest house tomorrow and hope I see something, or should I go out on the boat?" Asia asked Gray.

"If you stay on shore you will see wildlife. That's definite. There's a constant parade to the water hole behind the house. I can't guarantee you'll see a tiger though. Why don't you spend the morning on the boat and the afternoon watching the water hole from the house? We'll make sure a guard is close by at all times. "

Julian agreed with Gray that Asia should take advantage of both locations. Gray told them he and Ali would be on shore, in the general area of the rest house all day, unless called away. Another of his team would be on the watchtower, in case Timur came back that way. Either way, Asia would be well protected on the boat and on shore. After dinner Gray escorted Asia and Julian to the rest house. To allow them privacy he planned to sleep on the boat while the couple were with him. He knew he could not sleep in the room next to them under any circumstances. He showed them where the lights were situated and put an oil lamp on a table, explaining the generator went off at 10 o'clock. Once they were inside he shot the bolt on the wire screened door to the veranda. At the garden gate he raised three more planks of wood, slotting them in the posts over the waist high gate, to discourage any attempt at entry by inquisitive jungle dwellers. Alone and suddenly lonely, he walked back to the boat.

CHAPTER 23

Timur ran with his stumbling gait until he was well out of range. The noise of Rezaul's gun still echoed in his ears. Limping awkwardly he slowed and forced his way through thick undergrowth until he felt safe. He surveyed his chosen concealment and crawled under a bush to sleep, his chest heaving from his exertions. When he awoke it was night. His paw ached. There was blood seeping from the wound again. Timur licked it clean, taking his time. He was thirsty and, as usual, he was hungry.

Taking care not to put pressure on his injured paw he wriggled out of hiding and limped in search of water. The first creek he came to was salty, as most were in the Sundarbans. Timur was not averse to brackish water, he drank it often. This night he wanted fresh water and that could only be found a long walk away, behind the rest house at Kotka. Other creatures would drink there too; he could possibly find food as well. Knowing full well that man was near the water hole, Timur avoided the straight line approach. That would have taken him past the fishermen's huts and the boats pulled up on the beach. He needed to drink before he ate. He moved slowly, half hopping on three legs much of the time, keeping to the thickest parts of the forest.

There were no lights on at the rest house when he emerged from the trees by the water hole. Just the row of bulbs, which illuminated the path from the jetty to the garden gate, were still glowing. In the background the generator hummed mechanically. Voices could be heard dimly in the gloom.

Timur was patient; he eased himself to the ground, using his right front paw as a prop, and waited. Eventually the generator went quiet and the lights by the path went off. Timur waited another minute or two then, keeping the pressure off his injury, he walked down the bank to crouch at the water's edge. Still he didn't drink. His eyes burned into the blackness. Nothing was there to cause alarm. He lapped hesitantly at the cool water. Gaining in confidence he drank thirstily. Not once did his caution leave him. Ears twitched, finely tuned for any sound. Two eyes roved back and forth, assessing the night.

A sudden murmur, perhaps a human sound, filtered through the walls of the building silhouetted against the sky. Loud enough to have strength, it rippled across the water to Timur's ears. He stopped drinking, listening intently. A sudden cry in the night sent him scurrying back up the bank to the refuge of the trees. Among the shadows he turned, standing erect he looked towards the building. Another cry, followed by a moan and a rhythmic drumming reached him. It sounded like an animal in pain, gasping, begging for release.

Another sound merged with the first. Timur put his head on one side, trying to identify the noises. A creature in pain meant an easy meal. He smelled the air, expecting to taste blood. There was none. The sounds were confused. The drumming was faster. A deeper, heavier sound, like a big boar breathing heavily after a long run, grunted at him.

Timur trotted around the water hole, favouring his left paw, his head held high, until he was right outside the back of the rest house. The sounds came from there, inside the house. Above him a window, covered by wooden shutters, rattled in the night. He listened. The drumming was louder, like an injured deer thumping its legs in its death throes. The cries got stronger. Timur stood up on his hind legs, stretching his fore paws up to the shutters. They were just out of reach. His claws scratched down the wall as he dropped heavily to the ground. He remained where he was, his eyes and ears tuned to the window.

"Ah! Ah! Oh yes! Now! Now!" The cries rose to a new height, the drumming reaching a crescendo, ceasing suddenly, replaced by a long drawn out moan. Then silence. The drumming, the cries, the moans, all were gone. Heavy, hoarse breathing was all that was left to disturb the night.

Timur let out a deep low 'Awoom' and blended back into the jungle.

In his sleeping bag, on the boat's upper deck, Gray was wide awake. He heard a tiger's rich growl and sat up, staring into the darkness in the direction of the rest house.

"Timur." He said under his breath. Instinctively, he crawled into the damp night air. He pulled his jeans and shirt from under his pillow and dressed. For much of the remaining hours of darkness he sat alone and still, a blanket round his shoulders, his eyes turned towards the rest house and the tiger that he knew was close.

CHAPTER 24

Rezaul thanked the fishermen for carrying he and Marshall across the river and gave them a few taka each. Leaning heavily on his crutch, he pushed the bow of their boat back into the current. Marshall didn't offer or attempt to help. He was busy working out their location and taking a compass bearing on the nearest point of Jawtoli. Marshall estimated two and a half, perhaps three, kilometres to the open meadow. It would take at least two hours to walk that far; Rezaul was in pain and slowing down. The ground was soft and his crutch sunk far in at every step. Darkness would be on them before they could go much further. Marshall still pushed Rezaul into going on for another hour.

Gradually the forest thickened. There were more trees, more bushes. Creepers dangled from tree to tree. Thick vines snaked from high branches to trip the unwary. Marshall had to use his machete to cut a path for Rezaul and for himself. He too was tiring. He slashed at the undergrowth, tearing the cut foliage from his path and shoving it out of his way. With a reasonably clear, though narrow, lane extending some twenty five paces he stopped and helped Rezaul negotiate the next stage. Then he started cutting once more. And so the painful process went on. Before the hour was passed, he called a halt. He could do no more without rest.

"We'll camp here for the night; I'll go on alone in the morning to get help."

Rezaul was too worn out to care. He sipped some water, made himself as comfortable as he could with his back to a tree trunk and fell asleep. Marshall dozed intermittently, his rifle in his hands, his forearms aching with the strain of wielding the heavy machete. Weary though he was physically, Marshall's mind was active. He thought carefully about the next day. Not much more to go. Five kilometres, no more, probably less, to be abreast of Kotka. Someone was sure to see him and cross the river to investigate. Once he had sent a rescue party for Rezaul he could, he would, go on by himself to find Timur. Marshall had no fear of the wilderness; he knew now he could still survive in the jungle alone. He knew, somehow, somewhere, soon, he and the tiger were destined to come face to face.

For a while he slept fitfully, chasing fleeting images of his family. A tiger kept getting in his way, blocking his mental view, mocking him. With a start he woke. A sound in the night, or was it part of his dream? Rezaul was awake too.

"What is wrong?" he asked Marshall. "Why are you shouting?"

Marshall realized he'd been talking in his sleep, shouting as Rezaul had said. He was sweating and aware of a deep rooted fear. The tiger in his dream had become a lion, with a huge bushy mane and a striped body.

◆ ◆ ◆

Unknown to the denizens of the jungle, the sky was about to change. The sun climbed higher in the sky. The moon, keeping station with its Mother Earth, revolved through space as it did every day. This day, however, would be different. Today the moon's passage through the cosmos would take it across the face of the sun, creating a temporary false darkness. Only visible in a narrow band stretching from Iran across Afghanistan, Pakistan, India, Bangladesh, Burma, Thailand, Cambodia, Vietnam, Malaysia and Indonesia, the phenomenon would be short lived.

In India, for the first time in over two hundred years, Hindus celebrating Diwali, the festival of light, would see the light go out for a fragment of time. Millions of people across Asia, knowing the eclipse was a natural event, prepared to watch through special glasses to avoid eye damage. Many others, lacking the education or understanding, would take the darkening of the sky as an omen, either good or bad. In the Sundarbans of Bangladesh, it started as just another day.

Julian and Asia boarded *Fatima* to breakfast with Gray. He seemed preoccupied, lacking his usual attention. For much of the time, his eyes wandered from Asia to the forest by the rest house. He spoke little, concentrating on his food.

"Did you hear the tiger in the night?" he asked suddenly, "not long after you went to bed."

Julian flashed an amused glance at Asia, she looked down at her plate.

"No, we didn't hear anything. Where do you think he was?" Julian replied for them both. Asia took another piece of toast, studiously avoiding Gray's eyes.

"It sounded to me as if he was over by the waterhole, behind the rest house. He could have been further away, but I don't think so." Gray finished his meal in silence. Putting down his tea mug he called for Ali.

"We'll take a look round the waterhole; I'm sure we had a visitor last night."

He got up and wished Julian a successful day. With a half smile at Asia, he went ashore where Ali waited with the guns. As they strode along the old wooden jetty, stepping over the gaping holes where planks had broken, Asia heard Gray say, "I think he's here. I can almost feel him. I'm sure he's here."

Asia and Julian told Abdul they were ready. Julian decided to continue his search at the spot where he found the iron band. While Julian was diving, Asia was quite content to sit on deck and read. The crew would soon let her know if anything exciting happened. As *Fatima* turned and steamed past the shore, Asia waved to Gray and Ali in front of the rest house. They were too absorbed in something on the ground to notice.

"What do you think made these tracks Ali? It looks like a tortoise to me."

Ali told him, but the Bangla word was unknown to Gray. With a stick, Ali drew a rounded shell in the dirt.

"Yeah, that's a tortoise. I've never seen one here. Have you?"

Ali told him there were a few. Still talking about the tortoise, they strolled round the outside of the rest house garden. Where the back of the house overlooks the pool an uncut field of grass, perhaps twenty five metres across, separates the two. A footpath cuts across one corner where the fishermen carry drinking water from the pool to their boats. One pace from the path Ali stopped in mid-sentence and crouched, the tortoise forgotten. Gray went down on one knee beside him. Ali's hand hovered over the pugmark. He looked sideways at Gray.

"Timur!" they said in unison.

The tracks were clean and they were fresh. They led from the forest, round one side of the pool, to the house. Gray ran his hand lightly over the vivid new scratches on the wall, where the white paint had been scored. Running from a little below the window, the scratches gouged the wall to a point waist high above the ground, where they ended abruptly. Gray stood where Timur had stood, taking care not to damage the pugmarks. At full stretch he could not reach the window. Timur had come much closer to it. Involuntarily Gray shivered. The man-eater had seriously considered making a meal of Asia or Julian, or both. They were fortunate, he knew, that the shutters were closed.

He remembered Julian's laugh at breakfast and the way Asia had avoided his eye. Gray knew, without being told, why the pair had not heard Timur. He began to suspect why Timur had been attracted to the house in the first place. He accepted that he was unreasonably jealous, thankful that he had slept on board. He would continue to do so he decided.

They tracked the tiger back round the pool to the edge of the forest. A water carrier tossed his urn into the water and held the rim under to fill it. Ali told him there might be a tiger nearby. The man finished his job as quickly as he could and left hurriedly, passing on the warning to others on the path.

"Let's see where he went, Ali."

Timur, his tracks told them, had stopped inside the forest and turned back to the water hole. He had almost certainly wanted more to drink; his later tracks overlaid his initial stop at the pool. Gray wondered if, perhaps, his curiosity about the people in the house had prompted the return. From the faint mark left by his injured paw, it was apparent that he was favouring it again. The deeper sign from his right was more proof. It was evident the tiger was in pain and limping. He would have little chance of catching fleet footed game. Pain and hunger would make him more aggressive – more likely to try for human prey. The departing tracks led into the forest. Gray and Ali went with them, with their safety catches off.

Timur did not go far from the water hole at first. He rested part of the night near a trail worn by countless wild feet over many long nights. The hours of darkness were not kind to him. A deer caught his scent and announced his presence to the world with short snappy barks. The customary nocturnal drinkers either found other sources to refresh themselves, or held their thirst in check until the threat had passed. Timur, hungrier than he had ever been, made his way through the woodland on a large circular route. Quiet and cautious he crept from tree to bush. From bush to tree.

Downwind from grazing deer, he contained his hunger and exercised his talent for patience. He couldn't catch them on the run, but, if he was lucky, they might come to him. The deer were skittish, not concentrating on their stomachs. They nibbled and looked up. Nibbled and looked up again. With infinite slowness Timur went to them. A healthy tiger could have taken its pick of the deer. One lightning spring and a short run would suffice. Timur no longer had that capability. He stalked them closer.

Out of reach on a branch of a sundari tree, a black sentinel watched the drama unfolding. As the tiger bunched his muscles ready to spring, the crow shrieked its warning. The deer didn't wait to ask questions, they turned in a body and pranced out of sight and out of reach. The crow flew off, calling derisively to the discouraged tiger.

Timur limped along known game trails, finding no sustenance. The guardians of the Sundarbans noted his direction and passed the news ahead of him. Every creature in his kingdom avoided him, watching, unseen, from safe havens. The further he walked the more his paw hurt, the more energy he wasted, the hungrier he became. His ramblings took him back inexorably towards the coast. Out of sight of those on and in the water, he looked for somewhere to lay down.

In the thicket where his mate preferred to dine, he found a safe, obscure den. Timur sighed and sagged to the ground, toying with one of her left over bones. There was no meat on it. No marrow left inside. It was simply an old dry bone. He crunched it hungrily, but without enthusiasm. It was better than nothing.

On *Fatima*'s deck, Julian adjusted the clinging rubber of his wet suit. Out in the sun he was getting hot, the sooner he was under the surface the better. With a thumbs-up sign to Asia, he stepped off the boat's lower deck and splashed noisily. He checked his regulator again and upended himself, rapidly becoming lost to sight in the murk. Asia moved her deck chair under the awning and relaxed with her book. Directly underneath the boat Julian turned on his lights and fished around on the sea bed among the empty munitions' shells. He worked methodically, trying not to stir up any more silt than he had to. As he widened his search area he moved further from the boat, closer to the shore. A deck hand and a cook's helper watched his bubbles rupture on the surface to mark his course.

Halfway to shore, where the sea bed commenced its casual rise to meet the land, Julian's probing hands touched a hard object. He dug around it with his fingers, carefully prising it loose from the insistent mud. In his hand he held a circular band of metal, smooth along one edge and carved into sharp peaks and valleys on the other. It was heavy, even in the sea. He wiped off the clinging mud, agitating the find in the water, his excitement rising. He had found – he was sure – a single part of Diego's treasure. A small golden tiara. He stuffed it in the sack tied to his waist and kept looking. If there was one piece, there had to be more.

Gray and Ali read nature's description of Timur's wanderings. The place where he had taken rest near the water shouted of his brief stopover, the grass still bent from his weight. His three-legged stance told them how much he must hurt, reminding them of their danger. They followed, Ali tracking the tiger and Gray, mindful of Timur's tactics the day he killed Hassan, keeping watch all around. Ali found where Timur had narrowly missed the deer. The signs gave no explanation for his failure. Gray guessed, only half right, that the wounded paw bore the responsibility. There was nothing to tell them of the talkative crow's timely intervention.

Gray found himself becoming increasingly uneasy. Timur was hunting in a circle. If he continued he would end up back at Kotka, or nearby. Gray prayed Asia and Julian were still at sea. He was tempted to bisect the circle and get there ahead of the tiger, if he was in fact going to Kotka. If, however, he changed direction again, to go west or north, there was but a slim possibility of catching up with him before he killed the next time. Gray, hoping he was right, stuck to his original plan.

Julian kept himself close to the sea bed, running his hands through the fine silt, breathing easily through his mouthpiece. As the water became shallower he rose with it to the surface. Excited by his find, he stood up in thigh high water and splashed towards the land like a giant upright frog. A watching deckhand on *Fatima* called out.

"Missy, look." A voice carried through Asia's slumber. She picked up her book, which had fallen to her feet while she dozed, and looked round for Julian. He was floundering ashore, his great flippers sending sheets of water in all directions. She saw him take off his mask and swing the oxygen cylinders off his shoulders. He then turned to look at the boat and waved to Asia. He put one hand in his sack and pulled something out. Facing the boat he held up a large shiny ring, waving it back and forth at arm's length. He studied it for a second or two then held it above his head with both hands, before slowly lowering it to crown himself like a comic court jester. Asia started to laugh.

The happy sound choked off as a large gold and orange and white blur, slashed with black stripes, came into sight. Asia rose to her feet, trying to find her voice. The boat's crew shouted in panic as Asia finally screamed in horror, "JULIAAAAN!"

From his hide, Timur saw the black apparition materialize out of the water. For a second he was still. Then he rose and, keeping to the shadow of the bushes, he crept forward. Twenty paces from Julian's back, Timur began his ungainly charge, covering the ground in huge strides in spite of his wound. Julian heard Asia's scream and turned instinctively. Seeing the tiger bounding towards him, he launched himself full length into the water. Before he could take one over arm stroke and kick his feet twice to find deep water, Timur landed across the back of Julian's legs. His claws curled and gripped Julian's thighs as massive jaws crunched through his hips. Timur's weight carried them both under.

On *Fatima*, Abdul too heard Asia scream and grabbed the rifle. He fired the two blanks as Timur came out of the water in a shower of spray. Julian, still alive fought him with his bare hands, trying to get at one of his knives. Abdul risked a shot at Timur, sending a spout of water skywards near his tail. The brown sea water turned a ruby red as Timur lifted his struggling and bleeding burden from the sea.

Gray and Ali heard the screams and started running. As the shots echoed loudly around them they moved apart for safety, not wanting to be hit by stray bullets. Bursting out of the trees, Ali fired a blank, ejected the spent cartridge and rammed a live round into the chamber, while running at full speed. Out of the corner of one eye, he saw Gray to his right and a bit behind.

Gray held the dart gun in one hand, the strap trailing near the ground. In the other he carried his rifle with the strap over his shoulder. They saw Timur and Julian directly in front of them as Timur saw them. Ali skidded on the wet mud, almost losing his balance. He recovered, stopped, raised his rifle and fired. Timur shook himself and Julian at the same instant, moving a fraction to his right. Ali's bullet fanned Julian's face and tore a strip off Timur's hind quarters. He roared with pain and a terrible rage, dropping Julian in the mud.

Gray tripped on a root and fell heavily, winding himself, his index finger involuntarily pulling the trigger of the dart gun. The tranquilizing dart streaked uselessly over the water, skimming the surface until, its speed exhausted, it slowed and sank. Before Ali could fire again Timur bowled him over, slashing at him with razor sharp claws, leaving a long gash the length of his arm from shoulder to wrist. Gray threw the dart gun from him and let off a wild shot with his rifle, but Timur had reached the trees and was out of sight. On the sea *Fatima* was at full speed aiming straight for the dock. Gray's dart gun was under water.

Gray pulled Ali to his feet and ran to Julian. Feebly the valiant scuba diver inched himself up the mud with his hands. Behind him, his lifeblood ran in living streams back to the sea. Gray reached down and, with some help from Ali, who was himself bleeding profusely, carried Julian from the water's edge. The wet suit, from the waist down, had been almost completely ripped apart by the fury of Timur's attack. Julian's body was terribly injured, the blood pumping out of savaged arteries. Ghostly pale, he clung to Gray as the zoologist tried to stem the flow with his shirt.

"Asia!" Julian called with fading strength.

Asia came running along the path, her pashmina streaming behind her. Past the rest house and over the mud she raced, her sandaled feet dodging this way and that to avoid tripping on the roots. Abdul ran with her, guarding her with Gray's spare rifle. Behind them, wielding a boat-hook, came a deckhand. The three skidded to a halt where Gray sat in the mud holding the dying Julian across his lap. Asia dropped to her knees and took her husband from Gray. She sat crying softly in the mud, holding Julian in her arms as he died.

Gray, fighting back his own tears, held them both. Ali, still bleeding heavily from his lacerations, leaned against Abdul. The deckhand faced inland, his boathook ready to defend them all. Down at the water's edge, where the sea spread and diluted Julian's gore, the golden tiara lay forgotten, half buried in the mud.

"Let me take him, Asia."

Easing Asia away, Gray picked Julian up in his arms and led the sorry procession back to *Fatima*. Under Asia's stunned supervision, he cut the ripped shreds of the wet suit from the body. The dreadful wounds he uncovered reminded him of Kumar and he had to fight to keep his stomach in check. Asia took a clean white sheet and covered Julian's torn remains. As she pulled the cloth over his chest, she bent and kissed his lips, then gently laid the shroud over his face. Pulling the curtains together to keep the light out of the cabin, she closed the door, locking it from the outside. Then, with tears streaming down her face, she went to help Gray dress Ali's wounds. As she finished cleaning and bandaging the long cuts she turned to Gray. Her husky voice, harsh with pain, was strong and clear.

"Go find your tiger, Gray Pendennis. Go. Get him now, before someone else has to die."

In the sky, the moon was aiming its cheerful visage at the sun. In the forest, Timur, unnerved by the repetitive explosions and hurt by a second bullet wound, staggered away to distance himself from man. For the moment his hunger was overridden by fear and pain. Instinct called him to one place where he knew he could hide. The thicket of bushes on Jawtoli would give concealment while he licked his wounds. There he could find food and peace.

He limped the length of a shallow creek, making for the shoreline north of Kotka. The river, which he must cross to get to Jawtoli, narrowed at a bend. He plunged in after ensuring he was alone. The cool water soothed his body, though it stung the bleeding wound on his rump. On land again, he shook himself, spraying the bushes with river water and flecks of his own blood.

The boat Marshall had chartered arrived back at Kotka while Asia cared for Ali. The captain had cruised extensively on the rivers and streams without seeing any sign of Marshall or Rezaul. He had come back to wait as instructed.

Gray ordered Abdul to prepare *Fatima* for departure. As soon as Asia and Julian's belongings had been packed and collected from the rest house, they would leave for Mongla. Ali would go with them to get professional attention for his arm. Knowing that Timur had been hit by at least one of Ali's bullets, Gray planned to stay behind until he found him, with the help of the local guard now on the tower. When he was ready he could hitch a ride out on Marshall's boat.

A crew member loaded the dingi with food and water, plus a red can of gasoline. Gray hugged Asia to him wordlessly. He embraced Ali, shook hands with Abdul and lowered himself over the rail to the dingi. Without looking up, he pulled the starter cord. The motor ticked over, running smoothly. Gray waved once in farewell. The engine clicked into gear, and he headed up stream. In sight of those on *Fatima* he turned for the jetty in line with the watchtower. Gray was gambling that Timur had been hurt and would come home to Jawtoli. He and the guard would be waiting at the tower.

CHAPTER 25

Even though they had little in the way of preparations to take care of, Marshall and Rezaul were slow to get moving that morning. Soon after they started Marshall raised his hand for silence. He listened carefully.

"Did you hear that?" he asked Rezaul. "It sounded like shots."

Rezaul nodded. "It's far away," he began, when more shots carried to them, dulled by the density of the forest. Marshall worked with renewed energy, convinced Timur was the cause of the shots and praying he still lived. Finally Marshall hacked through the last of the branches, coming out into a substantial natural clearing. On one side the trees thinned out. The sunlight was brighter there. Marshall went back to help Rezaul, who he could hear talking loudly to himself some way behind. Determined to go on alone, he saw his partner comfortable in the shade, with the sunshine reaching for his feet.

"I won't be long," he told him encouragingly as he left.

Marshall hurried through the waist high grass, his rifle loaded and ready, the safety catch off. Kotka was, at

last, within reach. He could just see the top of the watchtower outlined above the trees at the far end of the field.

Rezaul untied the shirt from his ankle and examined his ankle. The swelling was getting worse. Tenderly
he re-wound the makeshift bandage, attempting to ease the
pain and prevent his ankle from moving. For a while he
dozed. As the sun moved and changed the shadows, Rezaul
awoke. Instinctively he reached for a cigarette. He stopped
suddenly and strained his ears. He thought he heard a faint
noise on the path Marshall had blazed for them yesterday and this morning. He listened. The sound of laboured
breathing was weak, but it was there.

Rezaul, forgetting about his smoke, climbed up his
crutch until he was standing. The breathing was louder. A
large animal was coming slowly down the track. Rezaul
didn't wait to find out what it was; he had a fairly good idea
anyway. He hopped on one leg and the crutch to the field,
his shirt bandage unravelling and falling from his foot.

Marshall was far in front. Rezaul could see the
brown of his safari hat but little more. He shouted to Marshall as he cocked his rifle, making sure he had a live round
in place. Marshall did not turn round. Rezaul forced himself to keep moving, looking back over his shoulder every
few seconds. Walking on one leg, with a stick for a crutch,
was difficult on the uneven ground. The thick grass at this
end of the field hampered Rezaul even more.

Timur was close to exhaustion. His breathing was
rough; his wounds hurt like fury, but he was almost home.
He smelled man again, between himself and his hide. He
smelled fear. He felt his own hunger. Timur came to the
grassland downwind from Rezaul. A slight breeze blew
in from the sea, carrying the dual scents of Marshall and
Rezaul to the tiger. Despite his wounds, the gnawing in his
belly gave him the strength to hunt cautiously. He trailed
Rezaul through the grass, his natural camouflage rendering
him invisible. The man was slow. The tiger gained on him
with each step. With a full throated growl, Timur switched
into high gear, bounding, hurting, stretching, with all the
skill of the trained killer his mother had raised.

Rezaul turned at the growl. He threw his crutch down and transferred his rifle to his right hand as he tried to keep his balance on one foot. Timur was fast, too fast. Rezaul was in the act of bringing his rifle up when he and Timur collided. Rezaul jerked his finger, sending off one wide shot, which smacked harmlessly into the ground, as the tiger took his life.

Marshall heard the rifle report and looked back. There was nothing to see, except the meadow, the trees and a movement in the grass halfway between himself and the trees. He shouted and ran back the way he had come.

Up in the heavens the moon took a bite out of the sun. Timur took a bite out of Rezaul, raising his bloody muzzle at the sound of another voice. He snarled a warning to stay away. The running steps came closer. Timur stood over his human prey, his tail lashing the air defiantly. Marshall, his lungs near bursting, held his rifle high as he ran. Without warning Timur attacked. One second he was on Rezaul, the next he was up to full speed. The two old enemies faced each other over a rapidly diminishing gap. On the run, Marshall squeezed the trigger as Timur flew through the air at him. From somewhere in the deepest recesses of his mind, Marshall saw a lion outlined on a boulder at sunrise. As his imagination replayed the scene, culled from a different time and a different place, he pulled the trigger again.

Timur screamed and jerked sideways as the bullet carved a scorching line down his body. His forward momentum was such that it would have propelled him past Marshall, as the rifleman dodged left. Timur, however, was not to be cheated by a sideways feint. One good paw, with claws extended, reached out and tore into Marshall's bare chest, swinging them both in a circle. The rifle was knocked from Marshall's hands as he fell. The breath slammed out of him by the blow. Badly hurt by the sharp hooked claws, he was dazed. He had no chance of getting back to his feet. Before he could move, Timur was on him. Marshall died, with Tracy's name on his lips, facing the tiger which had killed them both.

The moon darkened the sky as it covered the sun with its blackness, leaving a ghostly bright halo. The jungle went quiet. No birds sang. No creature moved. Confused by dark when there should be light, nature's children cowered in fear. Timur was no exception. He pinned Marsh under him while he strove to understand what was happening to his world.

Gray heard the first shot as he reached the tower. Sprinting up the steps to the top observation platform he scanned the meadow, desperately searching for its origin. As the moon crept over the sun, laying an artificial twilight over the jungle, he found Marsh's back in the gloom. He was running to greet his destiny. Coming to meet him through the grass was a tiger. Gray heard the second shot as he went down the steps four at a time. With his new guard hot on his heels he raced to where he had last seen Marshall.

Crashing through the long grass Gray could see the tiger and he could see Marshall. He stopped well within rifle range. The tiger straddled Marshall, who hadn't moved. He glared at Gray in the half light. His breathing coarse and his chest heaving and thumping. He was covered in blood, his own and that of the two who had stood in his way.

Gray shouted and raised his rifle to his shoulder as the tiger roared his dominance. Face to face with Timur for a second time and, knowing there was only one option open to him, Gray still held his fire, unable to bring himself to pull the trigger.

"You fucking stupid, arrogant cat," Gray raged. "Why couldn't you be normal, Timur? Why did you have to become a killer?"

Timur snarled in reply, guttural, defiant, threatening. Close to Gray the guard sighted along the barrel of his rifle. He was shaking. He flashed a momentary look at the professor.

"Shoot, sir, please shoot," he begged.

Gray wiped his eyes with the back of his hand. He and Timur glowered at each other. Through his sights, Gray studied the tiger. He had devoted so many years of his life to the preservation of this tiger and others like it. For more than seven years he had searched the Sundarbans, from north to south and from east to west, to study the tiger with the unusual pugmark. Now he, the man who had taken on the responsibility of safely removing the man-eater from the wild, had to take his life. He took aim on Timur's head, blinking tears from his eyes. Dimly he could see Marshall's body under the tiger.

Timur kept growling, the sound rumbling up from his belly. Gray took a deep breath to steady his hands, his nerves and himself. He pulled the trigger. The bullet rocketed out of the muzzle. Crossing the intervening grass, it sliced through a dozen or more strands, reaching its target before they started to fall. It hit Timur on the first black stripe over his nose, right between his beautiful golden eyes. The impact pushed him back a pace. His hind legs collapsed, leaving him half sitting, half laying down. Slowly the anger faded from his eyes. His weak forepaw gave way; he toppled over with a deep final sigh.

Gray knelt where he had stood to fire the shot. The tension of the last few days and, in particular, today, had his nerves whining like violin strings. He found himself praying as the adrenalin, like the tears, flowed from him.

Fatima was in mid-stream, beginning her funereal voyage to Mongla, when the shots rang out. Abdul, at Asia's insistence, altered course for the Jawtoli jetty. With the injured Ali and the deckhand by her side, Asia ran to the tower. Ali located the tragic scene with his binoculars and led her to it. In a clearing of flattened grass, the forestry guard who had spent the night on the tower stood with head bowed, his rifle butt resting on the ground. Gray knelt alone, His hands over his face, a rifle on the grass in front of him. Beyond, a tiger lay on its side as if sleeping. Cradled protectively in its paws, was another man. In the background a third body was barely visible through the slowly waving grass. Asia stopped beside Gray and placed one hand on his shoulder.

"Is that Marshall?" she asked.

Gray took his hands away from his face. He looked at Asia, then to the bodies in front of him. He nodded.

"That's Richard Marshall, Rezaul and Timur. They caused each other such bloody misery. Perhaps it's fitting that they should meet their combined fate in the jungle where it all began."

Ali kept his rifle ready as Asia checked for signs of life on the man Gray referred to as Marshall.

"He's dead, Asia. They're all dead."

Asia ran to check the other man anyway. He too was dead as Gray had told her. She looked long and hard at the tiger which had killed her husband.

"His reign of terror is at an end," Gray said, more to himself than to anyone else. "He was a magnificent old cat though. Absolutely magnificent."

Asia shivered. In the sky the moon was leaving the sun. Natural light was coming back, speeding across the grass blowing lightly in the field. Gray still had not moved. Asia reached down and held his tear streaked face in her hands. Somewhere on the edge of the forest a kingfisher hesitantly whistled, then began to sing.

"It's over, Gray. It's over," Asia whispered.

"No, Professor Pendennis, it is not over."

The sudden intrusion of the deep voice startled them all. Asia jumped back, almost tripping over Gray's rifle. Gray looked up to see General Rahman and a soldier standing close by, their rifles pointed at him. The soldier had a net slung over his shoulder.

"I will take the tiger, if you please," Rahman signalled the soldier to collect the dead tiger.

Gray looked up at Rahman angrily, his hand on his rifle. "No, you poaching bastard. You will not have the tiger," he hissed. "I will see you jailed for this."

Rahman motioned with his rifle. "I'm sorry, Professor, but you are not in charge. I am. And your usefulness is at an end. Now get up slowly and leave the gun on the ground."

Exhausted from his injuries, Ali leaned against the deckhand, unable to use his rifle. The forestry guard had frozen. He stood apart, fear lining his face; his rifle forgotten. Gray snatched at his own weapon and pulled the trigger without aiming. General Rahman fell on his back, his rifle flying out of his hands; blood spurting from the livid hole where his left knee had been. Rahman's soldier dropped his net and turned to fire at Gray, but he was too slow. Gray tackled him and took him down hard. With the help of the forestry guard he tied the soldier's hands behind his back with part of the net. Next they did the same with the general.

"You two are going to jail for a long time," Gray told Rahman.

Asia stood in silence, her face a mask; her eyes roaming from Gray to the tableau of two dead men, two prisoners and one dead tiger. Gray went to her, putting his arms around her.

"Come on, Asia," he said, "it's time to leave this place."

EPILOGUE

Ten years later

"Ladies and gentlemen," the master of ceremonies spread his arms wide to encompass everyone in the great ballroom, "it is my privilege, and my pleasure, to announce this year's recipient of the society's Gold Medal. This annual award goes to an explorer/scientist whose career, in the highly educated opinions of our board of directors, has opened up new fields for further study, has answered previously unanswerable questions, has broadened our scientific horizons, and has had a positive ecological effect on a significant segment of our planet."

On the wall behind the podium and the honoured few on the dais, a portrait of a noble Royal Bengal tiger expanded into view. From speakers situated around the auditorium a thunderous 'Awwoomm' reverberated from wall to wall: the proud voice of the Emperor of the Jungle expressing his agreement with the imminent announcement.

"This year's Gold Medallist has dedicated his professional life to the study and preservation of the tiger," the M.C. looked back at the huge portrait. "That booming tone you just heard might well have been a belated 'thank you' from one species of the animal kingdom. For three decades, since he was a teenager in fact, one man, backed for much of the time by a loyal and highly skilled staff, has given his all to understand and save tigers in general – and the Royal Bengal tiger in particular. Not content with successfully introducing measures to increase the population of healthy tigers in the jungles of India and Bangladesh; our recipient undertook a most hazardous task in the field. He deliberately set out to study the man-eating tiger. Those dangerous studies were not only successful in increasing our understanding of the factors which turn a wild creature into a man killer, but also they have been instrumental in reducing the number of fatal attacks on humans by tigers in the wild. In the course of his research in the field, he also found time to discover a previously unknown archaeological site in the Sundarbans. Two grateful governments have already honoured this man for his endeavours. His own country has seen fit to confer one of its highest honours on him. Tonight the Exploration Society is proud to bestow its supreme accolade on a man who has gained the respect of his peers, not only for his scientific achievements, not only for his impressive and courageous expeditions, but for his conduct as a gentleman.

Ladies and gentlemen, it is, I am sure, no surprise to any of you to learn that the Gold Medal for this year is awarded to our immediate past president, Professor Graham Pendennis."

Gray stood up and ruffled his shaggy mane of silver curls. He raised his eyebrows at a smiling Rab Choudhury seated in the middle of the front row of tables and went to the podium. As the medal, with red and gold striped ribbon attached, was placed around his neck by the current president, Gray bowed deeply to him. He turned and bowed again to the dignitaries behind him. Walking to centre stage, he clasped his hands together in front of himself, and repeated the gesture to the audience in the main hall.

Staring up at him from the central table in the front row, Asia's eyes filled with tears of pride. She flicked a long braid of jet black hair over her shoulder and let it run down the back of her golden sari. With her eyes fixed on Gray, she rose to her feet and put her hands together in applause. All around her chairs were being moved back as the assembly broke into a standing ovation. Asia turned to Rab on her left and hugged him. She then turned to a seven year old boy at her side. Her son smiled up at her, his black curly hair framing deep brown eyes flecked with blue. He looked up at his father on the stage. With a broad grin on his face, he raised two thumbs in the air.

"Well done, Dad," he called.